K. BROMBERG

Combust
By K. Bromberg

ISBN: 978-1-942832-10-2

Published by JKB Publishing, LLC

Editing by AW Editing and Marion Making Manuscripts
Cover Design by Helen Williams
Cover Photography by R + M Photography (Reggie Deanching)

PRAISE FOR THE NOVELS OF K. BROMBERG

"This book will have you CUFFED to your chair until the very last page of this high-flying tale."

—*#1 New York Times Bestselling author* Audrey Carlan

A poignant and hauntingly beautiful story of survival, second chances and the healing power of love. An absolute must read."

—*New York Times Bestselling author* Helena Hunting

"A homerun! The Player is riveting, sexy and pulsing with energy. And I can't wait for The Catch!"

—*#1 New York Times Bestselling author* Lauren Blakely

"An irresistibly hot romance that stays with you long after you finish the book."

—# 1 *New York Times* bestselling author Jennifer L. Armentrout

"Bromberg is a master at turning up the heat!"

—*New York Times* bestselling author Katy Evans

"Super charged heat and full of heart. Bromberg aces it from the first page to the last."

—*New York Times* bestselling author Kylie Scott

OTHER BOOKS BY K. BROMBERG

Driven

Fueled

Crashed

Raced

Aced

Slow Burn

Sweet Ache

Hard Beat

Down Shift

Sweet Cheeks

Sweet Rivalry

UnRaveled

The Player

The Catch

Cuffed

The hero is commonly the simplest and obscurest of men.

—Henry David Thoreau

PROLOGUE

Dylan

"WHOA. WAIT A MINUTE. WHAT DO YOU MEAN, *I HAVE to pretend*?"

"Your contract has a penalty for not finishing the songs on time." My agent's calm, coddling voice comes through the line but has the opposite effect of what she's hoping for with it.

"Finishing the songs on time—which I'll do—is not the issue. It's you telling me I have to pretend to still be dating Jett; that's the problem. You know," I say with a voice dripping with sarcasm, "*the Jett* I found screwing Tara-Perfect-Tits in *our* bed." My words hang on the line with so much conviction, yet my heart is imploding.

"Yes, *that* Jett." Her voice is quiet now. Resigned. "I know I'm asking a lot of you, Dylan. I know it's going to be hard, but you know how hesitant the label executives were to sign him on for another album with his history."

"History?" I laugh. "You mean trashing clubs and being unbearable to work with in the studio? That history?"

"Dylan." She sighs my name. "They know he's on his best behavior, but they also know it's *him*. The change from bad boy to good guy has never lasted long for him in the past."

"And his crappy reputation is my problem . . . why, exactly?" I cringe, already knowing the answer.

"Because you're the only reason they signed him on again. You're the only person who could calm him down. You're the—"

"*Jett whisperer*," I mumble, hating the term I once thought cute. Now I realize it made me look like a naïve fool. Silence falls as I pinch the bridge of my nose. How am I supposed to make this work?

"I know it's only been a day since it happened, but maybe once you calm down—"

"I'm pretending I didn't hear you say that, Ava. There's no way you just insinuated that I should overlook what Jett did because he's Jett Kroger. That I should stand by and suck it up. Tell me I'm wrong."

"That's not what I said."

"That sure as hell is what it sounded like."

"Look, Dylan . . . both you and Jett are my clients. I want the best for both of you, even though I currently want to kick Jett in the balls for what he did . . . but what is best for you is to finish this album."

"Like I said, that's not the problem—"

"And to do so without the label knowing you're not together anymore."

"But why?" I throw my hands up as a frustrated tear slides down my cheek.

"Because it will make them nervous. Nervous executives might delay or even table the album for another singer who's more of a sure thing, because let's face it, as successful as Jett has been for them, he's a pain in their asses. And them delaying the album—"

"Means I don't get paid," I finish for her, thinking of my mom and her mounting bills. Just one more piece of the fucked-up puzzle added to this chaos my life has become.

I blow out a breath and roll my shoulders, hating every single thing about my life right now.

"It won't be easy. I know that. But think of it this way . . . finishing the songs, pretending you and Jett are still a team . . . it will keep you in a favorable light with the label. I've already been working with them on expanding your writing collaborations outside of working with Jett, so it's in your best interest to bite the bullet for a bit."

I sink into my couch, close my eyes, and tighten my hand on the phone at my ear. She's right. I know she's right . . . but hell if I want to admit it. And hell if I want to have to sit face to face and write songs with the man who just broke my heart.

"Fine." There's a bite to my tone. Every part of me revolts against what that word agrees to.

When I open my eyes, Jett is everywhere despite his side of the closet being empty and his house key sitting on the credenza by the front door where he left it. His Dodgers hat he forgot hangs on the back of the kitchen chair. The odd-shaped coffee mug he swears makes coffee taste better is beside the Keurig. The rumpled throw on the couch is where he left it from the last time he fell asleep there.

His cologne lingers. The strum of his guitar still echoes. His laughter still fills the halls.

"Dylan?" Ava's voice snaps me back from thoughts I shouldn't be having. From the ache in my heart, I'd give anything to go away. From the ridiculous thoughts edging my mind that maybe it was a mistake when I know full well it wasn't. "What do you have to lose?"

My dignity.

"I'm good. Fine. You'll get your songs, but I have to go."

Literally.

I shove up off the couch and head to the one room I've been avoiding. The bed is bare—mattress without sheets, pillows on the ground from when I threw them in a fit of fury—and I head to my closet for my suitcase. As I grab its handle, I dial my brother.

"Hey stranger." His voice breaks the dam against the floodgate of tears I've been trying to hold back.

"Da-Damon."

"What did that bastard do to you?"

"I need your help."

ONE

Dylan

I AWAKE DISORIENTED AND LOST IN THE SILENCE. IT FEELS WEIRD without the usual sounds—the loud honking of cars and music floating up from the dance studio across the alley. It feels like I'm naked.

Just absolute and complete silence.

Then I hear the giggle. A *thump* against the wall. A swear following the thump.

And I know he's finally home.

Crap.

This isn't how I planned on meeting him, but what am I going to do? Hide away in this bedroom and pretend I'm not here when my car is clearly parked on the left side of the driveway?

I scramble out of bed and throw on a robe, pull the sash on it as tight as it can go, and prepare myself to meet my new housemate. *Of sorts.*

There's another giggle. A murmured sound of satisfaction. Both make me cringe to open my bedroom door.

But I do. Curiosity gets the best of me.

I'm blinded momentarily as the sun from the open front door reflects off one very sexy, slinky, and *daring* silver sparkly dress. A pair of sky-high strappy heels is in one of her hands. Her other is threaded through the hair at the base of the neck of the man whose back is to me.

I shouldn't stare, but I do.

And not because I'm being rude but because of the immediate sense of inadequacy I feel when I look at her. My frumpy robe admittedly makes me feel out of place next to her in her party dress.

"I've gotta go," she murmurs against his lips and, of course, her voice sounds like she looks, sultry as all hell.

"Mmm. You sure?" His laugh is a deep rumble that fills the hallway.

Another kiss. The run of his hand down the side of her torso until it rests squarely on her ass.

"No . . . but yes."

They both chuckle as their lips meet again before she steps out of the open doorway, their arms stretching between them, giving me a full view of her for the first time.

Mussed, brown hair that makes bedhead look sexy. A body I'm used to seeing in the Los Angeles perfection I escaped but know I'll never have: long legs, subtle curves, defined arms, great boobs. Simply put, *she's gorgeous.*

I don't even fear she'll see me, because her eyes are so completely focused on him that I fade into the background.

They look like an Abercrombie & Fitch ad. Their positioning—her body turned toward his, the pout on her lips, the undeniable attraction between them.

Dear God. Is this what I've moved into? Perfectville?

After one more hesitation, she walks away with him staring after her and me looking at the back of him.

A car door shuts. An engine starts. His focus still on her.

"Are you just going to stand there and stare? If you were interested in joining, I'm sure Mal would've been all for it."

His words blindside me, but nowhere near as much as the sight of him when he turns to face me.

Wow.

I open my mouth to speak. Close it. Open it again. Sputter. "I don't—I'm not—she—" I manage to get some words out, but they come off sounding just how I look: frumpy. In my white fluffy bathrobe—that I'm holding closed at the neck—I look like someone's aunt Gertrude while he looks like . . . *that*.

Perfection with a little bit of grit thrown in.

Those aqua eyes of his pin me motionless as they narrow and stare. "Well?" He lifts his eyebrows as he folds his arms across his chest and leans his shoulder against the wall. The hardened expression on his face transforms instantly when his mouth turns into a carefree smile. "Relax, McCoy. I'm just teasing you, but I have to admit, the look on your face was worth it." In the same amount of time it takes me to breathe a sigh of relief, he crosses the distance of the foyer and reaches a hand out to me. "Grady Malone."

"Dylan McCoy." I look at where our hands meet, and my attention is hijacked by the abs in the background, peeking out from behind his unbuttoned shirt. All eight of them. "But you knew that. Thanks for letting me . . . uh—"

"Don't worry about it," he says as he walks past me and into the family room. "Sorry I didn't know you were here or else I would have"—he shrugs in an adorably sheepish way that is in complete contradiction to the pure, heady maleness of him—"not made so much noise."

"My car's in the driveway. Can't be much more obvious than that," I say, fully aware I'm being sarcastic when he doesn't deserve it. But, he opened the door with his initial comment.

And frankly, I'm sick of taking shit from men. After Jett . . . ugh. *After Jett* is all I need to say to remind myself why I'm allowed to be snarky.

"I never use the driveway." He looks at me and lifts his eyebrows unapologetically.

"And I'm supposed to know that, how?"

"Are you always this combative?" His tone sounds as if he's irritated, but his smile says anything but.

It stops me from saying more, and I remind myself he isn't Jett.

Grady Malone isn't the man who broke my heart. He's not the reason I've set off for the next few months to lick my wounds and gain some distance to grow immune to his charms before I have to face him again.

"No. Sorry. I . . . it's just been a long few days." I hang my head for a moment, swallow my pride when I'm so used to being strong, and then lift it back up. "Thank you for letting me stay on such short notice. I appreciate it."

"You needed a place to stay. I have an extra room in a house where I'm gone several days of the week. And it's Damon." He shrugs as if letting a friend's sister stay in his house for a few months is something he'd do any day of the week. "I'd do anything for your brother."

"Thanks. Like I said, I appreciate it more than you know."

"We all need to get out of Dodge sometimes. I get it." He opens the fridge and pulls out a bottle of water. I shake my head when he holds one out to me.

The scanner on his bookshelf comes to life—codes dispatched to Fire Station Thirteen—scaring the shit out of me, and brings back the bittersweet memories of my childhood. I must jump a foot because Grady laughs. "Sorry 'bout that. I have a habit of turning it on the minute I walk in the door."

"It's fine. I'll get used to it." *I was used to it once.*

"You can always turn it off if I forget when I leave for a shift." I nod in response. "Make yourself at home. Did you find the Wi-Fi code?"

"No." I remember my fruitless attempt to find it. "I didn't want to snoop." I rest my hips against the back of the couch as he walks out of the kitchen and mirrors my posture against the counter a few feet across from me.

"Snoop all you like. I've got nothing to hide. Besides, I made sure all the really embarrassing and equally pleasurable sex toys were put away before you arrived." He flashes that grin, and I stare at him, mouth agape, wide-eyed and innocent when I'm far from it.

All I can do is choke on air.

He shakes his head. "Jesus. You're as easy to rile up as your brother. If you're going to live here, Dyl, you're going to have to learn to relax. I like to joke. Life's too serious not to joke. So get used to it."

"Dyl?" I'm so used to Jett and his broody ways that Grady's humor is going to take some getting used to.

"We're roommates now. It's normal to shorten each other's names, isn't it? You'll call me Grade. I'll call you Dyl. See? Perfect."

"Are you always this cheerful?"

"Depends on the day. *Or the morning.*" He rubs a hand over his unshaven jaw and grins as his eyes flash toward the door. *Ah,* Mal, the source of his happiness.

My mind is moving a million miles an hour. Living here seemed fine twenty-four hours ago when I had the house to myself, and he was on shift. But now he's home, and I have to get used to the fact that he's going to be everywhere. Him *and* his cheery demeanor. Or rather, him *and* his girlfriend.

"Is your girlfriend going to have a problem with this?" My mind flashes to Jett. And walking in on him and Tara. *In my bed.* Not that I'd do that to Mal. *Not that Grady would want* that *with me . . .*

"Who?"

He has to ask? "Glitter-dress girl."

"Glitter dress? Oh, no. She isn't my girlfriend."

"Oh."

"And she won't be around again."

Could've called that one a mile away.

"Ah, you're so sentimental." My voice drips with sarcasm.

"At least I'm honest."

"Does she know that?"

He rolls his eyes like a little boy. "Yes, she knows that. Mallory and I used to have *a thing*. She moved away and was home visiting some family . . . so we, uh—"

"Reconnected?"

"If that's the term you want to use." He chews on his smile.

Every part of me wants to find fault with him for being so cavalier, but I can't. There's something about the roguish look on his face and dead honesty with me, a woman he's never met before, that makes him seem almost adorable . . . in a grown man kind of way.

"I'm hungry. You hungry? Let's go get breakfast. Break bread . . . or in our case, break pancakes."

I scrunch my nose and study him. The messy brown hair, eyes laden with humor that probably see more than they should, and that body. If I were to base my opinion solely on what his abs look like, well, hell . . . at least I'll have something good to look at when I get writer's block.

"Breakfast?"

"Yeah, that stuff you eat in the morning. Fuel for the day. The must-have meal. Breakfast."

My stomach rumbles at the thought. "Sure. Yeah. You have some, uh"—I let go of where my hand is holding my robe together and point to a smear of red on the side of his face—"lipstick on your cheek."

"That isn't the only place I have it." He flashes me a devilish grin before unapologetically walking out of the family room. "Be ready in ten to leave."

And I stare after him. Of course I do. My eyes wander over his retreating back and I picture things I shouldn't be thinking. What he'd look like naked with a strategically placed kiss of lipstick.

Then I groan.

I can't think like this.

Besides, he said he likes to joke.

He's probably joking.

Then why can't I get the visual out of my head?

TWO

Grady

"AREN'T YOU GOING TO EAT?" SHE'S BEEN LOOKING AT those pancakes like she's starving but hasn't made a dent in them.

Her eyes dart to her plate and then back to mine.

"I'm not that hungry."

Bullshit.

My coffee scalds my tongue, but fuck if it doesn't taste like heaven . . . and clears the cobwebs from my head that too much whiskey allowed to grow.

"That wasn't what your stomach was saying in the car." Not even a smile. Just a blush of her cheeks. *Frickin' women.* "Is it that you aren't hungry or more that you're afraid I'm going to see you eat?" The quick blink of her eyes says I've nailed it on the head. "If that's the case, it's going to be pretty miserable having you sit on the couch next to me, starving to death and all."

She meets the lift of my brow with the clench of her jaw. Still not even a crack of a smile.

"I'm watching what I eat."

"Why?" I reach forward and help myself to a forkful of her pancakes. There's no way I'm letting Bertha's pancakes go to waste. They're legendary.

"Because I need to."

"*Need to*? You women are too harsh on yourselves."

She opens her mouth and then shuts it as I study her. Raven-colored hair, kind of short, kind of edgy, kind of hot in a rocker girl way. Gray eyes so light they're almost clear. A set of lips—*damn,* a set of lips that have *blow job* written all over them. Her shirt is baggy and earlier her robe covered her, but her body seems normal. No third leg growing out of her hip or anything.

But she's self-conscious. A bit shy. Very uncomfortable in her own skin.

This isn't the same woman I've seen in pictures in Damon's house. That girl was full of fire and brimstone and a whole hell of a lot of rebellion.

No doubt the ex-boyfriend did this to her. From what Damon hinted at, it's been a rough few days for her.

"Do you mind?" I reach my fork out again, and she pushes her plate toward me. I take another bite and smile. "You haven't lived until you've devoured Mama Bertha's pancakes." Her eyes watch as I chew her food. "If you get hungry, your fork is right there. Your stomach will thank me."

"I'll keep that in mind."

She'll be eating them by the time we leave. I'll make sure of it.

"So what brings you to Sunnyville?"

"Damon didn't tell you?"

"Bits and pieces, but he's a guy. We aren't known for being real observant or forthcoming."

"I needed a break." Her eyes flit over my shoulder to where Bertha is chatting up the old-guy crew who come and occupy the counter every morning for a few hours. "Somewhere I could go and finish a project I'm working on."

"Project?"

"Album. Songs. Whatever you want to call it."

"I'm assuming having a studio helps. Wouldn't it be easier to do that at home?"

Her eyes harden. "I wouldn't be here if I thought so, now would

I?" Ah, there's the fight in her. "I can write lyrics anywhere. Besides, my place was kind of stifling my creativity."

Hm. They must have lived together.

"Is 'I needed a break' code for 'my boyfriend's an asshole'?" Might as well lay the truth out there.

"*Ex*-boyfriend."

"You *or* him?"

"Me but only because I was blindsided."

I hiss. "Ouch. That sucks. What happened?"

"You don't hold back, do you?"

"What's the point? It's going to come out sooner or later." I shove another forkful of her pancakes in my mouth. "So?"

I get a glimpse of a smile as she shakes her head.

"It wasn't working."

"For him, right? It wasn't working for him, but it was for you?"

"Something like that. Working together can make things tough at times."

"Wait. Oh . . . do I know who he is?" Damon said she was big time, but he didn't say who she worked with.

She shrugs. "Jett Kroger."

Her eyes hold mine, waiting for recognition to fire, but hell, there's no need to wait. Everyone knows who Jett fucking Kroger is. The bad boy of rock with an incredible voice, a killer instinct for trends, and who's produced an endless stream of hits over the past few years. That and a reputation for being a hothead who causes trouble.

"You look too damn innocent to be with him." The words are out there as I realize she's the one behind the number one hits. She's the lyrics to his beat.

She stutters a laugh. "I'm not sure if that's an insult or a compliment."

"I just—"

"I've heard it all, so just say it. At this point, I've learned to have tough skin. Nothing will offend me." She laughs and finally gives me a genuine smile, but her eyes show the truth. She's been hurt. "She's trying too hard to fit into his crowd. She isn't his type. Jett could do better, so much better. Don't sleep with the hired help. And the list goes on—"

"Actually, that's not what I was thinking." I lean back in the booth and stare at her, immediately feeling the need to protect her from the snarky comments. No doubt the assholes were just jealous. "I was going to say his music is killer, but he comes off like a dick, and you deserve better than that."

"Yeah, well . . . it didn't stop me from loving him."

"The heart's blind. It's the head that causes all the trouble."

Her body pauses for the briefest of seconds, an internal struggle waging a silent war across her expression. "Sometimes both are stupid," she murmurs, shifting her gaze from mine so she can stab a piece of pancake with her fork and eat it.

"So, is this the whole *distance makes the heart grow fonder* thing?"

"What do you mean?"

"Obviously, you still like the guy or else you wouldn't appear so miserable—"

"I am *not* miserable."

"Just like you're not hungry." She stops mid-chew and rolls her eyes at me.

"What's your point, Grady?"

"Is this one of those situations where you leave so he sees what he's missing? Then in a few months, you go back with a new haircut, a careless attitude, and your cleavage and curves on display so he falls madly in love with you all over again." I get the death glare from her. Guess that means I'm closer to the truth than she wants to admit. Either that or she's pissed I'm even suggesting such a thing.

And she takes another bite.

Hell, if I piss her off enough, she might forget she isn't *hungry* and eat the rest of the food.

"I highly doubt that will happen."

"You didn't say no."

"Let's just say the woman riding him in *my* bed *told* me that even if I showed up buck naked with a portable stripper pole, he wouldn't give a second glance my way."

"Well, shit." Not much I can say to ease the assholery he did to her.

"Pretty much." She draws the words out.

"And yet you still love him?"

"I didn't say that."

"You didn't have to." The hurt in her eyes said it all for her.

"Being with someone for almost two years doesn't make it easy to turn off the feelings, no matter how much he screwed me over."

"*Literally*."

Her eyes, storm clouds of emotion, flash up from where she's pouring syrup on her pancakes. For a minute, I think she's going to cry, but then she surprises me when she throws her head back and laughs.

"I walked right into that one, didn't I?"

"Yep." I take a sip of my coffee and watch her. She's pretty. No, not just pretty, but *sexy*. There is a difference between the two. And not in the classic sense, but there is definitely something about her that would make any man look twice. The bitch riding her ex was completely wrong. "So . . . the project you're finishing . . . is it his?"

"It's the label's, but yeah, it's with him."

"That must suck, having to write music for someone you hate."

She shrugs. "To put it mildly, but that's the problem, we write good music together. And even if we didn't, we're bound by contract to get twenty songs turned in over the next four months."

"Twenty? Christ. Why so many?"

"Labels like variety. They like to decide what song is the best fit for the current musical climate. In the end, they're the ones who have the ultimate say over what songs make the album."

"You can write the lyrics without him, then?"

She nods as she chews. "Each song is a different process. Sometimes, it's the lyrics first and then the music, sometimes it's the music and then the lyrics . . . other times it's side by side, verse by verse. I'm hoping we can avoid that last one this time around. The less I see of him, the better."

"Why?" I ask, prompting her to look at me as if I've grown two heads. "You're either running from him because you're pissed and never want to see him again, or you've taken off because if you stay, you know he'll wear you down, get you to forgive him, and then start your relationship song and dance all over again."

She glares at me for a beat. That's all it takes. "Maybe I just want to check the box for all of the above."

"Understandable. There's no judgment on my part for whatever box you check. Hell, maybe you can write a song about a jerk musician who cheats on his girlfriend and then falls off the face of the earth. That might let him know where he stands with you."

"Such an active imagination."

"Funny. Mallory said the same thing last night." *C'mon. Turn those lips up.* "And she finally smiles . . ."

Her eyes soften, her smile widens, and she shakes her head before eating the last forkful of pancake.

Mission accomplished.

THREE

Dylan

"I feel like such a prick. The one time you really need me, and I turn you away." My brother's voice warms me with his sincerity and makes me snuggle deeper into my spot on the couch.

"You didn't turn me away. You have twin baby girls in a two-bedroom house. I think you have your hands full as it is. Besides, this is more than fine. I needed somewhere to crash long enough to give me a breather, get my work done, and clear my head before I head back and figure shit out. If I were at your house, I'd probably be so distracted playing auntie that I'd never work."

"I appreciate you trying to make me feel better, but I still feel helpless. I'm your big brother. Between you taking the burden with Mom—"

"You have the twins. The last thing you need to be thinking about is Mom and—"

"And now this with Jett—"

"I'll be fine, Damon."

"I still feel like I should be doing something. More. I don't know."

"You did do something. More," I repeat with humor in my voice to try and put him at ease that I'll be okay. That it will all be okay. "You found me exactly what I needed. A place to stay where I could tuck my tail between my legs and lick my wounds for a bit."

"Yeah, but it's four hours away from me here in Lake Tahoe." His guilt tinges the edges of his tone.

"And I'm normally nine hours away from you when I'm in Los Angeles . . . so think of it as me moving closer for a bit," I tease. "Look, Damon, I appreciate all your help. I was upset, in a hurry to leave, and you helped me out by thinking of somewhere I could go and get my head—and heart—straightened out without living in a hotel for months on end. I'm thinking of it as a personal Airbnb."

"With a firefighter." And there it is. The one thing he neglected to mention when he called and told me about the old friend he had who lived away from my beaten path. Said friend also happened to have an extra room, an abundance of quiet at his house, and would leave me be so I could work.

A firefighter. Faded memories of our dad flicker through my mind. Ones I'd rather forget. Ones that have left me always waiting for the man I'm with to walk out the door one day and never come back, because his love for his job, his friends, his freedom, his whatever-the-hell excuse is more important than his family.

"It's fine, Damon. I'm okay with it." Except for every time the damn scanner goes off I'm left thinking of our mother. How she left the thing on for months after he left us, hoping to hear his voice . . . making her feel close to him even though he didn't want anything to do with us. And then how in the absence of the scanner came the alcohol. "I am. I promise."

"I'm not sure I believe you."

"Believe me." My smile pulls tight even though he can't see it.

"How are you holding up otherwise? I mean, it all happened so fast, it has to be hard."

"It sucks. It stings . . . but that's Jett." And I wish everyone would stop asking that because it does more than suck. It's a dagger in the heart.

"Don't I know it."

"Look, I don't need you to start in on me about him."

"I was right, wasn't I?" And that's why I didn't want to stay with him even if he had the extra room.

"You aren't making me feel any better. It's my heart that was hurt, so at this point, does it matter if you were right or not?"

Silence eats up the discord between us. "You're right. I'm sorry . . . I know you still love him, and I know you still have to work with him, so please promise me you won't fall for his shit again."

I think of Grady's comment about the heart versus the head and grit my teeth, hating that he's pegging me as the helpless female. "My life. My choices." There's a bite to my tone he doesn't deserve, and yet, it's still there.

"I know . . . I just . . ."

"I'm not sixteen anymore, Damon. Heartbreak is a thing, and it's part of life. You can't protect me from it or go around punching guys to prevent it."

"You know I would if I could." There's softness in his tone. A resignation that his defiant little sister is going to do what she wants regardless of his big brotherly warnings against it. "Are you getting settled in?"

"Were you going to warn me that Grady is a manwhore or is that part of the man code not to?"

"Grady is Grady." I can see him shrugging as he opens his mouth and closes it to try to make up a better excuse even though he knows it won't work with me. "He's a good guy. I wouldn't have let you stay there if he wasn't. Wait . . . tell me he isn't being a dick?"

"No." I think of everything I've learned about him so far. The funny. The sweet. The perpetually cheerful. The total guy part. "He's just unexpected."

"He's had a rough go of it lately, so let me know if he's being an ass, and I'll put him in his place."

"What do you mean he's had a rough go of it?"

"Almost two years ago he . . . you know what, never mind. It isn't anything other than knowing he's not your type, and he's not the staying kind because of it. It makes me breathe easier as a big brother, knowing nothing will be happening between the two of you."

"I'm a grown woman, Damon. I'm more than capable of deciding whom I do or don't sleep with . . . so tell me again, what's going on with him?"

"Nothing. Forget I said anything."

But I don't buy it. I find it hard to believe the man who hasn't been anything but happy and welcoming is having a hard time.

I hear cries beginning in the background and smile when I think of my brother being a dad—to twins no less.

"I've got to go . . . Tessa is starting up."

"Give her a kiss for me."

"Hey, Dyl? I know you like to be left alone while you work, which is why I figured Grady's place would be perfect for you, but don't be a stranger."

"I won't."

I end the call and wander through the house aimlessly. It's decorated in warm colors with the sparseness that bespeaks of a single male living here. There are touches of his personality here and there in pictures of who I can assume by resemblance are his family or his brothers at the fire station, but it's missing that feminine touch. There are rugs on the hardwood floor but there are no random tchotchkes cluttering the space. No throws on the back of the couch to add a touch of color. No candles half-burned on holders.

And yet while it is void of those little touches, Grady's house still screams comfort to me. It feels like a place anyone can walk into and feel at ease.

I run my hand along the back of the brown leather couch as the squelch of the scanner becomes background noise I don't think I'll ever quite be comfortable with.

It's the view that pulls me to the kitchen window. Past the fenced-in backyard where the half-built shed is on one side of the yard and a small covered patio with a fireplace is on the other. There are acres and acres of fields with grapevines growing. Their rows line the hills and their stakes make an optical illusion I stare at for some time, lost until the parachutes in the far distance near where I saw the airport on my drive into town catch my attention. Then I notice the space. Wide-open space without high-rises, or neighbors nearby, or the constant sounds of the city.

It's beautiful. It's foreign.

I stare as the tears burn my eyes and the emotions I continue to bury try to fight their way to the surface.

I'm so lost in my thoughts that I yelp when something wet and warm hits the back of my leg.

What the hell?

When I whip around, I'm met with the ugliest, cutest thing I have ever seen. All fifty-or-so pounds of her.

The pig is whitish-pink with black spots. She has a fine layer of wiry hair coating her skin, and her pink snout is wet and quivering as she sniffs the air.

I know what I'm seeing, but it actually takes me a few seconds to really believe that I'm standing in Grady's kitchen having a staring contest with a pig.

"And who, may I ask, are you?"

She shifts her feet, but her eyes stay fast on mine.

"Do you have a name?" I look for a collar, but then realize how stupid that sounds to be treating a pig like a dog . . . and yet, there is a pig in front of me. One that is very comfortable in . . . I bend over to check out the pig's underside just to be sure of her gender . . . *her* surroundings.

Her tail twitches some, and I laugh. I've resorted to speaking to a pig. Maybe I'm going crazy.

"Well, I'm going to eat some breakfast," I say. "No worries though. It isn't bacon. Just cereal."

Yep. Definitely crazy.

It's when I set the phone on the counter behind me that I see the handwritten note.

Dylan,

Don't be alarmed by Petunia. I forgot to warn you about her, but the vet dropped her off this morning. She's perfectly harmless . . . mostly. She has a doggy door so no need to take her out.

Grady

I stare at the note for a few seconds as Petunia grunts from the floor.

"Well, Petunia . . . it's just you and me today."

FOUR

Dylan

"How are you?" Jett's voice rasps through the line like a fine whiskey over ice—smooth but with a burn to it.

I fight the threatening tears. I refuse to let his sudden concern for me make me fall back into the black hole being in Sunnyville is trying to pull me out of.

"Do you like the lyrics so far? I think they work well with the track you laid down." I try to sound all business and wonder if he can see right through it.

"Dylan . . ." His voice is part apology, part concern, and I don't want to believe either is sincere. "It feels like it's been forever since—"

"Weeks. Not forever." *Twenty days to be exact.*

"Too long."

"The bridge sits perfect with the riff you have on there—"

"I didn't call to talk about the songs," he says.

"Then I guess I'll be hanging up about now."

"No. Please, Dylan. Don't—"

"You're going to show up for your scheduled session in the studio on Wednesday, right?"

"Of course, I am."

"And you're going to be on your best behavior? No tantrums. No—"

"Christ, Dylan, I'm not a kid."

Then stop acting like one. The thought rushes through my mind. Why did it take me so long to see how immature he is? How his temper tantrums were not artistic frustration but rather him being spoiled rotten?

"Don't screw this up for me, Jett. I need the label to think everything is good. I don't need them worrying if the album will be completed in time. From the get-go of this contract they threatened to table it if you weren't behaving, and I can't risk that. I need the—"

"*Money.* I know, I know. And I told you I'd give you the goddamn money to help your mom. It's not a problem."

"I don't need shit from you," I say through gritted teeth. "All I need is for you to do your job and not screw up."

The quiet vibrates across the connection.

"And if I don't? If I miss the studio time, maybe that will force you to come home and actually talk to me face to face."

"You wouldn't dare." My hand fists on my phone, and I hate knowing that I wouldn't put it past Jett to pull a stunt like that. His threat is real.

"I wouldn't." There's amusement in his voice, and I can all but see the cocky smirk on his face. "I don't need the money. I'm more than good. Then again, we *do* need to talk."

"Actually, we don't." Images flit through my mind like the snap of a camera: the light under the closed bedroom doorway, Tara straddling him, their mutual moans, their shocked faces when I gasped. How he shoved her off him and chased after me. The words, the promises, the apologies. Her stalking after us in all her naked glory. *And then* the nasty words she said that fed every insecurity I feel about myself.

"I made a mistake. I don't know how many ways I can apologize to you before you believe it."

"Apologizing doesn't take the hurt away." Neither does the photo I saw of them in *People Magazine* sitting outside at Starbucks where they knew the paparazzi would snap a shot of them.

"Have you seen her again?"

"I miss you, baby. I miss—" *I'll take that as a yes.* His change in topic is classic Jett Kroger. If he doesn't want to admit to something, he shifts gears without a second thought.

"Let's focus on the song I sent you earlier. I'm still not sold on the opening verse, but—"

"I stopped by our place the other day—"

"You mean *my* place. It's *my place* now. Not ours."

"You were gone," he says, completely ignoring my correction.

"Yep. Sure was." I hate that my heart aches. I hate that I miss him. And I hate that I even wanted to see him.

"You packed up and left in such a hurry that—"

"I think once we're in the studio and hear the whole thing put together, I'll be able to pinpoint what needs to be changed."

"You could be in the studio with me on Wednesday . . ."

"No, I can't." *I won't.* For so many more reasons than just the physical distance between us.

Needing to abate the emotion rioting within me, I walk to the open window and look out at the darkness beyond. The warm night breeze blows gently against my skin, and it smells so clean. I'm so used to being able to watch the city come alive as the day fades to night that it's unnerving to look outside and see silhouettes of trees against the moonlit sky.

"You're not going to budge, are you?" I don't respond. I can't. There's always been something about Jett that has made me melt, and I can't melt this time. Yes, he cheated on me. Yes, I swore if anyone ever cheated on me I'd turn my back on him and never look back, which is exactly what I've done here. I called Damon, told him I needed help, packed my shit as fast as I could, and came to Sunnyville where he had helped me find a place. Just because it was easy to hold up to my own promise, doesn't mean I can turn off the emotions or tell my heart not to hurt. That part is a lot harder than it seems.

But I'm here. I'm here because I knew it would be much easier to cave—to be weak—if I was in my place where his things surrounded me. Where he and his charm could wear me down.

"Dylan?"

"No, I'm not going to budge, Jett." I clear my throat.

"Well, if you're not going to come here, then I'll come to you. Where are you?"

"I've already moved on. *Found someone new*." The words come off my tongue without thought, and I hate the need to lie just to get him to stop.

"I don't buy that for a goddamn minute."

"You should."

"You want to tell me where you're staying?"

"No. It's none of your business."

"Are you staying with *him*?" As much as I'm not trying to play games here—and lied just to end the topic of conversation—a part of me enjoys hearing the shock in his voice.

"It doesn't matter who I'm staying with. Get to the studio on Wednesday. Don't be an asshole to Kai and the rest of the guys," I say, referring to the audio engineer. "And listen to the lyrics I put over the track. Let me know what you think. I'll move on to the next song until I hear from you."

"I love you, Dylan."

I close my eyes and let my head fall forward as I hear words from him I know he doesn't often say. "If you loved me you wouldn't have fucked someone else."

And with that, I end the call and sink onto the edge of my bed. My phone is clutched to my chest as the reel of me walking in on him and Tara plays over and over again in my mind.

I glance at the clock to see that it's two in the morning. We always worked best when it was late and our brains were fuzzy and that kind of delirious state kicked in . . . I guess not even distance can change that.

Picking up my guitar, I hum the lyrics and play the chords, my mind trying to pinpoint where the song is off.

A sound breaks through my process. At first, I assume it's the scanner, my telltale sign that Grady is home from his shift, but just as I strum the guitar, I hear it again.

"Help. Please. Oh. God."

Grady's voice is filled with anguish and need. I drop my guitar and am out of my room within seconds, heading down the hall to where I can hear him waging a verbal struggle. His bedroom door is open, and when I enter, he's sprawled across his bed, asleep.

He's dreaming. Not in trouble.

My heart slows a beat, but the deep mewl of agony he emits as he bucks his body on the bed has me moving to him without a second thought.

"Grady! Grady! Wake up!"

He flings his arm back as I try to shake his shoulders and jar him awake. He struggles against me while that horrible keening sound continues in the back of his throat. I climb onto the bed, uncertain of what to do but positive I can't let him continue with this nightmare.

"No. Please. No," he murmurs as he writhes from side to side and I struggle to calm him. He's too strong and shifts suddenly so I fall somewhat on top of him. I can sense the minute he wakes and comes to. His body tenses. There's a quick intake of breath. His hand holding my wrist relaxes.

"Dylan?" It's a question, as if he needs to understand why I'm sitting here, straddling him in his bed.

The light from the hallway casts light over his face and makes the sheen of sweat covering his chest noticeable. Our eyes meet, his glassy and curious. "You were having a nightmare. I tried to . . ."

He clears his throat, and I can see him try to shake off whatever ghosts of the dream still cling to him. "I . . ." He brings his hand up to scrub over his face. "It was just a bad dream. Sorry to wake you." The unbothered tone in his voice contrasts with the struggle of emotion in his expression.

When he lowers his hand and meets my eyes, there is more in the depths of them—vulnerability, fear, shame, confusion—but he blinks it away as quickly as it flashes.

"Are you okay? Can I do anything to help you?"

"No. It's . . . I get them often."

And it's in this moment—the one where his eyes try to avert from mine so I don't see too much and slowly run their way down my torso—that I'm more than aware of what pajamas I have on. A tank top and flimsy shorts that could double as panties.

His breath stutters again, but it has nothing to do with his nightmare. His dick stirs to life beneath me. There is a moment of suspended disbelief that passes in slow motion as we realize what is happening and neither of us is sure if we should stop it.

And then, just as quickly, his hands are on my torso pushing me as I'm scrambling off him. Standing beside the bed, I cross my arms over my chest to hide my nipples, which are hard and needy and reflect exactly where my thoughts went.

"I'm sorry." We both say in unison and then laugh, nerves tingeing the edges.

"I didn't mean . . . I hope you're okay." There is a long, awkward pause before I stammer out, "I'm just going to go now."

I make my way to the door, embarrassment staining my cheeks and modesty having me wish I had my robe to cover up.

"Dylan. Wait."

When I pause and turn to face him, Grady is sitting up in bed, a sheet draped over his waist, his hair a total mess. My first coherent thought is: *I was right.* He looks every bit as mouth-wateringly perfect as that eight-pack of abs beneath his shirt hinted at the other day. "What is it?"

"I'm sorry . . . for waking you up . . . for, you know." He motions his hand at the space between him and me as a sheepish smile tugs at the corners of his mouth that has me wanting to bolt when my feet want to stay.

"It's, uh, natural."

Oh my God. Did I actually just say that?

He chuckles. "Something like that. You wanna turn around for a sec?" He motions his finger in a circle.

"For what?"

"Because I'm naked beneath the sheet, and since I'm planning on grabbing a drink of water from the kitchen, you might get an eyeful when I do." He bites the side of his cheek, trying to fight the arrogance in his smirk. "I couldn't care less . . . but, uh, you might."

"Oh, yes. Sure."

Feeling like an idiot, I walk from his room and down the hall to mine. My mind keeps reliving the thought of him naked with his dick hardening beneath me. My body does too.

"Christ," I murmur as I grab my robe and pull it tight around me.

It's normal to have that simmering ache in my lower belly after straddling a man, an extremely good-looking man, right?

He's already in the kitchen when I make my way out, T-shirt and shorts on, and a glass of amber liquid in his hands. The lines of his face etched with the unknown.

"I needed something stiffer than water. Want some?" He holds his glass out to me, and I take a sip, fighting the urge to swear when the burn hits my throat.

"That's good for me, thanks."

He chuckles, but it sounds absent of humor as he moves to the window and stares at the darkness I found solace in earlier. His shoulders are broad, his hair is a mess, and his bicep tenses as he brings the glass to his lips.

I debate leaving him be, giving him the peace he's most likely used to living on his own. Yet, there is something about him that has me sinking onto the couch and watching him from afar. Maybe it's that he looks as lost as I feel right now.

The scanner sparks to life and holds both of our attention as codes are given and 10-4s are responded.

I try to push away the riot of memories the sound brings up. The muffled sound of the dispatcher I'd hear as my mother would sit and listen to the scanner long after my brother and I had gone to bed. That and the clink of the neck of her vodka bottle as it hit the rim of her glass.

"Car accident on the outskirts of town with a passenger trapped," he deciphers the codes for me when the radio falls silent, almost as if he's not sure what else to say.

I close my eyes and say a silent prayer for the person trapped. When I open them, he's standing in front of me, head angled to the side, staring. "What are you doing?"

"Saying a little prayer for the person in the car to make sure they are all right."

He smiles softly and sits on the edge of the coffee table that faces me. "My mom used to do that when she'd hear a call on the scanner. She'd also say one for my dad's safety. I forgot that until right now."

"Was your dad a firefighter too?"

"A cop. Then the chief of police."

"You didn't want to follow in his footsteps?"

"For a while, but my oldest brother ended up going that route, and I ended up falling in love with fire." His eyes darken some, and I'm reminded of the nightmare he's just woken from and wonder if it has anything to do with his work.

"Your nightmare . . ."

"Nothing big really. Just a reminder to keep me on my toes when I'm at work."

"You said you have it often," I say, curious if he'll tell me more.

"It's late." He shoves up from his seat and moves around the back of the couch toward the hallway. "Thank you for trying to help, but I need to get some sleep." I freeze when he places a kiss to the top of my head. It's unexpected. It's sweet. It makes me want to snuggle into the couch and stay right here with him.

"Good night," I murmur, unable to think of anything else to say.

"Sleep sweet."

I remain seated, listening to dispatch for who knows how long, wondering if my dad is on the other end of that code somewhere.

And if maybe my mom does the same thing even after all these years.

FIVE

Grady

"WHAT GIVES, MAN?" GRAYSON ASKS AS HE TIPS THE neck of his beer toward the house.

"What do you mean?" I swing the hammer and pound the nail into the two-by-four.

"Hottie songwriter," Grant fills in the blanks for him.

"How do you know she's a hottie?" I ask.

"I have my sources," Grant says with a lift of his brow.

"So, that means Emerson must have seen her somewhere and given him the rundown," Grayson says about Grant's wife. "So, is she?"

I think back to the other night. The heat of her pussy with nothing separating us but a thin sheet. The way her nipples pressed against her tank top. She was warm and real and inviting when everything about my dream was cold and dark and debilitating.

I line up another nail on the two-by-four I'm holding over my head and pound it into place. "Aren't you assholes supposed to be helping me?"

My older brother chuckles as he takes a sip of his beer before rising to help. "He isn't answering, Gray. You know what that means."

Grayson chuckles as I swing the hammer, and I know what's coming next. "He likes her."

Yep. Had that one right.

"I do not like her." I take my frustration with them out on the nail.

"So she isn't hot?" Grant asks, pushing my buttons when they're already pressed after a few nights of restless sleep.

"That's not what I said."

"So . . . are you getting any yet?" he eggs on.

"Asks the man who probably isn't getting any since he tied on the old ball and chain." I chuckle and step back to grab the next piece of wood Grayson has cut for me on the table saw.

"I have no clue what you're talking about." Grant smirks a cat-ate-the-canary grin as if he's remembering something I don't want to imagine him remembering. "It's only gotten better since the wedding, so no complaints here."

"Dude, she's pregnant," I add.

"So? She's still hot and everything still works the same. *Duh.*"

"He's still punch-drunk on love." Grayson rolls his eyes and sticks a finger down his throat like he used to do when we were little, and I laugh. "Seriously . . . how is she?"

I glance to Dylan's bedroom window and think of the string of music that was coming from behind her closed door earlier. The guitar playing the same chords over and over, her muted voice barely making its way through the cracks. The oddly comforting rhythm of start, stop, repeat.

"She keeps to herself mostly," I say as I flip the top of a fresh beer off and let the taste cool me off.

"She's a songwriter?"

"Yeah," I say with a shake of my head, still trying to wrap my head around her lyrics. "For Jett Kroger."

"No shit," Grayson says, but I don't elaborate on their situation. "So?" He draws the word out.

"No. God. No." I say the words a little too quickly as if I'm trying to convince myself that's how I feel.

"She's that bad?" Grant asks as he looks toward the house.

I picture her standing with her hands holding her robe closed and that shy smile on her face. The woman has an amazing body but is so damn afraid to own it. Such a contrast from the others I've dated who use it to their every advantage.

It's refreshing. And kind of a turn-on since I finally got a peek of just how hot those curves are.

"No. Not at all. She's pretty. Sexy more than pretty. She's just quiet and reserved. Not my type at all."

"As opposed to open and willing?" Grayson asks then chokes on his own laughter.

"Fuck off. This coming from the serial dater."

"Like you're one to talk. I heard Mallory stopped by your place on her way through town," Grant says and smirks.

"Jesus Christ. Do you guys have cameras watching me?" I flip my brothers off and shake my head but know I'll talk anyway. "Yeah. You know Mal—"

"A guaranteed good time so long as that time only lasts less than twenty-four hours."

"Those are her terms, not mine." *Glitter-dress girl.* I hear Dylan say the words and smile.

"Must be tough having someone want no strings, no rings, and just your ding," Grayson says as we all start laughing.

"What are you?" Grant asks throwing his bottle cap at him. "Twelve?"

"Some days," I mutter as I swing the hammer again and secure the crossbeam on the outdoor room I'm building. "Dylan's cool. She doesn't get in the way. She's more than easy on the eyes. She grocery shops."

"Sexy and domestic. *Damn*."

"Yes. Happy? Now, can you stop being so damn annoying?"

Grant smirks in victory. "Never. It's my job as the oldest to keep you in check."

I mark the next board with my yellow chalk to show Grayson where to cut it. "Do you think Mom's going to be pissed we bailed on Sunday dinner?" I ask to try and change the topic off Dylan. Last thing I need is for her to open her window and hear us talking about her and sex . . . especially when she knows damn well my dick hardened when she was on top of me.

"Nah. She was cool with it. She said it was too hot to cook so she's taking Luke to the movies for Nana time instead," Grayson says referring to his son.

"Maybe she's the smart one and we're the dumb ones sitting out here in this heat. It's fucking hotter than hell. I thought it was supposed to be a mild summer," I gripe as I pull at my shirt where it sticks to my skin.

"Take your shirt off, then," Grayson says right before the whir of the saw begins and then ends.

I ignore his comment, hating that it still bugs me when it shouldn't, and grab the beam a little more forcefully than he deserves. "Help me hold this, will ya?" I ask Grant, but he just stands there and stares at me like I'm about to get a big brotherly lecture I'm not in the mood to hear. "Don't start this shit. It's been a rough couple of days, okay?"

"You having dreams again?" Grayson asks while Grant's eyes remain locked on mine.

"I'm good." I shrug off his stare and walk to the farthest end of the concrete pad to ignore the shit he wants to address. I want to be left the fuck alone.

"Then take your shirt off. Show the two of us up with your definition since I know you've been lifting like a son of a bitch at the gym at all hours of the night."

Goddamn small town.

"So what? I can't sleep, so I go and lift. Is there a problem with that? It's better than going out and drinking like I desperately want to some nights."

"True. It might heal the scars in your head but—"

"But what?" I snap at him, hands fisted, temper tested. "*Not the ones on my back*?"

"Do you think I give a flying fuck about the ones on your back? I've seen your ugly ass more times than I care to count. Even parts of you I need a microscope to see," he says for the laugh, but I don't feel like smiling. "Do you think it bugs me what your scars look like? Do you think I'm going to look at you differently or love you any less? It's the ones in your head I worry about, you stubborn asshole. Take your shirt off, keep it on, it doesn't fucking matter. What does is that you know none of it's going to get better until you realize the only thing we fucking care about is that you're here and whole. Got it?"

I stare at Grant, jaw clenched against the shit in my head I don't want to think about. Drew. Shelby. Brody. The sleeping pills I've been taking again just to keep my head above the water. The exhaustion from trying to pretend like everything is normal. I nod my head ever so slightly, letting him know I've heard him but not wanting to talk about it right now.

I don't think I'll ever be able to.

"Keep your shirt on, Grady. At least that way I'll get a chance with the ladies," Grayson says, always the one to play moderator.

Fuck that.

"You happy?" I yank my shirt off over my head, hating the immediate urge to turn my back from them so they can't look, and swallow down the churning in my gut.

"Not anything we haven't seen before," Grant says as he turns to grab his beer without a stutter in his stare.

Christ. Why does it bug me so much? These are my goddamn brothers.

And yet, it still does.

"Are you guys going to help me, or are you going to stand there with your dicks in your hands all day?" Anything to shift the topic. To get the look on Shelby's face and the request she made when I saw her at the station earlier this week out of my head.

"Says the guy who strokes hoses all day long for a living," Grant says with a laugh.

"If firefighting was easy, cops would do it," I reply and dodge the roll of duct tape he throws at me.

"Fucker," he mutters but sets down his beer and picks up a hammer.

It's about fucking time.

This room isn't going to build itself.

SIX

Dylan

LORD, HAVE MERCY.

To think I've been in my room this whole time, struggling with lyrics when all of this has been sitting outside my window.

Three stunningly handsome men. All with brown hair. All with the same build. All with the same mannerisms. Grady mentioned he had a brother who was a cop, but he didn't tell me there was a third.

Who would turn down a Malone sandwich like that?

I feel like I've just walked in on a Diet Coke commercial. Three shirtless men with carpenter belts on, a sheen of sweat on their skin, and grins on their faces.

If that isn't one of the best distractions from writer's block, I'm not sure what is. Or to keep tucked away for a memory during ménage à moi time. But now the problem is how in the hell do I pull my eyes away from the visual and back to lyrics about anger and heartbreak?

Get back to work, Dyl. Finish writing the song and strike one more off the list of twenty tracks. One more link broken in the chain tying me to Jett.

Their laughter floats in the open window above the cadence of the hammer and pulls my eyes to admire the sight one more time.

And that's when I see them. The angry red lines marring Grady's back. He's too far away for me to make out how bad they are, but they're enough to give me pause, to make me wonder if they have anything to do with the nightmares I heard him fighting off.

I stare longer than I should, curious and jealous of the ease between the three of them. Even when they seem like they are razzing each other, there is a light-hearted nature that bespeaks of affection.

Back to work.

After one more look.

It's when I pull my guitar onto my lap that I realize I was so blinded by the sexiness outside, I forgot the one reason I had gotten up, to get sustenance. A soda. Licorice. And some grapes to add to my other two essential food groups: carbonation and sugar.

Preoccupied with a text on my phone from my agent, I walk into the kitchen and suck in a breath when I come face to back with Grady. He's standing with his hand on the refrigerator door, head leaned inside, and his back fully exposed to me. It's broad and strong and scarred immeasurably.

I stare.

I can't help it. The marks are a dizzying array of dark and light and ridged and smooth. Horrific burns. Goosebumps chase over my skin as I imagine the pain he must have endured when he got those. I think of his habit of wearing unbuttoned shirts but never going shirtless and the hint of scars just visible above his collar that I never could have imagined led to this roadmap to hell on his back.

A part of me instinctively wants to reach out to touch them, bring some kind of comfort. It sounds ridiculous, even to me, but that doesn't abate the urge.

"Not pretty, huh? Get a good look while you can." His voice is gruff as his spine stiffens and body stills, emotion woven through the words.

"Thank God not all of you is pretty. I was beginning to feel majorly insecure having to live with perfection like you," I say off the cuff, trying to make this situation less awkward. My attempt to settle the sudden tension sparking in the air around us.

"Perfection?" he asks as he turns to face me with a smile that masks the emotion swirling in his eyes.

"Yeah. You have scars. I have mermaid thighs."

"Mermaid thighs?" He laughs. "What in the world are you talking about?"

"Thighs that touch from the top all the way to my knees." I shrug as if it doesn't bug me, as if I'm not highlighting one of the insults Tara threw at me. It's a whole lot easier to make fun of myself so long as it puts him at ease.

"Do you ever give yourself a break?"

"*Do you*?" I ask the question, sparking a silent battle of wills as we stare at each other and wonder what to say next about the other's insecurities. Coming up empty, I shift gears. "I think there is some type of rule about how many abs are fair for a guy to have when the rest of us are just struggling to find one of them."

His smile rings more genuine as he steps toward me, and I step back, my hips leaning against the counter now.

"Is that so?" His voice lowers as his eyes flick to my lips and then back up. "I'm sure you have some under your shirt there."

Why does the simple action make it seem so hard to swallow?

He takes another step.

"What are you building outside?"

"A playroom."

A nervous chuckle falls from my lips as I think of all of the versions of playrooms I've read about in my romance books. My cheeks stain red as I imagine Grady with a flogger in one hand standing beside a St. Andrew's Cross.

"A playroom?"

"Yeah." He takes a step closer so we're breathing the same air, his voice husky enough to cause every part of my body to grow alert. "A playroom. You know . . . a pool table. Foosball. A real man cave."

I exhale a shaky sigh, suddenly more than aware that he's so close, shirtless, sweaty, and smelling like sun and soap mixed together. But it's his eyes that make my thoughts falter. There's an intensity to them I don't expect from the perpetually cheerful Grady Malone.

"Ah, that kind of playroom . . ." But my words trail off as he steps even closer and braces his hands on the counter on either side of my hips. I can hear his intake of breath. The music floating in from outside. The pound of my pulse in my ears.

"Hey, Dyl?"

"Yes?" Our eyes hold, my lips fall lax.

"I need you to open up."

"*What*?" I question as his hand brushes against my hip and his fingers pull on the drawer handle I'm standing in front of.

"I need the bottle opener. You're standing in front of the drawer it's in." His lips spread into a full-fledged grin as I scramble away from the counter and, of course, run smack dab into the hardness, all six foot plus of him.

And then I rebound off him again in a flustered state that has him laughing and me stuttering. "Sorry. I wasn't—I didn't . . ." His arms hold on to my biceps to steady me, which prompts me to look up and meet his eyes.

"We need to stop meeting like this," he murmurs, the heat of his breath hitting my lips.

"We do." *Brilliant, Dylan. Freaking brilliant response.* "I've gotta . . . I've gotta get back to . . . to writing."

"Okay," he says, that lopsided grin deepening and forcing his dimples to spark to life. Still, his hands remain where they are just as my feet do.

"What's the holdup, Grady?" The words come seconds before feet clomp on the hardwood floor and then fall silent.

We shock apart as if burned by lightning. "I was just leaving." I'm met with an expression so similar to Grady's that the two may as well be twins.

"Not so fast." He walks into the kitchen as Grady opens the drawer behind me and grabs the bottle opener. "Grant Malone. Nice to meet you."

He extends a hand, which I shake. "Dylan McCoy."

"You look like your brother," he says.

I quirk an eyebrow. "Well . . ."

"Not like that." He laughs when he realizes telling me I look like a guy isn't exactly flattering. "I just meant coloring, expressions, and . . . okay, I'll stick my foot in my mouth now."

"No, it's okay. I know what you mean. How do you know him?"

"We had a boys' trip a few years back."

"Oh. Okay. Well, it's nice to meet you." Grant looks at Grady and then back to me as awkwardness settles into the room.

My cell rings.

It's loud and echoes off the granite countertops of the kitchen and from the ring alone I know who it is.

Jett.

My eyes flash to Grady's as if I've been caught doing something I shouldn't be when there's no reason to feel that way at all.

He lifts his eyebrows as the ring sounds again, but I make no attempt to answer it.

"Don't you need to get that?" he asks with a casual glance to the illuminated phone screen where I'm certain Jett's name is plastered across the front of it. He looks back to me and lifts his eyebrows. "It might be important."

I'm not sure why I feel like I'm being challenged to see if I'll answer or not, so I stare at Grady, my own eyebrows raised to match his as my cell rings one more time before it goes to voicemail.

"Huh," he murmurs.

"Huh," I reply.

"Sure is a lot of huh'ing going on around here," Grant says from where he stands in the doorway causing me to laugh nervously.

"I've gotta get back to writing songs about love gone wrong," I finally say.

"Don't forget to call Jett back," Grady says as he grabs my cell off the counter and holds it out to me.

A part of me doesn't want to take it. I want him to think I'm stronger than I am and that I'm not the least bit curious why Jett is calling me. I want him to think better of me than I do myself right now.

"Yeah, sure," I reply and grab my phone from him. "You guys go have fun pounding your wood or something."

"*Or something*," Grady murmurs as his eyes meet mine one last time before I leave the room.

My mind's still on him.

On how that's twice in the past couple days he's deferred to his sexuality to avoid talking about whatever plagues him.

The bad dream and his nakedness the other night.

His scars and the flirting today.

There's definitely something beneath the sexiness of Grady Malone.

Question is, do I want to get invested enough to find out what?

I'm reminded of the feel of his body against mine, which tells me I'm already invested. I think that happened the first morning I met him.

Grant and Grady laugh at something in the kitchen before the door slams and their voices carry outside.

And I'm left contemplating the contradiction that is Grady Malone.

SEVEN

Dylan

THE KNOCK ON THE DOOR COMES MOMENTS BEFORE THE handle pushes open, and Grady stands on the threshold staring at me.

"How's it going?" His voice is quiet as if he's afraid he's intruding.

I look up from where I'm sitting on the floor, my guitar resting on my lap and several pads of paper in front of me. He looks fresh from the shower and is wearing a pair of khaki shorts and a blue Sunnyville Fire Department shirt, which makes his eyes look like they are translucent.

"It's going." I sigh. "Slower today than others, but I've had some distractions."

Like you.

"Petunia and I were about to have a BLT, do you want one?"

"There are so many things wrong with that statement I don't even know where to start." I laugh.

"Can't protect the children from the world's tough reality all the time, now can we? It would be a disservice to them." I shake my head all the while loving the humor lighting up his eyes. "So yes, no, I don't ever eat, I'm still on that hunger strike . . . what'll it be?"

Glancing around at the crumpled pieces of notebook paper strewn around me, and the nearly blank pages in front of me, I heave a silent sigh. If I take a break for a bit and get some fresh air, it isn't as if it will impede my nonexistent creative process right now.

"Sure."

His smile lights up his face and makes me feel good. At least I can make one person happy. "I'll give you a minute to get ready."

"Get ready?"

"It's Farmers' Market Thursday."

It's Thursday?

Wow. I guess the past few days filled with little sleep and even less creativity have melded together. I definitely need to get out.

"Oh."

"Yes, and it's four in the afternoon." He shakes his head as if he's worried about me. "You need to get out more."

"I guess I do." I roll my shoulders. "And you go there to get BLTs?"

"I do, yes, but Petunia passes on the sandwich." He glances toward where she is rooting around. "We always go when I'm not on shift."

"Your pig is your date?"

"No." He lowers his voice. "She thinks she is, but we don't want to hurt her feelings. Burnt bacon is never a good thing."

And lucky for Petunia's feelings, they're fresh out of bacon at the BLT stand when we get there, so Grady and I opt for corn dogs and French fries to eat while we walk around.

"I finally got you out of the house," he says as he holds out the container of fries to me.

"I've left before."

"When?"

"When we had breakfast. Then, the other day, I went to the store, and last night, I went for a walk. I've ventured," I say, feeling like an idiot having to admit that's about all I've done since I've moved here.

"Living the high life, are we?" he teases, and the smile comes easily to my lips.

I glance at him, and he meets my eyes, a soft smile on his own face as we stroll through the crowded downtown district of Sunnyville with a pig walking begrudgingly on a leash between us.

Something stirs in my belly, and I push it away. The kind of stir full of equal parts giddy, hopeful, and lustful that you feel when you realize you would be more than okay if the man took an interest in you.

Not here. Not now. Not a rebound.

A rebound, Dylan? Like he's even offering.

And if he were to, it isn't as if I would even be in the right mindset to acquiesce. Sure, his smile warms my insides while the sight of his body heats between my thighs, but c'mon, after seeing glitter-dress girl, it's very doubtful he'd want anything to do with me, the antithesis of everything she is.

I glance his way as he smiles at a little kid who stops to pet Petunia, and I shake my head. Someone would have to seriously have a screw loose not to think he's attractive. Not to be attracted to him.

But then again, I probably have more than one screw loose since I'm standing here in the middle of a farmers' market, debating whether I'd allow something to happen between us when that something is nonexistent in the first place.

"Do you know everyone here?" I ask as yet another person calls out his name and waves to him.

"Not hardly. But it helps that I'm Chief Malone's son. Growing up, everyone wanted to know me because they had this notion that if they got in trouble, being my friend would have made it easier. Like my dad would've given them a free pass if they said they knew me. Plus, it doesn't hurt that everyone loves Petunia."

"So, that's how you reel the ladies in then."

"If that were my game, I'd definitely need more help." He laughs at himself and nods in greeting to another person waving from afar.

"I doubt you need any help with your game or the ladies."

"Oh yes, me and my eight abs." His laughter fades as his attention catches on something in the crowd ahead. I can't see who or what it is, but the lines on his face deepen with concern. "Can you hold Petunia for a minute? I need to go talk to someone."

"Sure." I watch him jog through the crowd and refuse to admit that I'm being nosy when I shift my feet so I can get a better view of where he's heading.

About the time I get a clear line of sight, Grady is dropping to his knees and letting a little boy—I'd say around four or five—tackle hug him so that he falls back onto the grass beneath them. Grady wraps his arms around the child and presses a kiss to the top of his shaggy brown hair. I can't help but smile at the connection between the two, but then my gaze is pulled to the woman standing there watching.

She's petite, pretty from what I can tell, and is standing with her arms crossed over her chest, almost as if she's guarding herself.

Something in my chest clutches at the visual, and my mind begins to whirl. A little boy thrilled to see Grady, the woman he's with not so much. Her expression reflects a sadness that's almost palpable, and it wears on me despite the distance between us.

Is Grady divorced? Is that his son? Is this the "a lot" Grady had been through that my brother refused to expand on?

I don't know why the idea of Grady being a dad has me so confused. Is it any of my business? No. Should it matter? No. Maybe it's that I'm hurt that he didn't tell me.

Or is it that I thought better of him than my dad, the only other firefighter I've known, and now I see that he isn't. If he's a father, how come he hasn't mentioned his son to me? How come he has zero pictures on the bookshelves or walls? Is it because he doesn't want to claim his child like my dad didn't want to claim us? Is it because it's hard to seduce a woman when you take her back to your place and she sees you have a kid and all the baggage that comes with one?

Memories, moments, shame—they all flood back as I watch the emotional exchange between the three of them. The baseless resentment bubbles up, still as strong as it's always been.

I'm jumping to conclusions. I'm being sensitive and letting my past and my current emotional upheaval make speculative assumptions.

I'll just ask him. It's that easy. Decision made, I stand in the middle of the farmers' market between a stall selling organic produce and one selling cheap sunglasses and hate that Grady is the same type of guy I had as a father.

My heart wrenches for the little boy, who is so desperate for Grady's attention that I have to avert my focus so I don't choke up. I turn to a newsstand, pluck the first magazine I put my hand on, and start to flip through the pages. My mind registers that it's *Rolling Stone* a split second before Petunia tugs on her leash.

"Sorry about that," Grady's voice invades my thoughts and simultaneously strikes a nerve.

"Who was that?" I ask, trying to sound casual.

"Who?" He looks over his shoulder where the lady and her little boy were and turns back to me with a pained look on his face. "That was no one," he says and effectively shatters the notion of him being a good guy. He's *exactly* like my father.

Despite knowing it's none of my business, every part of me sags in disappointment, and I have to take a minute to come to terms with the riotous and unfounded feelings bouncing around inside me.

Of course, being reminded of one man who hurt me isn't enough, because life decides to slap me in the face with the other.

There in full color between the pages of *Rolling Stone* is Jett. The bad boy of rock is in a dress shirt, tie, vest, and slacks, looking every bit the part of everything he isn't. His handsome face stares back at me, wearing that cocky smirk of his and I'm-a-rock-god expression.

My heart aches.

I know I should close the magazine, put it back, and walk away, but my eyes wander and roam over the interview. Skimming the questions about his upcoming album. About his home life and long-time girlfriend. Where she fits in his everyday, and how she gets him when it seems no one else does. About how he sees a good thing in his girlfriend and would never purposely screw it up, although he unintentionally has many times before. I scan his answers and then read them again, slower this time.

He's talking directly to me. The dichotomy of it all makes my head spin. On one hand, he's in *Rolling Stone* apologizing to me, and on the other hand, he's saying everything I needed to hear before. Everything he negated to utter when he screwed Tara-perfect-tits.

"Dylan? Everything okay?"

I hear his question, but by the time his words register, he's taking the magazine from my hand.

"Christ," he mutters as he scans the article before looking up to meet my eyes. There's concern in his, compassion, and the sight of it from a man I'm currently mad at has me fighting back tears. "I'm sorry. Just when you need someone to be nowhere, they're everywhere. Let's get out of here. We need to drop Petunia at home, and then I know the perfect place to go."

"Why are we here drinking again?" I laugh as I tap my glass to his for what feels like the twentieth time.

"Because your boyfriend's an asshole and because I'm . . . because I need it too."

I stare at him as he tosses back the amber liquid, and the sights and sounds of the bar buzz around us. He doesn't give me more than that, and I accept it without prying further.

"You want to tell me why Jett was speaking about you as if you were still together?"

I sigh and finish off my drink. "Our agent wants us to keep our split under wraps."

"You have the same agent?"

"Yeah." I snort. It sounded good at the time to have the same one. I can only hope that's still the case once this project is done.

"Why would they want you to keep quiet?" He looks as confused as I felt when Ava made the request.

"While Jett's bad-boy reputation may play well with his audience, the label isn't too fond of it."

"Why do they care so long as he sells albums?"

"Selling albums is one thing. Being manageable is a whole other matter. Jett is *far* from manageable. When an artist has a hard time recording an album, let alone promoting it, because his antics get in the way, it's a problem." I sigh. "Temper tantrums where he's trashed the studio when a song isn't working. Refusing to show up and record a song because I'm not in town to be there. It's just—"

"He sounds like a real winner, Dylan."

I glare at him, feeling like I'm being judged while justifying in my mind that he doesn't know Jett like I do. He doesn't understand him. And then I roll my eyes at myself. *How stupid does that even sound*?

"There's a part of him that's all image. Then there's the guy he was before he hit it big."

"Uh-huh." He doesn't sound convinced. "So where do you fit in all of this? Why does your agent need you to keep up the charade?"

"Because I was told I 'soften' his image. I'm the only one who *tames him*. The label knows I'll deliver. The producer will work with me, not Jett. Ava fears that if they know we've split, they're going to delay or table the album like they threatened to from the get-go."

"So let them table the album. Maybe he deserves to be taught a lesson," Grady says, giving the most logical commentary .

"I'm not sure anything will change him. It's obvious he hasn't learned from any of the repercussions he's faced before, but when he's punished, I'm punished. Tabling the album would damage my career and livelihood too."

"How so? It's not your fault he's unmanageable."

I think of the contract Ava constantly reminds me about. I think of the billing statement in my inbox from the rehab center. I think of this surreal bubble bursting that I've actually made it in this business when Jett fucks up and the album isn't delivered on time.

But I don't say any of those things. Instead, I toy with the edge of my cocktail napkin and refuse to meet his eyes.

"You know you don't owe him anything after what he did to you, right?"

"You're right. I don't." I mentally shake myself from my thoughts. "I sound like a doormat agreeing to our agent's request, but I assure you, I'm not."

"You're the furthest thing from being a doormat, and yet . . ." He lifts his eyebrows as if he's disappointed in me. It's a look so very similar to one my brother would give that it has my back straightening.

"Look, I'm not proud that I misjudged him. I'm not proud that I agreed to pretend to still be with him." I take a sip of water before I look up to meet his eyes. "What I am proud of is that I'm a damn good songwriter, and I have the reputation to match it. I'm proud the label knows it can depend on me to deliver the songs it asks for, quality songs, as well as songs for their other artists. The last thing I want to do is jeopardize that relationship because of Jett. I'm between a rock and a hard place, and the only way to survive is to try to climb up using the only hand I have extended to me. Swallow my pride and pretend for a little while, so in the end, I'm the one who wins. I come out with songs that will net me royalties, and I get to keep the door open to keep my career going beyond him."

He stares at me for a beat, and the intensity of those aqua eyes bearing down on me makes me shift in my seat.

"You finish the album with Jett, then what?"

"Long-term? I sell songs to other singers. I make a name for myself beyond Jett's cowriter." I shrug. "But for now I need to get through this current mess."

"And you think you can do that and come out the other side unscathed?"

I angle my head and stare at him, hating being questioned but knowing it's a valid point. "I can play the game that needs to be played while at the same time protecting my heart. But it doesn't make seeing the things he said in that interview any easier. All the things he never said to my face but that I needed to hear."

"I'm sure it's brutal."

"It's hard not to feel like a coward for heading for the hills, but I couldn't stay."

"Nah. I get it. You gravitate to comfort. To what's familiar . . . even when that familiar has done you wrong and is now saying all the right things."

"Hmm. True."

"Did you fear you'd get back together with him if you stayed?" Grady asks the question I've asked myself a million times. When Jett calls. When he texts. When he's mentioned on the radio.

Because I've taken him back before. Not for cheating though . . . this time was a first. *That I know of.*

"It isn't something I'd admit aloud because feminists would be in an uproar . . . but, yes."

"At least you're honest. So many people say they wouldn't put up with it but then end up taking the person back. Hell, I've done it."

His admission takes me by surprise, but I appreciate that he's trying to put me at ease with my decisions. "You know what the best way to get over someone is, don't you?"

"Drink?" I ask and laugh as I hold up my empty glass.

"That's a start, but no." A mischievous smile curls up the corners of his lips and his eyes fill with amusement. "Sleep with someone else."

His eyes hold mine as my mind spins. Is he offering to be *the* someone else? Is he feeling okay? Is he . . . *holy shit.*

"Wh-what?" I stutter the word out as embarrassment floods my cheeks. "Are you—?"

"There are plenty of guys in here who wouldn't hesitate to spend the night with you."

Thank God he cut me off. Thank God he just saved me the embarrassment of asking if he was offering.

It has to be the alcohol making my brain fuzzy.

"C'mon, Dyl. What would it hurt? You have some fun, clear your head for a bit, and realize there are other guys besides Jett Kroger who want you and think you're attractive."

"We're in a bar with a few dozen drunk men. I don't think my looks factor into anything after a certain number of drinks have been consumed." But I laugh at the notion anyway. "Besides, you're crazy if you think I'm going to pick up some random guy and take him home with me. Like that's safe."

"First off, it's *my* home, so no need to worry about your safety.

Remember? Chief Malone's son, here. And secondly, he wouldn't be a random guy. I know everyone around here, so I'll make sure he's a good fit."

"A good fit?" I laugh.

"Yeah. Someone who's not clingy. Who's not a dick—"

"This sounds so promising already."

"A guy I don't have to worry about being—"

"You're actually serious, aren't you?" I ask as he stands some from his seat and cranes his neck to survey the patrons of the bar.

"I never joke about getting laid." He laughs while all I want to do is shrink in my seat and vanish.

"I have to keep up pretenses that Jett and I—"

"Fuck Jett." He rolls his shoulders. "This is a small town. No one's even talking about Jett being here so that means he's keeping a low profile. And his low profile means that no one has connected the dots that the two of you are together. Or rather, *not* together."

"This is a bad idea," I groan.

"You didn't say no." He stares at me, eyes alive.

"Fine."

"Fine?" he asks as he scans the crowd.

"No firefighters," I say, prompting him to whip his head my way.

"What's wrong with firefighters?" he asks. If I could kick myself under the table I would.

It's a one-night stand, Dylan. One. Night. It isn't as if I need to worry about them staying around long-term. It isn't as if I have to worry about them leaving like my dad.

His eyes narrow, and the look he gives me demands an answer. "No firefighters," I reply and lift my eyebrows as if to say that's the only explanation I'm going to give him. "You're crazy, you know that?"

"And you are *so* getting laid."

EIGHT

Grady

SLEEP WITH SOMEONE.

Did I actually encourage her to get laid?

Christ, I'm sure Damon would chew me out if he knew what I did tonight. What I encouraged.

But Wes Winters isn't all that bad. I can think of worse guys for her to sleep with. Besides, he's nice and polite and not the kind to stick around.

So, he's perfect.

But fuck if I'm not questioning why I suggested this. Why I called him over and initiated small talk between them. Bought them a round or two of drinks and then subtly made my exit.

The front door bounces back followed by a giggle and a laugh. There is a trail of thumps of body parts hitting walls as they make their way down the hallway.

Her door shuts, but I can still hear her.

Giggles turn to moans.

And dear fucking god. Those moans. *Her moans.*

Throaty and sexy and . . .

They're enough to make me hard instantly.

Yeah, I'm definitely questioning why I did this.

And even more so, I'm questioning why my dick is in my hand and my thoughts are on Dylan and how she felt straddling me the other night. The hazy look in her eyes. The weight of her tits against the fabric of her shirt.

She's moaning for someone else, and fuck if I'm not pretending she's moaning for me.

The taste of her. The wine on her tongue. The buds of her nipples against my lips. Licking my way up her inner thigh.

I work my hand up my cock. Rub it over the head. Tighten my fingers and slide it back down.

Imagining her.

The heat of her tongue as those blow-job lips of hers wrap around me. Tease me. Taunt me. Suck me dry.

I squeeze the base of my shaft and work my hand up and down. Listening to her moans. Audible sex. I work myself so precum drips off the tip, and I use it as lube.

The pink of her pussy. How tight it is. How wet I make her. How she stretches around me as I pull out and then plunge back in.

Faster. Heat and pleasure. Harder. Friction and desire. Over and over.

The tense of her thighs around my hips. The scratch of her nails down my back. Her arousal coating my cock and dripping down my balls as I bury myself in her over. And over. And over.

I close my eyes and throw my head back against my pillow as my legs tense and my body begs to come.

The pulse of her muscles as her pussy comes around me.

And only for me.

Heat surges through me. Out to my fingers. Then slams back into me as my head grows dizzy and I come all over my hand, a groan on my lips.

Jesus Christ, I'm going to hell.

I just jacked off thinking of Dylan.

My roommate.

Damon's little sister.

But fuck if she wasn't incredible.

NINE

Dylan

I STARE AT THE CEILING OF MY BEDROOM AND A TEAR LEAKS silently out of the corner of my eye. I can feel as it makes its way through my hair and onto the pillow beneath my head.

Last night replays in my mind. The good, the bad, the ugly of it. Each thought reinforcing the insecurities riddling my self-esteem.

Wes's rushed goodbye.

The shame that followed.

The embarrassment I feel as I wait for Grady to leave the house for whatever plans he has today.

The clink of the dish in the sink.

The slam of the front door.

The sound of his engine shifting into gear and slowly retreating down the driveway.

Drawing in a deep breath, I pick up my cell and dial.

"Serenity Acres, how may I direct your call?"

"Francis McCoy, please," I say.

"Let me check and make sure she's able to receive phone calls," the receptionist replies.

"She should be. She finished detox the other day." For the sixth or seventh time. Or is it the tenth? It's been so many I can't remember.

"Mmm, yes, and you are?"

"Dylan McCoy, her daughter."

"Yes, I have you on the list of approved contacts. Ms. McCoy, she's still in a very fragile place so please don't say or do anything that will upset her." *What about all she's said or done to upset me?* "She's allowed five minutes on the phone."

"Yes. I know."

"Hold, please. I'll connect you."

The electronic beep of a ring comes through the phone. One. Two. Three. "Hello." She sounds so frail.

"Hi, Momma."

"Dylan?" Her voice is cautious.

"How are you?"

"Miserable. Do you know what they do to you here? Detox is hell. Friggin' hell. And they try to pretty it up by using the term abstinence, but it's still the same damn thing. My hands shake and my mouth is dry, and I'd give anything for a drink right now. And—"

"You promised me you'd try." *Again.*

"I am, but you know it's your father's fault, right? I loved him but obviously not enough for him to love us back."

"I know, Mom."

"Do you have any idea what hell this place is? Do you . . ." She drones on, complaining about the same damn things she always does, never letting me get a word in edgewise until an electronic voice comes over the line.

"You have one more minute," it warns.

"Dylan, I'm sorry. How are you? I've been selfish, prattling on this whole time and I haven't asked a single thing about you." *Because alcoholism makes you selfish.* "How are you? Did you need me for anything?" she asks as a tear slides silently down my cheek.

"No. I just wanted to hear your voice is all," I say, trying to find comfort in her the only way I know how. In the only way this disease has allowed me to over the years.

"You're okay, then?" she asks when she's in no place to offer any kind of solace for my bruised ego.

"Yes," I whisper.

"I love you. I'll try harder."

"I love you too." *Please try harder.*

The line goes dead.

And this is what it comes down to. *Five minutes.* That's all I get. This seems to be all I can remember getting from her.

Me needing her when she still craves something else.

First it was my father.

Then it was the alcohol.

Maybe it's still my father she still craves.

I'm not sure. All I know is it has never been me.

Seems to me I always come in second place.

TEN

Grady

"ARE YOU AVOIDING ME, McCOY?"

My boots clomp on my wooden porch, and I take a seat beside her on one of the steps. She doesn't respond, and I don't push as I look at the progress on the playroom. It isn't pretty, but it's a work in progress.

She takes a sip of her coffee, and I bump my knee to hers to prompt a response out of her. "Not avoiding, no."

"I think you are. I didn't see you at all yesterday."

"I was writing." She says the words but there's an underlying tone. Something is bugging her.

"And you aren't talking to me now."

"I just said three words to you."

"You know what I mean." I take a sip of my coffee and turn the handheld radio in my bag down when dispatch begins to chatter. "So are we going to pretend that I didn't hear you bumping into walls the other night when you brought Wes home. Or giggling." *Or moaning.*

"No, it happened. Believe me, it happened," she murmurs, and a part of me is instantly pissed that Wes Winters was that good she's still thinking about him.

"That good, huh?" There's a bite to my tone when there shouldn't be.

Her laugh is unexpected when it rings out and the self-deprecating sound to it rubs me the wrong way.

"None of your business," she says with a playful smile that seems more forced than genuine.

"There's no need to be embarrassed," I say, trying to make her feel more at ease when I realize she's most likely not used to talking to other men about her sex life. At least, I hope she's not.

She splays her hands over her face for a second and shakes her head to try and clear the confused emotions from her expression. "No. I'm not—that isn't what—I've never done that before. You don't understand. Just . . . just never mind."

Well, at least I know Wes isn't a stallion in the sack.

"You've never had a one-night stand?" I try not to sound so surprised, but I don't think I pull it off.

"No. God. No."

"What's wrong with them?" I ask with a partial laugh, trying to figure out how she lives in the Hollywood fast lane and is still so damn innocent.

"Nothing. It was just . . . you know what? It's super weird discussing this with you."

At least I called that right—it was embarrassment—not anything else that had her shying away from me.

"Look, there's no use in regretting it. It was fun. It was one time. It was a way to get your mind off Jett the fuck face and back on you and your needs. There is no shame in it."

"Says the man who probably lives at the One-Night-Stand Café."

I pound my hand to my chest as if I'm clutching a dagger. "And she thinks so highly of me."

"You had another nightmare last night, didn't you?"

"You're changing the subject."

"And you're not answering," she counters with an impenetrable stare.

I shrug. "Not sure. I was asleep."

"Do you want to talk about it?"

Do I ever? No.

"If I did, I don't remember, so there isn't much to talk about."

"You were screaming for an Andrew. I think that was the name."

No. It's Drew.

"Huh. That's weird. I don't know any Andrews." I stand abruptly. "I've gotta get to the station."

After I take a few steps, she calls my name. When I turn around, there is a sympathetic look in her eyes and concern on her face. "Don't think I don't notice how you always change the subject when it circles back to you."

"I don't know what you're talking about." With that, I turn and walk to my truck without looking back.

I'm frozen.

Smoke billows out of the old warehouse, and all I can do is stand and stare. *And remember*. The crackle of the beams and the whooshing sound they made as they fell from above. The panic in Drew's screams. The smell of the burning wood and plastic . . . *and flesh*.

"Goddamn it, Malone!" Dempsey rips the line out of my hands and glares at me as if I've lost my mind. The problem is, I fear I have. And it isn't the first time. "We need you. Either engage or get out of the fucking way," he growls.

But I don't move. I feel like I don't even breathe. The smoke is gray and thick and ashes rain down on everything around us. Embers. Papers, half charred and glowing against the darkened sky, float around me like a ticker tape parade of disaster.

The guys from our engine and Swift City's are laying down pipe and breaching the building from the west side. A crew is on the front, breaking the windows to control the fire's fuel. Another crew is putting on their air packs to prepare for a second entry.

And I still stand here, frozen in memory, hearing the PASS sirens going off in my head when there are none sounding off around me.

Everyone is moving. No one is stuck in the fire. No one is trapped.

No one is dying.

"Malone! Malone!" I'm yanked from my trance, and Bowman is in my face demanding my attention. "Take command, until the chief comes, will ya?"

"What?" I shake my head, trying to figure out why he's giving up his command.

"Get to it, Malone."

And then I get it. He doesn't trust me. I'm out here, and they're in there, and he knows I still can't bring myself to step foot into the beast and get over the past. The fear. The bullshit weighing me down.

He looks at me, eyebrows raised, impatience in his expression. The figurative helping hand extended, yet again.

"Yeah. Sure. I've got it." I jog over to where he stands, momentarily snapped from the living hell in my memory and into the present one. I grab the clipboard and radio from him. "*Two-in. Two-out,*" I murmur without thinking.

His body jars from the words. From hearing the phrase Drew and I twisted to make our own.

Christ. I just proved his hunch right. That I'm thinking about Drew and what happened instead of the here and now. Instead of doing my job. That the memories are in fact what is holding me back.

He meets my eyes and nods as a slight smile curls his lips. "*Two-in. Two-out,*" he repeats before jogging toward danger, and as I start the personal accountability record for the guys on scene, I can't help but think of the last time I went in it was two-in. *One-out.*

Hours pass.

Each one marked by the charred contents of the building being gone over and over to make sure no hot spots flare up. The scene preserved for the arson detective to investigate the cause of the blaze.

"You want to tell me what happened earlier?"

I look to where Dixon stands with his fire hook prodding something, but he doesn't meet my eyes. He just keeps looking down, letting me at least keep my pride.

"Nothing did. I froze. It was no big deal."

"Sounds like burnout to me."

I don't flinch at the term now that I know his eyes are studying me. Waiting. Expecting. Questioning. "Nah. I'm good."

"You think I don't realize that you haven't actively participated in a fire since the accident?"

"What do you mean?" Fucking Christ. I roll my shoulders and turn my back to him to investigate a pretend stream of smoke that needs to be stomped out.

"I mean, there's always a reason, an excuse, or something keeping you from going into the flames. It's kind of hard to be a firefighter when you're afraid of fire, don't you think?"

"I'm not afraid of shit," I say as I turn back around and force a chuckle. "I had a shitty dream last night about a fire, and it felt like fucking déjà vu standing there. That's all."

"Is that what happens every time? Seems like a coincidence to me."

"Look, Dix, I get your point. I know where you're going here. The same place the other guys have gone. Were you the one elected this time to broach the subject? If so, thanks but no thanks. I'll say it again, I'm fine."

"We all lost him, Grady. You aren't the only one."

But I was the one who couldn't save him! I scream the words in my head but on the outside, I nod while my insides churn with a guilt no one understands. *It was my job to watch him and make sure he came out. But he never came out.*

"Yeah. I know."

ELEVEN

Grady

"THIS IS ONE HOT MOTHERFUCKER."

I look over to where Drew stands in the doorway, the flame's fingers licking all around him and smoke billowing like a son of a bitch above us and from the windows we've broken out. His voice sounds like it's in a tin can as it echoes in his helmet and then through my radio.

"We need to knock down that head over there and then get the fuck out of here."

"I've got a bad feeling about this, Malone."

I glance over to him again and wave my gloved hand his way. "We're fine. Hitch and Collins have the other side of this. Johnson's holding down the escape route."

"Are we sure this place is cleared?"

I can't see his face as I search through the smoke. "Why?"

"I swear I keep hearing someone calling for help."

I stop what I'm doing and hold up my fist to tell him to be quiet. And I listen. There's the crack of the fire. The snap of wood as it twists and pops under the pressure of the heat. The rush of the smoke as it pushes and pulls against the oxygen before devouring it. The roar of my own heartbeat in my ears.

But I don't hear anyone crying for help.

"I don't hear it, man."

I take my axe to break apart a pile of burning debris, trying to dissipate the fire's fuel. But it isn't going to help. This place isn't going to stop burning anytime soon.

"Listen."

I stop again at Drew's command, but the flames are closing in on us, roaring and spinning and whipping around in a vortex of heat I can feel through my turnouts.

For the life of me, I can't hear shit. There's a whistling somewhere, but I swear it's the oxygen sucking through wood.

When I turn around to look back at Drew, he's pushing deeper into the building. We should be getting the fuck out.

"Drew? Drew, c'mon. We gotta get out of here. We've been in here too long."

"Just let me look in here."

"Malone. Drew. We need to pull out. The roof's unstable," the chief commands over the radio.

"Goddamn it, Drew!" I move after him. My boots hitting debris I can't see. My eyes are straining from searching through the dense smoke, and I'm just clearing the doorway as I hear the crack.

A portion of the ceiling falls in and lands in front of me and at his back.

Panic flickers and flames just as brightly as the fire raging around us.

"Grady? Where are you?"

"I'm here. You okay?"

"I can't see you. I can't . . . shit . . . I can't find a clear line out." The same panic I feel laces the edge of his voice.

"I'm here. I'm here," I yell as my body heats with fear.

Another crack.

Then slam.

A beam falling.

A scream.

"Drew!" I shout. "Drew!"

Sweat coats my skin as I wait for an answer.

Seconds.

Tick.

Tick.

"I'm trapped." His voice is almost quiet. *Pained.* "I can't . . . I can't." *Fearful.* "Grady." *Terrified.*

"I'm here. I'm coming, Drew. I'm coming." Every part of my body shakes. Scared. Afraid.

Seconds feel like minutes. Minutes feel like hours. And neither of them are things we have.

"There's no way in. There's no . . . Fuck." His breath is labored. With fear. With exhaustion. With smoke. "I can't . . ."

"Don't you fucking give up on me. Don't you dare!" I scream and then radio back to dispatch that I need help. "Mayday. Mayday. Drew's down. He's trapped." I look back into the flames where I last saw him, but only see black. And orange. And yellow. I give our location in the building and then turn my attention back to my partner. "*Two-in. Two-out*, man. Get over here so we can go two out!" All I hear is his breath laboring through the intercom. "Get through a wall. Push back and swim through it. Goddamn it, Drew, answer me!"

Another crack of the ceiling. Another deluge of burning debris rains down on us.

"Grady!" His voice is packed with every kind of fear I've ever imagined in my life, and I can't do anything but cover my head and ward off the flames as they fall on me.

"Hold on! They're coming for us."

"My mask is cracked. I can't breathe."

Fuck. Fuck. Fuck.

"C'mon, Drew. Hold on." I take my axe and start hitting anything I can in a blind panic to try to get to him.

His gasps are in my ear. Each painful draw, coming more and more infrequently.

"Tell . . . tell Shelby I love her . . . tell her I'm sorry." Each word is labored exhaustion as the carbon monoxide drugs him. As the fire takes over.

"No!" I shout the word at the top of my lungs, as if it's going to help me get to him. "Chief, where the fuck are you guys?"

"Tell . . . tell Brody . . . I love him . . . promise me . . .Grady . . . you'll take care of him. Please."

"No! I won't. You tell him. They're coming for us, Drew. Any minute. Hold on. Hold the fuck on."

I try to pass through the fallen beams. I try to get to him. I try to save him.

"The whole west side is gone. We're breaching from the north." The chief's voice breaks through the panic ricocheting around inside me but does nothing to abate it.

There is a roar from Drew in my ears, and in that moment, I know it's a sound I'll never forget as long as I live.

If I live.

Because I'm not leaving him.

I can't leave him.

And then the siren starts. The PASS alarm that tells me he's no longer moving.

"Drew! Drew! Get up. Fight! Fucking—"

Crack.

I hear it before I feel it.

It's deafening.

The loudest sound I've ever heard.

There's a split second of pain. Of pressure. Of sparks.

There is sweat on my lips.

Or is it tears?

The Nomex of my jacket gives under the flames.

Two-in. Zero-out.

"No!" I wake up, bolting upright in my bed. My sheets are soaked with sweat. My room smells like fear. My back feels like it's still on fucking fire.

It takes me a moment to realize it was only a dream.

But it'll never be a dream.

It was a nightmare.

A fucking night terror that never ends.

Especially when I have to look into Brody's eyes and try to hide the guilt of not saving his dad that is rotting me from the inside.

That I didn't do the job I'm tasked to do daily.

Save lives.

What kind of firefighter am I when I can't save anyone, not even myself?

I throw on some shorts and head toward the kitchen. To the bottle of whiskey that is becoming way too comfortable in my hands, but fuck if I don't need it to get through some of these nights.

Bracing my hands on the kitchen counter, I look out the window to the half-built playroom. How stupid was I to think building a place for Brody to come and hang out someday would be enough to teach him what it's like to be a man? After everything my parents have done for me, taught me, how did I ever think that would be enough?

And yet, when I pick up that hammer, I feel like I'm doing something instead of doing nothing. Like I'm trying, when every fucking time I look at Brody, my goddamn heart breaks in my chest from the guilt weighing it down.

Because I couldn't save his dad.

It's after my second refill—the burn chasing away the cobwebs of memory—that I hear Dylan's voice through her closed door.

It's soft. It's haunting. It sounds just like how I feel. When she adds her guitar to the words, I sink down into the couch to listen.

To lyrics about loss. Hers are about losing love but they're so fitting to where my thoughts are after my dream. They make me feel less alone. Almost as if she understands.

And I fall back asleep to the sound of her voice and the comfort she oddly brings.

TWELVE

Dylan

I PLAY THE SAME SET OF CHORDS OVER AND OVER, MAKING MINUTE adjustments with each strum to see which one works best with my lyrics.

"We drive into the dark.

Crash into the wall.

How do we find our way back from this endless free fall?"

I write down notes as I go on my three pads in front of me: one for the music, one for the lyrics, and one for anything else that comes into my mind that doesn't work for this song but might work for another.

I move my fingers on the neck of the guitar and start to sing again. Just as the first line passes my lips, it dies off when I look up to see Grady standing and watching me from the doorway.

Did I forget to shut it?

"Hey." His voice is quiet, his smile is soft, and there is sadness in his eyes when they meet mine. Or maybe it's exhaustion. I can't tell.

"Hey. I'm sorry. I didn't realize you were home or I would have shut the door. Did I wake you?"

"No, you're fine. I got home a while ago. I had some stuff to take care of after my shift." He takes a step into my room, and once he's in the light, I can see how tired he is. It's in his posture. His expression. He's spent.

My mind whirls back to the little boy from the other day at the farmers' market. Was that where he was? Why is he so secretive about it?

"*He's had a rough go of it lately.*" I hear my brother's words and bite my tongue to keep from outright asking him about the child and overstepping my boundaries.

"Did you have a good shift? Hopefully, it was uneventful."

He shakes his head as if he's mulling over the answer. "A house fire that burned itself out before we got there. Some medical assist calls. Nothing much."

His words are simple enough, dismissive even, but there is something that has me taking note. "Everything okay?"

His expression—part confusion, part conflict, part uncertainty—tugs on every part of me that wants to fix whatever is wrong. "Yeah. Just . . . I went to the gym for a while to deal with it. Came home. Fell asleep exhausted, but now I can't sleep at all." He steps farther into the room, and I set the guitar down. "Don't stop because of me."

"What do you mean?"

"There's something comforting about listening to you sing as you work through lyrics. I can't really hear through the door, but I know you're singing," he explains, throwing me for a loop and making me suddenly self-conscious. "You have an incredible voice. Why aren't you the one who sings?"

He moves to sit on the bed beside me, and for some reason, it causes the nerves to jitter inside me. "Because I don't like the limelight. The attention."

"Don't like it or don't want it?" He pokes my leg to prompt me to lift my head and meet his eyes.

"Aren't they the same thing?"

"Not hardly. If you don't like it, you don't like it. It isn't your thing. If you don't want it, it's because you know you're good enough to sing but you don't believe in yourself enough to take the chance." He lifts his eyebrows as if to ask me which one I fit into.

I stare at him for a moment as I mull over my answer, hating that he's probably right about all of it, and I don't want to admit it. "I've always been a songwriter. Not a performer . . . so that's all I know how to do."

The thought of being on stage makes me want to break out in hives. The staring eyes. The criticism. The constant feelings of inadequacy.

"Hmm," he says, making my back straighten. "I think you know how to do both quite well. Aren't singer-songwriters all the rage these days?"

"If that's your thing." I try to be vague so he'll drop the topic. Just the thought of throwing myself out there to be torn down by fans makes my stomach churn.

"Can I sit and watch you work for a while?" The rejection is on my tongue immediately. No one has ever watched me work, except for Jett, but the words die when I see the look in his eyes. It's as if he doesn't want to be alone right now.

"It isn't very interesting to watch."

"I'd like to, though." He scoots over before I consent and rests his back against the headboard. "I'll close my eyes if that makes it easier. That way, I'm not really watching you."

"Semantics," I say with a laugh.

"Semantics are important."

Our gazes hold for a moment before he makes a show of closing his eyes and leaning back on my pillows as if he's settling in for the long haul.

"What does two-in, two-out, mean?"

I told myself I wasn't going to ask him and yet there it is. Out in the open. Me and my big mouth.

The hand he's bringing to put behind his head jerks momentarily, but he never opens his eyes. "Where'd you hear that?" His voice lacks all emotion.

"You yelled it last night in your sleep."

His sigh fills the silence and weighs it down. I study him. The fan of lashes against his cheeks and the way he purses his lips.

"It's just a saying I used to say to someone." His eyes remain closed as I debate whether I should speak or let it go. "Technically it means that when two firefighters go into a building, two more remain outside to initiate a rescue just in case shit goes south. Two-inside, two-outside."

"Oh. Okay."

"But my old partner and I . . . we would say it to each other before we entered a fire. We used it to mean that the two of us were going in together, and the two of us were going to come out together, safe and sound. It was our way of saying we had each other's back *no matter the cost*." He pauses and his Adam's apple bobs as he swallows. "The rest of the crew used to razz us over it and say we sounded like an old married couple when we said it. That's all. There's nothing else to it."

But the emotion swelling in his voice and the fact that he hasn't opened his eyes at all says there's so much more to the story.

"Grady . . ." *Thanks for sharing. Who was your old partner? Is he the one your nightmares are about?*

He clears his throat but doesn't speak. As the silence stretches I battle my need to ask more, but figure I'll leave it be. So I turn my focus to my work. To my notes and my guitar. And the moment I strum my fingers over its strings, the tension in Grady's shoulders eases some.

Music is my therapy, so I offer the same to him.

I look at him often as I work through the lyrics. Words about love and loss pass over my lips, run through my head, and are jotted down, and yet, he's the one I keep looking for a reaction from. His fingers thrumming to an imaginary beat he hears in my work the only response he gives.

I'm self-conscious at first, worried he's judging me or laughing to himself as I repeatedly work through verses and chords. Then, after a while, I almost forget he is there—if you can forget a six-foot-plus man sitting on your queen-size bed as you work.

And who knows how much time passes before I look up from my guitar, lyrics on my lips, and find Grady's eyes open and watching me. My words falter, but he shakes his head and tells me to continue. And so I sing and play and keep my gaze locked on his.

"Your tongue on my skin,

My head begins to spin.

Your heart in my hand,

Falling like endless quicksand.

Words are spun and lies are told,

But in the end it's you I hold."

The connection causes that ache in my lower belly to simmer to life. It's sensual. It's intimate. It's as if he's hearing the very inner workings of my mind and heart and soul, and as much as I tell myself I need to look away, I can't.

"That one," he murmurs when I finish. "I like that verse better."

My pulse pounds in my ears. How can he hear anything when my heart is beating so loudly I can't even hear myself?

"Why?"

"Because love is rarely pretty. It's messy. It's complicated. It's often ugly, but that's how you know when it's right. Pretty doesn't always last. It's the things you have to work at that make the reward that much sweeter."

"And you've been in love and know this firsthand?"

He falls silent but never averts his gaze. "I've loved a lot of things in my life. A lot of people. But I can't say I've ever been so head over heels in love with someone that I'd want to stay with them no matter the cost."

"*No matter the cost*?" There's that phrase again. "That's your criteria?"

"No matter the cost." He nods, and our eyes hold across the dimly lit room as seconds tick by. "Unfortunately, when it comes to me, the cost is too great to ask someone to pay to be with me."

"What do you mean by that?"

The muscle in his jaw pulses as he chews over the answer I can sense he knows but isn't going to verbalize. Then, without warning, he shifts and sits beside me. "Show me how you do it, will you?"

And once again, he changes the topic.

"Show you how to do what?" I ask to buy time and make my heart settle since it has decided to use my ribs as a bounce house.

"Play. Write. I don't know. Just show me how you work. I'm interested."

I laugh nervously as his arm brushes against mine and he takes my guitar from my hands. "It takes an awful lot more than me telling you where to press the strings to make a song."

"I'm good at manipulating things to make them sing my praises, Dylan."

My breath shutters. I hope he doesn't notice, because I think he just made an innuendo I really don't want to touch, given how close we are and how much closer we're about to be.

"So . . . hold it like this," I say as I avoid responding and show him how to hold the guitar. After a few attempts, I realize it's impossible to teach Grady without being more hands on. I shift behind him so my arms can shadow his and my fingers can help him press the correct strings when needed.

He laughs as he messes the chords up over and over, but I just keep my hands where they are and guide his.

"You need to be patient," I tease.

"Patience is not something I'm good at." He groans in frustration as the notes fall flat again. "You need to sing."

"Is that the problem?" I laugh.

"Yes, if you sing, it will mask my horrible guitar playing skills."

I press my forehead against his back as I laugh some more before I agree. "Okay. Hands in the ready position." I guide him back to them when he doesn't get it right the first time. "Your tongue on my skin . . ."

And we play through the lyrics I've been working on. It isn't pretty but it's the break in concentration I didn't realize I needed. We end with a laugh, and right when I shift to the side of him, he turns to face me.

It's a sudden movement that neither of us expects and leaves us closer than expected. So close, I can feel the heat of his breath feather against my lips.

Everything zooms in and out of focus in those first few seconds. The hitch of his breath. The scent of his soap. The zap of his touch where his fingers rest on my forearm. The firestorm of want burning through me, which is nothing at all like I felt with Wes Winters last week.

There can only be distance.

There can only be adjusting to a life without Jett.

There can only be not wanting this.

And yet, he's right here. A whisper away. With piercing eyes and full lips and that body that begs to be touched. *Explored. Tasted.*

"Thanks for showing me," he murmurs, his eyes flicking to where my tongue darts out to wet my lower lip.

"You're welcome."

And still, neither of us moves.

"You've shown me yours, when are you going to let me show you mine?" His voice is a suggestive murmur, but for the life of me, I have no idea what he's talking about . . . and I don't care so long as he keeps talking to me in that tone. Hell, he could probably ask me to remove my panties, and I would without question.

"Grady?" I'm asking so many things when I utter his name, but I'm not quite sure which one I want him to answer. Show me what? *Why aren't you kissing me?* This is dangerous. Isn't this a bad idea? "What do you have to show me?" The words barely make any sound when they come out.

"Why don't you like firefighters?"

His question throws me, and out of reflex, I slide off the bed and busy my hands by putting my guitar in its case. Again, I'm left to feel like an absolute idiot when it comes to misreading Grady.

"Well?" he prompts as I straighten papers on my dresser that don't need to be straightened.

"My dad was one."

"How did I not know this?" he asks as if he's dumbfounded that neither Damon nor I have told him this before.

"Because I don't talk about my dad. That's why." Grady starts to talk, and I hold my hand up to stop him while making sure I have a soft smile on my face. "It's a long story for another time. Another night. What was it that you wanted to show me?"

Grady looks at me, fighting a smile until each dimple breaks through—one side at a time—before throwing his head back and laughing at something I'm not privy to.

"What? What's so funny?" I start looking at my clothes, at my hands . . . everywhere to see what is making him laugh so hysterically.

"Do you know how badly I wanted to say 'my fire pole'?" I scrunch my nose, still not understanding. "At the fire station. You showed me how you work, and I want to show you where I work. So I was going to say I wanted to show you my fire pole as a joke."

I roll my eyes because he's acting like such a little boy, but I can't help my smile. "C'mon, you can do so much better than that."

"I can?"

"You can. You're a firefighter. Don't women fall at your feet?"

"They fall at my feet?" He looks to his socks and then back up to me as if to say no one is there. "If you can do so much better, let me hear it."

I put my hands on my hips and purse my lips as I try to think of one. "How about, I'm a firefighter, I see your pussy needs rescuing."

"Can't deny having heard that before, but it sounds all sorts of hot coming from you."

"It's sad that I'm one-upping you, and I'm not a firefighter." I throw down the challenge and wait for him to think of one.

"Find 'em hot, leave 'em wet." His eyes are laden with amusement as those dimples of his wink. "Or two-in, two-out is the safest way to do it."

"Is that so?" I laugh as he rises from the bed.

"Definitely. It's important to hit your target with a loaded stream. It's always best to get yourself positioned on top of her when she's hot." That tone is back in his voice, liquid sex with a bit of gravel mixed in.

"Oh, the man *can* talk a good game."

He steps closer to me, and his smile falls a fraction as he chuckles. "It isn't talking a good game you should be worrying about. It's if a man can back it up with his actions."

"Can you?" No doubt he can.

"Wouldn't you like to know?" He lifts his eyebrows and then heads toward the doorway.

"Where are you going? To play with your hose?"

"Not as good as mine," he says but keeps walking down the hall as I step after him. "It's late."

"You going to bed?"

"Nah." He pauses and turns to face me. "I'm going to work on the playroom."

My neck feels like it just encountered whiplash. "It's almost two in the morning."

"And? It isn't going to build itself, now is it?"

"What's the rush?"

His feet falter just the slightest bit, but it's all I need to tell me there is something about his extravagant shed that he isn't telling me. "Sometimes it's easier than trying to sleep."

With that, he heads for the back door, and a few minutes later I hear the pounding of the hammer.

It isn't the sounds of the city I'm used to, but it's definitely a symphony of its own for me to write my lyrics to.

THIRTEEN

Dylan

MY EYES BURN FROM EXHAUSTION. FROM THE LONG HOURS I put in last night on two songs, only to be interrupted by Grady when he was at my door and then again when another nightmare ripped through him long after the hammer stopped pounding.

I'd been on my way to his room when he woke up, and I'd silently retreated back to mine to let him have his privacy.

I heard the clink of the ice in his glass.

And I'm the one who, at four in the morning, pulled the blanket over him where he slept on the couch after it had slipped off and fallen to the floor.

So now I'm doing the only thing I can think of to help him. The one thing my Italian mother would do if she were in my shoes. I am going to cook for him.

Antipasto. Lasagna. Cannoli.

My stomach rumbles at the thought as I unload my groceries on the belt at the checkout stand. Of course, the tabloids catch my eye with their outlandish tales that are so far from true it's laughable.

I know that.

Yet, I still stare when I see a picture of Jett. The hurt still real. The heartbreak still raw.

It's an old photo of a performance I remember, but *US Weekly* says it was from last week. At least that helps with the sting of the headline below it.

"Jett's Wild Weekend with Women Galore."

"Hey, aren't you the one who's staying at Grady Malone's house?"

The chipper demeanor from the woman behind me is enough to stop me from picking up that magazine and torturing myself with the article inside. I look over to an inquisitive expression set on round cheeks and wide eyes of a tall brunette.

"Yes." I'm not sure what else to say.

"I saw you with him at the farmers' market the other day." Well, at least there is a reason for her to know me. "And I'm his sister-in-law's best friend." She holds her hand out to me. "Desi Whitman."

"Hi," I say as I shake her hand. "Sister-in-law?"

"Yes. The only one there is. *Officer Sexy's* wife."

"Officer Sex—*oh*, Grant. I've met him." This time my smile is sincere.

"How can you forget meeting any of the Malone men? I mean, it's as if they were put here to show the rest of us we'll never reach their level of perfection."

I laugh as I remember my thoughts of a Malone sandwich the other day. "Ain't that the truth?"

Her grin widens. "Well, it's nice to meet the woman in Grady's life."

"We're not—" I begin to correct in an effort to keep up my I'm-with-Jett charade, but her next words have mine dying on my lips.

"He deserves the best after everything he's endured. Such a horrific thing to go through. I mean . . . they were best friends, and he couldn't save him. God, can you imagine?"

My head reels with this new information, but I keep my smile plastered on my face, feeling slightly guilty for wanting more details when it's obvious Grady would have told me himself if he wanted me to know.

"No, I can't. It's just terrible."

She loads a gallon of milk and a bunch of bananas on the conveyor belt behind my order. "Grant said he's been doing better lately. I'm thinking that's because of you."

"I can't take any credit. I haven't done—"

"Oh, shush." She swats at my arm. "If I was doing a Malone man, I'd declare it outright. Wave a flag over my head. Write it in smoke signals. Girl, you want to claim him fast before someone else does. If they do, I have a feeling they'll never let go."

"I'll keep that in mind," I say as I laugh and hand the clerk money for my groceries.

"Well, you keep that man of yours happy, and I'll stay over here and keep dreaming about one for myself."

"There's always Grayson."

She licks her lips and rubs her hands together. "I think I kind of scare him." She laughs and waves her hand. "I'm a bit forward if you couldn't tell."

"Didn't notice," I joke as I grab my three bags. "Nice to meet you, Desi."

With that, I leave the store, my mind buzzing about Grady Malone, my curiosity growing by the second. I think about him all the way home. The burns. How he couldn't save his best friend. The emotional scars I've seen. The gruff exterior hiding them.

Every part of me rails against searching Google, but the first thing I do when I walk in the door is drop the groceries on the counter and head for my laptop.

I can't resist.

I search Grady Malone and Sunnyville, finding page after page of accolades and charitable deeds by the youngest of the Malone boys. There are a few articles on the trouble he got into as a teen, but it's the newspaper articles from two years ago that have me catching my breath.

"Tragic Loss of one of Sunnyville's Finest."

"Today we are a city in mourning," says Mayor Dan Jensen.

Tragedy struck the Sunnyville Fire Department last night in the four-hundred block of Crosby Court. Firefighters entered the engulfed Cooper Warehouse to check for occupants and knock down possible internal accelerants. During the search, a section of compromised ceiling fell, trapping firefighters Grady Malone and Drew Brooks inside the building. Despite the efforts of fellow firefighters, they were unable to reach them in time. Drew Brooks succumbed to the injuries he sustained from the fire. Grady Malone remains in Sunnyville General Hospital, where he is receiving treatment for third-degree burns to his back.

The cause of the fire is still under investigation.

Drew Brooks leaves behind a wife and three-year-old son. Services for him will be announced at a later time.

I stare at the article from two years ago, my mind filling in assumptions that only answers from Grady can confirm. I click on the next article, which is about the funeral service, and then the next, which is an update on Grady's condition. One about the cause of the deadly fire—inconclusive. And yet another with a picture of Grady leaving the hospital with his brothers on either side of him and a man, who I can only assume is his father, pushing his wheelchair.

The nightmares make sense now. The words he shouts. The groans of agony. The discomfort with his scars. The glassy-eyed fear he wakes up with that takes time to clear away.

The little boy and the woman from the farmers' market—Drew's wife and son.

I immediately feel like an ass for the conclusions I jumped to. My unfounded anger at Grady for not owning up to having a child. My distrust of men rearing its ugly head from both my father's and Jett's betrayal.

Lesson learned. Irrationality stemmed.

The scanner goes off. I jump at the sound and reach to turn the volume down, but it only serves to reinforce the magnitude of what Grady's been through and how much he masks. Putting myself in his shoes, I understand the dark moments that glance through his eyes. His use of his sexuality to avoid talking about anything to do with it. The survivor's guilt that most nights I'm sure wages war against the memories competing for which one gets to take the biggest bite of him.

My stomach churns, and my heart hurts for him. Feeling like I've betrayed him by searching, I close my laptop but the pictures of Drew and Grady that accompanied the articles remain fresh in my mind.

Needing something to busy my hands as I process his hurt, I head for the kitchen and begin to unload groceries. With a quick check of the clock, I know I have about an hour before he'll be home from helping his brother. The least I can do is make him a nice meal as an apology for a judgment I passed on him that he knows nothing about.

"You really should lock your doors, you know."

The voice stops me in my tracks. *That voice*. The one that owned my thoughts and heart for over two years.

My heart wrings. My spine stiffens. "I'd only lock them to keep you out, and since I wasn't expecting you, I didn't think I had to. Don't worry, as soon as you leave, I'll run out and buy padlocks."

I turn to face him, and the visceral punch to my system is staggering. His dark hair is in his signature messy disarray. His eyes are brown and unrelenting as they stare into mine. And then there's that mouth of his. One side is curled in a cocky, you-know-you-still-want-me smirk.

It feels like months since I've seen him—smelled his cologne, heard the rumble of his voice as I lay my head on his chest, get that nod that he used to give me from the stage to let me know he knew I was there. At the same time, it feels just like yesterday—the hurt, the anger, and the disbelief all like a fresh wound bleeding inside me.

"How's Tara?" It's my only defense against the tumultuous feelings rioting around inside me.

He half laughs, half smirks. “I told you, there wasn’t anything there.”

I chew my tongue as I stare at him. Disgusted. Hurt. Confounded. “That’s comforting. So you threw away a two-year relationship with me for something where *there wasn’t anything there*?”

“That’s not what I meant. You know how it goes—”

“Actually, I don’t know. How does it go?”

His eyes harden at being questioned. At not having an answer on the ready. “C’mon, babe.”

“If she was nothing, then the picture in People Magazine of you two at Starbucks was . . .?” I need to stay on the defensive because the longer he stands there, reminding me of everything that has been familiar for so long, the more my heart hurts.

And the angrier I become.

“Nothing.” He shifts his feet and folds his sunglasses to hang from the top of his shirt. “It was an old photo from an innocent lunch meeting. The tabloids recycled it.”

“Innocent, my ass.” I lift my eyebrows. “And the *Rolling Stone* article?”

“You saw that?” Confidence returns to his expression in that one simple phrase.

“Yep. Sure did.” I cross my arms over my chest and rest my hip against the counter as it dawns on me that Jett thought I would read that and all would be forgiven.

“You read that part about—”

“Yep,” I reply without even knowing which part he is referring to, because it doesn’t matter. None of this does. What he did with Tara is what matters. Not his words after the fact. “Too little. Too late.”

He shifts his feet and looks around when I don’t budge on my glare. “Look at that, all the fixings for a real Italian meal. You did know I was coming, didn’t you? Ava promised she wouldn’t—”

“It isn’t for you,” I say to stop him while silently cursing my agent for letting him know my whereabouts.

"You always did like a good fight. Is that what we should do here to fix things? You yell and rage. Tell me what a cocksucker I was. Then I shout back and tell you I'm sorry and that I made a mistake but I know you still love me. Then we meet in the middle and have some of that earth-shattering sex I know you like to have when we make up."

I remember that sex all too well. The odd places we'd find ourselves with our clothes pulled up and shoved down, our breaths heaving, our anger spent into passion.

Putting my hands on my hips, I steel myself against the memories that the hurt can't wash away with so little time. "What are you doing here?"

"I've come to take you back home."

My laugh is instantaneous and strained. "Nice try. I'm not one to be taken. Besides, there's no home anymore. You ruined that. That one is on you."

"C'mon, babe. Don't be such a hard-ass. I made a mistake. I was caught. Now I'm here to apologize."

"Seems to me like you're only apologizing because you got caught. Dare I ask how many other times you made the same mistake and didn't get caught? Or do I not want to know?"

"You're being ridiculous."

Oh, God. There were more women than just Tara.

"And you should leave."

He takes a few steps toward me, that soft smile he knows always wins me over on his lips. "Let's just stop this charade and get back to our life."

His hands are on my hips and mine are pushing against his chest. I revolt against the familiarity of him and the natural inclination to sag into him. "It isn't going to work this time. I put up with a lot of your shit—your ego, your need to always come first, your mood swings. What I won't put up with is being cheated on."

He angles his head and stares, trying to judge if he should believe me or not. "You're serious, aren't you?"

"Believe it or not, Jett, not all women find you irresistible."

"Yes, they do." I groan at his arrogance. "Baby, you know I'm joking."

"Don't 'baby' me and don't insult my intelligence." He holds his hands up as he takes a few steps back. "I asked it once, and I'll ask it again. What are you doing here, Jett, because if it's an attempt to take me back to Los Angeles, you can turn around and go out that door you just entered without asking."

Ignoring me, he walks into the living room and takes his time looking around, picking up a photo of Grady and his brothers from the bookshelf and staring at it for a beat. I wait as he sets it down and moves to the window so he can check out the backyard where the trees are close and the hills covered with grapevines are in the distance. He walks toward the hallway and pushes open my bedroom door to peer inside before turning back and facing me.

Just like Jett to walk around like he owns the place.

"The label wants to know our progress," he finally says and runs a hand through his hair. The D major note tattooed on his inner bicep jumps at the motion and draws my eyes. The one he got because he said he never would have hit the big time and become "major" if it weren't for me. The D note is for my initial.

"You could have called. We can discuss our progress over the phone. Just like we did when you were touring while we were writing the last album."

"Nah. You know I prefer to write with you face to face. Plus, I wanted to see you."

"Jett . . ." My voice trails off when I see his bag dropped by the front door. "Why is your bag here?"

"I can't stay in town."

"Why not? There's no Four Seasons you can trash and get kicked out of?"

"That's not it. There isn't really anything here that compares to—"

"Oh, I forgot. You're too good for the little people these days, just like you were too good for me."

"Bitter much?" He clenches his jaw. "Don't be a jerk, Dylan."

"Pot meet kettle." I raise my eyebrows.

"I can't stay in town because it will attract press, and then the press will figure out you're here and wonder if we're still together. I mean, why would you stay here while I'm staying in a hotel?"

"That isn't my problem. You're a big boy. You can figure out how to smooth it over."

"So what? You want me to let the press know, and then I can field more questions about where you are like I had to the other day?"

"What do you mean like you had to the other day?" Now he's got my attention.

"Kai was asking where you were. Callum stopped by to check in and was surprised he didn't see you. Then he called Ava. I think." He shrugs, referring to the label's very hands-on CEO.

"Why was Callum there?"

"Because they have a shit-ton of money riding on me delivering and the person they're depending on helping deliver it wasn't there?" He chuckles. "That would be my best bet."

Asshole.

"Were you pulling your usual *I'm Jett Kroger* bullshit and being difficult for everyone to work with?"

"You mean was I risking *our* album?"

We stare at each other as I ask without words and the slight curl up of his lips tells me all I need to know. Of course he was. A tiger can't change his stripes, and yet I'm still not convinced if Jett's telling me the truth or not.

I don't bite.

"I was on my best behavior, Dylan. If I'm trying to win you back, why would I purposely screw things up for you?" he asks, voice and smile softening.

"Why was Callum there?" I ask again, doing my best to ignore his attempt at charming me.

"Not sure, but he was asking a lot of questions about your whereabouts since no one had told him you wouldn't be there. When you were expected back in town. How our working together was going.

Fishing for info."

"And you told them what?"

"That you were off visiting some friends for a bit but promised you'd be back in the studio with me for the next scheduled session." I grip the edge of the counter and hate that I've been worked into this proverbial corner. "Then he pulled Kai aside for a whisperfest that didn't look good from my end."

I stare at him, trying to figure out if I'm being played or not. "Ava didn't call me." It's the easiest response I can give as my mind whirls over this information.

"Exactly. She called me. And now I'm here."

Son of a bitch.

"I'll get you a room at the hotel in town." I reach for my phone but Jett's hand is on my wrist stopping me before I can dial.

"No." The heat of his body is behind me. The scent of his cologne surrounds me. I buck my arms back to get him off me, hating the familiarity and missing it simultaneously. He steps back and when I turn to face him he's well within my personal space. "If we're staying in two different places, people will question if we're together. And if they question it, rumors will start and Callum will find out and—"

"You are *not* staying here."

"Yes, I am. C'mon. We can make a little music. Maybe a little love when we kiss and make up."

I laugh, but it holds no amusement. "It isn't happening, Jett. It's just like you to assume you rule the roost. Sorry, but it isn't my house, so I can't—"

The dispatch on the radio cuts me off. I thought I had turned it down when I walked in but I guess I accidentally turned it up.

Jett looks at the radio and then back to me. "It's true, huh?" His expression falls as he realizes I'm really in a house with another man. What did he think the pictures on the bookshelf were? Fake? "And he's a firefighter?"

"Yes."

"Really? After everything with your dad, you'd take the chance of being abandoned again by a glory-hound prick who needs the rush to boost his ego?"

Does he realize he could very well be talking about himself?

"It's none of your business."

He stares at me, and the hurt in his eyes is real. "Why him?" The way he asks it scrapes open the wounds he caused, but it only serves to remind me how deep they are.

"Why him? Because he's everything you weren't." The words are hurtful, but it could very well be the truth. I just hope that it's enough to get him out of here before Grady comes home because there's no way I'm going to be able to carry on this charade then.

"Are you happy, Dylan?" His eyes narrow as he studies me for any nuance to say otherwise.

"Deliriously."

He takes a few steps toward me. "You don't miss me?"

Yes.

No.

You hurt me.

"No." I hope my expression doesn't betray the conviction I use in the word.

"Yes, you do." He flashes another shy smile that says he isn't convinced. The one that used to win my heart over in an instant.

"Let me check with the hotel for vacancies. We can work a few days," I say when every part of me rails against the thought for the same reasons I left Los Angeles in the first place. "Then you can go back with more progress and let everyone know I'll make the next studio date."

He nods and his smile lights up his face. "There's my girl."

"I'm not your girl."

"Uh-huh," he says and chuckles as if he's not convinced. When he picks up his bag, my shoulders all but sag with relief that I've gotten him to leave. But just as I expect him to head to the screen door he walked in through, instead he heads toward my room. "So I can take this room, right?"

"*What*?" Whiplash. But I guess I shouldn't expect anything different when it comes to him. "No, Jett. The answer is no."

"It's no Ritz, but it'll do."

Frustrated with how he keeps ignoring me, I slip in my lie. "That's my room. You can't—"

"Deliriously happy?" He throws my own words in my face and lifts one eyebrow as a smile toys with the corners of his lips.

"That's what I said."

"Then shouldn't you be in that room?" Jett points his finger to the master suite.

"You are *not* staying here." I grit my teeth and avoid his question.

"Do you have something to hide?"

He thinks this is funny. He knows he's calling my bluff and is going to see how far I'm going to carry this.

"Honey, I'm home," Grady calls as he walks in the front door. He's totally joking, but he doesn't know how perfect his timing or his words are right now.

"I'm in here," I say.

You're lying, Jett mouths.

And the minute Grady turns the corner to the kitchen, I grab his face with both of my hands and press my lips to his.

I can feel the shock register through his body in the tensing of his muscles, but then, as I push my tongue gently between his lips, he reacts.

His hands slide around my waist and pull me against every firm inch of him. His tongue meets mine in a fervid dance of desire, and a groan that's so sexy I almost forget this isn't real slips from his throat.

His body startles as shock registers again.

And I know that he knows.

Jett's here.

FOURTEEN

Grady

CHRIST.

I can still taste her kiss on my lips.

Feel her tongue move against mine.

Hear the hitch in her breath when I stopped questioning *why* she was kissing me and went all in and kissed her back.

That's all I can think about as she stands in the kitchen and talks to me in hushed tones, her hands gesticulating wildly for emphasis.

Can't we just go back to her lips on mine before I noticed that fuck face was standing in my living room *attempting* to give me the death glare? It was almost as if he was accusing me of stealing his girl. *Idiot.*

"I'm sorry. I'll get him to leave," she says for what feels like the hundredth time as she looks out the window to where Jett paces in the backyard with his cellphone at his ear. I bet he's trying to look important to intimidate me, and there's no one on the other end.

Like that's going to fucking work.

"Are you really making me lasagna?" That's one way to get my mind off her kiss. And the feel of her tits against my chest. And the surrender of her body as she relaxed against—

"How can you think of food at a time like this?"

I laugh loudly, and I love that it puts a hitch in that fucker's stride outside. "You're the one who started it," I say. "So, we can either focus on food or focus on how we get to pretend to be madly in love." I shrug and grin. "Your call."

"I was cooking to be nice to you. That was my original plan. I haven't seen you eat anything but boiled chicken breasts and broccoli since I've been here. *Boring*."

"You saw me eat pancakes," I tease and lift my brows as she sighs in exasperation.

"Why are you taking this so lightly?" she asks.

Because it got you to kiss me.

"Taking what so lightly?"

She's definitely sexy when she's flustered.

"This. Jett. Being here. In your house."

I chuckle because I'm not really quite sure what I think of it yet. But, if him being here is netting me homemade Italian food *and* a kiss like that? I'm all for it.

"He's here. We'll figure it out. But let's get back to what matters. Food. Weren't we talking about chicken and broccoli?" I reach behind her and take a pinch of shredded mozzarella cheese from the bowl. "And why you were cooking for me?"

She twists her lips as she puts her hands on her hips and eyes me. I know she thinks I should be pissed at Jett and his ego taking up space in my place—and fuck yes, I am—but I'm still trying to figure out how I want to handle this.

"I was trying to be nice and give you a good meal. But now"—she looks out the window and sighs—"now, it's a peace offering."

My stomach rumbles just as Jett raises his voice, making sure we hear his fake laugh as it floats in through the open window. I stare at him. His dark hair and studded wrist cuff. His black jeans and tattooed sleeve. And every part of me bucks the idea of him and Dylan together. I just can't see it.

Maybe that's because I don't want to see it.

"He's a smarmy fucker, isn't he?"

She stops twisting her hands and nods her head. "That's one way to put it."

"What the hell did you ever see in him?" I can't stop the comment and don't want to. Just being in his vicinity makes me forget he's rock-god Jett Kroger and makes me want to bruise that pretty face of his.

"I don't know." Dylan sighs and the sound of it has me regretting asking the question. "I'm sorry. I never intended for him to know where I was. I'll figure out a way to get him to leave."

"Is he always this pushy?"

"More like inconsiderate. He's used to people doing whatever he wants. He says jump and they ask how high."

I can't ever imagine her bending to his whim. In fact, I can't see them together at all, now that I think about it. I glance outside again and watch him. Medium build, cocky-as-fuck attitude, and douchebag swagger as he walks around like he owns the place.

"How long?" I ask, and she angles her head as if she doesn't understand. "How long is he in town for?"

"I can go stay at the hotel—" My quirked brow stops her. "In a different room than him," she says as if she's exasperated I'd even suggest she'd be in the same room with him, "so he doesn't have to come around here."

A part of me likes the idea of not having to see him again. The other part of me hates thinking of the opportunity I'll give him with her in a hotel room nearby. *With a bed.*

Fucking Christ.

But if they stay here? If he stays here then I can torment the fucker by thinking Dylan and I really are together as she's told him . . . wouldn't that serve the fucker right for doing this to her? Nothing like wanting what you can't have once someone else has realized its worth.

Both are bad ideas.

One is just less so.

"How many days, Dyl?" I ask the question and reject my own mental warning.

"Three, four days tops." She glances at him again. "I can stay at the hotel. It's not a big deal."

"Let him stay." I spit the words out.

I'm going to regret this. I know it immediately.

And by the shocked look on Dylan's face, she is too, but for completely different reasons from mine. Hers? Ex-boyfriend in her face when she's still trying to get over him. Mine? It's twofold. First off, her in a hotel room near his. Not the scenario I want to picture. Second, who would say no to playing house for a few days with a hot female? Add to that knowing it would drive tantrum boy crazy with the charade is icing on the cake.

"What do you mean let him stay?" Her eyes widen and confused disbelief blankets her face.

He laughs again. The spikes on his cuff reflect off the sun and make me roll my eyes. "I mean just that. Let him stay."

"But why?" she stutters as confused to my reaction as I am.

"Because he deserves the torture of sitting here for a few days and seeing how deliriously happy you are. So let him stay while we play it up and make it so sugary sweet he leaves with a cavity."

"I don't think—"

"He needs to regret what he did to you."

She chuckles nervously and her hands mixing the ricotta fall idle. "Don't say this just to get more meals out of me because you haven't tasted my cooking yet."

She's goddamn adorable. "I'm certain that anything of yours will taste like heaven."

She stares at me—her eyes widen and head jostles. I love that I can fluster her so easily. She should be used to forward guys after living in Jett's world, so every time I can make her blush, I'll take it. It's the perfect mix of sexy and sweet, and fuck if I won't mind enjoying a bit more of both while we play house.

"How do you intend to make him see what he's missing?" she asks, ignoring my comment and the riot of uncertainty it brings her as she averts her eyes and starts mixing vigorously almost as if she knows the answer but is afraid to acknowledge it.

"We continue what you started." The stirring slows again, and it takes her a minute to lift those gray eyes of hers and meet mine.

"We're a couple. Isn't that what you told him? Boyfriend. Girlfriend. Kissing. Touching. The whole nine yards."

Fucking.

Her eyes narrow as she realizes she's just been screwed by her own game. "I know what I told him."

"Then what are you worried about?"

"That you're a firefighter."

"And you're going to be leaving in a few months. So?" I shrug as if she's making more of this than she is, but I won't deny I hate saying the words. I've gotten used to having her around. "This is make-believe, remember? Me being a firefighter has nothing to do with it, and even if it did, whoever you've pegged me to be because of my profession, I assure you, I'm not him."

I glare at her and see something pass through her expression that I don't understand. It almost looks like guilt, but she clears it away as soon as it's there.

"I'm not sure if we can pull it off." She shakes her head.

"You're a songwriter who writes about make-believe happiness. And a woman who I'm sure would love to see her ex be put in his place, so why won't this work?"

Why am I talking her into this?

"True." She's caving.

Because the woman *can* kiss. And that might just be a side benefit of this situation.

"What do you say, Dylan?" *Please. Use me.* "We can always make Petunia sleep with him too."

"Oh my God," she says through a laugh.

"Right?"

"He's going to die when he meets her."

"Well then, I guess we need to move her bed into his room." Her grin widens at my suggestion, and I know I've won her over.

I've also bought myself some time with the I-hate-firefighters Dylan.

It's when I hear the squeal—loud and scared and not from

Petunia—that I look outside and see her staring up at Jett. Dylan doubles over in laughter at the sight of Jett freaking out, and I know I've won.

Damn. This is going to be fun.

"Mmm that tastes like heaven," I say as I finish sucking the cannoli cream from Dylan's finger. I lick my tongue around it and then slide her finger out of my mouth with a pop.

I love watching her struggle with this. Acting as if she isn't affected by it and averting her eyes because she knows it's hitting her right between the thighs. "You want some, Jett? I know you have firsthand knowledge of how delicious her dessert tastes."

He looks up from where he's sitting on the couch with his iPad in hand, pretending to look at something when I've noticed his eyes darting our way every few seconds. With each laugh. With every kiss I press to her bare shoulder. When I leave my hand on her ass between helping her prepare the lasagna.

"No, thanks." His words are short. Agitated.

How does it feel, Mr. Rock Star, to want something you can't have?

"Your loss." I shrug and lift the bottle of beer to my lips as Dylan glances my way. The grin she's fighting is worth all of this.

I shouldn't notice her nipples. How they're hard against her shirt. I shouldn't look at her legs, the ones she calls mermaid thighs but are really perfect curves, and imagine what they'd look like spread for me.

No doubt my balls are going to be bluer than blue by the time this act is over.

My cell rings and I have no intention of answering it until I see Bowman's name flash across the screen.

"What's up, Bowie?"

"When you come in for next shift, can you head in a bit early?"

"Sure, but I'm not in till Thursday. What's up?" I ask the question, but the annoyed feeling is already hitting me deep. They're going to badger me about the damn calendar again. Might as well head this off at the pass. "Don't even think about it."

"Don't think about . . . oh. I'm not talking about the calendar, but that subject isn't dead yet, either."

Dread replaces my annoyance. "Then what's it about?"

His pause in response tells me it's shit I don't want to deal with. "We're just having a house meeting."

"Will Chief be there?" It's my way of asking if it's a procedural meeting or if it's about something that hits close to home, like my lack of performance.

"Nah. Like I said, it's a house meeting. No big deal." His nervous chuckle is all I need to know the answer. When you live with a man, even if only in twenty-four-hour shift increments, you learn his tells. And that was his.

No big deal, my ass.

"Sure. I'll be there early."

"Great. How's Brody's playroom coming?"

"Slower than shit," I say when all I want is to get off the phone so I can figure a way to avoid this meeting.

"Okay, then . . ."

"Later."

I hang up and stare out the window, forgetting the act going on around me, because this is real. This is now. And I'm fucking screwed.

"Everything okay?"

I already know what I'm going to do before my feet begin to move. She's going to hate it and so is he, but I don't fucking care. She's using me, and this little charade may be for her own benefit, but I might as well get something out of it too.

A way to release some of the pent-up chaos that phone call just brought. Fuck waiting for the dessert to be done. I want a taste of it right now.

"Grady?" she says seconds before my lips are on hers. Her hands are covered in cannoli cream, and she holds them out to her sides while I frame her face with my hands and do what I want.

Take.

Her kiss.

Her breath.

His patience.

My anger.

All four things are lost when my mouth meets hers. When my tongue darts between those lips. When my thoughts wander to what else I want to taste on her.

Yep. Blue balls, indeed.

FIFTEEN

Dylan

"If I were you, I'd make him wait until tomorrow," Grady says as he rounds the bed and moves to his dresser.

I stare at him from where I stand just inside his bedroom door, hesitant to go any farther in case that invades his space. "But the sooner we work on some songs, the quicker he leaves."

Grady stops where he is and narrows his eyes. "You can come in, you know. I'm not going to bite you."

"I know," I say, but all I can think about is those damn lips of his and how I just might want them all over me. The way he kissed me after he hung up the phone—as if his life depended on it—makes it impossible to deny that Grady Malone knows how to pretend to be model boyfriend material. "I just . . ."

With his body facing mine, Grady takes his shirt off, and the sight of his naked torso steals every last thought from my head. He looks up at the sudden silence to find me staring at him. "What's wrong? You do know we're going to have to sleep together, right?"

I choke on air as I think about everything that happened with Wes, and now . . . and now there is Grady standing before me, looking a hundred times more appealing then Wes ever did. How am I . . . if I couldn't make Wes . . .

"Relax, McCoy. I'm joking, *but not really*." He smiles wide, and I notice every movement he makes to pull the pillows from the bed is deliberate so his back, his *scars*, remain out of my line of sight. "We have to sleep in here if you want to sell this. You can take the bed. I'll sleep on the floor so that—"

"That's ridiculous. This is your room. I'll sleep on the floor." I hold up my hand to stop him from arguing. "Or we can sleep together in your bed. It isn't like we can't do that." When his grin turns mischievous, I correct myself. "That is if you wear pajamas."

His laugh is full and genuine. "You're cramping my style, you know that?"

I remember what his body felt like between my thighs, and I know this is going to be a horrible idea. "I'll stay on my side of the bed, I promise."

"I'm a cuddler. I can't make you any promises."

Our eyes hold. There's something about him—the unapologetic truth about himself he can't entirely hide—that makes him irresistible.

And dangerous.

It was all fun and games when I labeled him as just a firefighter. Keeping him at arm's length was easy while sleeping in my room at the other end of the hall. But tonight has been like some slow-burn foreplay I know both of us felt.

Either that or Jett being here has made me desperate for anyone who's nothing like him.

"Thanks for the warning." I lean my shoulder against the wall as Grady pulls a Sunnyville Fire Department T-shirt over his head. Now that our blatant attraction has been addressed in the only way we know how to deal with it—ignore it or joke about it—my mind fills with everything my Google search brought to light earlier. Every part of me wants to tell him I know about the fire but knows this isn't the time or place for this conversation with Jett just feet down the hall. Besides, a part of me wants to know he trusts me enough to tell me on his own. It sounds stupid, but it's the truth. "What are you going to do if I work on lyrics with him?"

"Since I don't think you'll be happy if I sit on your lap just to piss him off, I'm going to go work outside for a bit." He strides toward me and surprises me when he leans in and kisses my cheek. "Don't stay out too late with the enemy, dear."

That brush of his lips tells me Grady Malone may be as devastating to my heart as Jett, only in a completely different way.

"What do you think about those?"

I stare at Jett. He's in the glow of the lamp, his hair is ruffled from his hand running through it in frustration, and his eyes are tired. But when he looks over at me with the guitar across his lap and that soft smile on his lips, I remember why I fell in love with him. That hint of vulnerability behind the stage persona. The Jett I met in Excel Records' conference room four years ago. He was defiant and cocky. Pissed that he'd been dropped from his label, *and his label before that*, and frustrated that he had to ask someone else to let him have the chance to do what he was born to do.

He was such an asshole that day, but he'd reined it in enough for Callum, the label's head executive, to give him one more chance.

I sat and listened to Jett give the song and dance about how he'd made mistakes and wasn't going to pull any more public stunts like his other labels had sacked him for, but I could see straight through the lies. And I'm sure Callum could too.

The problem was Jett was the one Callum was giving me *my* chance with. A fledgling songwriter without a hit credited to her name was being tasked to write songs for the uber-talented but equally untamable Jett Kroger. The man who had yet to have a breakout, can't-get-out-of-your-head hit and who needed someone new to help him get that. A new songwriter.

Me.

I hated him instantly. He was everything I didn't fall for.

But he was my big shot with the label helping me make a name for myself and break into this tough world. And hopefully calm the hurricane that was Jett in the process.

I felt like I was selling my soul to the devil in those early days. Jett and I would argue over every lyric, every note, even the places we would meet to write.

And then one night it was late and we were loopy tired, and he admitted he was scared. That if this album didn't hit, he feared his shelf life was over. I had asked him why the antics then, and he'd shrugged with that cocksure smirk of his that told me he was either really smart at playing the part or equally as stupid . . . but a relationship was born.

Between us. Between us and Excel Records. And then when the album had a string of number-one hits, I felt a little more stable while Jett went and spun a bit more out of control.

Callum came to me, believing I could calm Jett down. He was the one who'd coined the phrase *the Jett Whisperer*. It was me he'd asked time and again to make sure Jett showed up when he needed to with a good attitude and compliant demeanor.

He was at the top of every chart, every sexiest man list, every free pass for wives to their husbands. And somewhere in there, we got caught up in it all and fell in love. Two people pushed together in a fishbowl bubble wrapped in excitement were bound to connect . . . and we did.

But even being with me couldn't stop the outbursts he'd promised wouldn't happen from happening . . . the difference was he was making the label serious money with songs—*my songs*—so it was easier for them to turn a blind eye.

Plus, they had me to center Jett.

The same me who is now stuck keeping a promise and wondering why I had been so willing to do so for the last two years.

Look where that left us. He was constantly apologizing for the bullshit he pulled while loving every second he spent in the spotlight, and I was hurt and upset but felt like I could breathe for the first time in forever.

Funny how I didn't realize I was suffocating until I walked away.

I shake from the memories and force myself to focus on the task at hand. "I think those lyrics fit with the beat," I murmur.

"You have so much anger in yours though."

I look over to him and furrow my brows in question. Does he not see the song was about him? How much he hurt me? "Yeah, well, maybe I have a right to be angry."

"Not this again," he mutters and reaches out to touch my leg but stops when I glare at his hand. "The song isn't about you."

"Every song I write is about me in some way or another," I counter as exhaustion tugs at the corners of my mind. "And this song is about anger and hurt and everything in between." There is no hiding my intention behind my words.

"Dylan. You know—"

"Don't. Just don't." I stand from my spot across from him. "I don't want to hear it anymore. Mistake. No mistake. Neither takes away the shitty things Tara said to me or the trust you broke with me."

"She didn't mean them."

"Don't you dare defend her!" I grit out as her words swirl in my head and spill from my lips in a mocking tone. *"Look at you, Dylan. Why would he choose you over me? Full figure went out years ago. Jett needs a woman he can wear on his arm. Someone he's proud to be seen with. You'd rather hide in the shadows than be in the limelight. You were good enough when he was up and coming, but he needs someone to fit his status now."* I watch him the entire time I spit her words back into the space between us and mark every flinch he can't hide.

"You know none of that's true," he says as he sets his guitar down and stands.

"No. I don't. Easy for you to say now, but I sure as hell didn't hear you stand up for me then, did you? You were too busy taking your condom off and cleaning up the evidence she wore on her thighs like a badge of honor. Just tell me, was she right? Did I not fit your status anymore and that was your way to try to break things off with me? Were you too chicken shit to say it to my face? How long had you two been fucking for her to think that? Because it sure as hell couldn't have been the only time given all she said to me." *And then that's when it really hits me. It couldn't have been the first time they'd fucked. He said the photo at Starbucks was an old one. How old? She knew her way around my house as she ran around collecting her shit. She thought Jett had already chosen her over me.*

"Don't you still love me, Dylan?"

"I can love you all I want, Jett. That's the hardest part. What I felt for you was real, and yes, I still feel it because I can't just turn it off . . . but that doesn't mean you're winning me back. That doesn't mean I *want* to be won back."

"We're still a good team." There is sincerity in his eyes, vulnerability. Resignation.

"I know." I take a deep breath and do what I need to do. "It's time for me to turn in."

"Dylan."

"We were doing fine until you brought up the past. Don't you get that's why I left town and came here? It allowed me to keep *us* out of *this*," I say, motioning to our guitars lying across the mess of notes. "The only relationship left is a professional one, and it needs to stay that way. We need to be able to get through these songs without muddying up the waters. We're no longer together."

"Not if I can help it."

I exhale a frustrated breath and shake my head. "Good night, Jett."

I walk out of the room and shut the door behind me. I rest my forehead against it and wonder how in a month's time we got here. I can't deny the sadness, but I can own my self-esteem and know I deserve better than that.

After I check on Petunia and make sure she has water, I head to Grady's bedroom. I'm cautious and exhausted all at the same time not to mention more than emotionally overloaded when I enter the room as quietly as possible. It's dark, save for the moonlight coming through the open blinds, and it takes a minute for my eyes to adjust. When they do, I see Grady on the left side of the bed, his breathing even and deep, and on the right side is a T-shirt and a pair of boxers.

When I slide my eyes to the empty spot beside him, I'm met

with a white sheet of paper standing out against the dark blue of the comforter.

Just in case you couldn't figure out how to wrangle your pajamas from your room without blowing your cover, here are some for you. And yes, Mom. I promise they're clean. — G

Sometimes it's the simplest thing that can cause the strongest of walls to crumble. His thoughtfulness. His ability to make my guarded heart swell without splitting open the old wounds that never healed. The way he somehow likes 'the me' I continually try to hide from.

I stare at him, and the part of me that was convinced long ago that his profession only breeds selfishness in the men called to do his job, slowly buckles under the weight of the moment. Between "his want to show Jett what he's missing" to now this, leaving me pajamas, he's starting to make me see him in a different light.

The kind of light that shouldn't be anywhere near my thoughts. Neither should reliving the feel of his kiss on my lips, but some things are hard to forget. Kind of like this thoughtful gesture.

Without thinking, I pick the T-shirt up and hold it to my face. It smells like Grady. Like soap and softener, and I hold it there for a moment before I realize what I'm doing and feel silly. I tiptoe to the en suite bathroom to change and brush my teeth before heading back to the bedroom.

Now or never, Dylan.

I slowly slide into bed beside Grady and swallow back the nerves that rattle around, whispering that I'm doing something wrong. I hold my breath and try to be as still as possible. Then, after a good five minutes, I realize how stupid I must look lying here stiff as a board on the very far edge of the mattress as if that will make me forget that Grady's beside me.

My mind is too alive with everything that has happened over the past few hours for me to fall asleep. So, I turn my head and study him in the darkness. The lines on his face have relaxed. His lips soft. The stubble he has to shave before the start of every shift starting to show. His dark lashes fanned against his cheeks.

He's definitely not a bad sight to drift off to. But about the time I do, I'm shocked back awake when he reaches over, hooks his hand over my hip, and pulls me against him. He murmurs something dreamily, but I don't catch it because I'm too busy noticing how our bodies fit together. I'm too busy fighting the urge to press my lips against his chest, which is dangerously near them. I'm too busy telling myself I should remove his hand from where it heats my skin, because it's causing other parts of me to heat up too.

But I do none of them.

Instead, I close my eyes and let myself enjoy feeling close to someone when I've felt nothing but alone since Jett and I broke up.

SIXTEEN

Dylan

COFFEE.

I need coffee.

Half asleep, I roll out of the empty bed and shuffle toward the bathroom, my head down, my body sluggish from a sleepless night spent pressed against—

Oh.

My . . .

A very hard, very wet chest cuts off my thoughts as Grady opens the bathroom door the same time I put my hand on its knob.

"Whoa," he says with a laugh as I look down to avert my eyes, only to end up looking right at the bulge in the towel. Flustered, I look up. His eyes are amused. "Fancy meeting you here."

"Sorry. I wasn't paying attention." I pull at his shirt I have on.

"No biggie." He shrugs. "It's bound to happen in such close quarters."

We stare at each other longer than we should. I'm embarrassed but still standing there, and he's amused, obviously enjoying my mortification.

"Thank you for the clothes last night."

"It was either that or let you sleep naked. I thought you'd prefer the former."

"It was very considerate. All of this is. You letting me stay here.

You not telling Jett to get out, even though you should have. You pretending—"

"Not a problem." He shifts his feet, and his eyes flicker to my T-shirt.

"Are we done here?" For some reason I follow his hand as he holds the towel together. But it isn't his hand that wins my attention. It's his dick, which is starting to fly half-mast against the thin piece of terrycloth.

"Yes. Sorry. I'll let you go." I snap my eyes up as his chuckle fills the room when he walks around me.

"Tonight I'll make sure the window stays closed. That way you're not so, uh, *cold* in the morning," he says over his shoulder as he skirts past me and over to his dresser.

Cold?

It's then that I look down to find my nipples hard and more than pressing against the fabric of his shirt.

With the buzz of coffee in our blood and the fresh air surrounding us, I've been able to shove down the tumult that Jett being here has caused and focus solely on the music.

If I keep my head down, if I don't meet his eyes, if I don't remember our past, I can keep this professional.

That's a whole hell of a lot of *if I's* and yet it's what I need right now.

And so far it's been successful since Jett and I have already powered through our second song of the morning.

It feels just like old times.

And yet nothing like it at all.

"I think we leave that one be, and we'll polish it up when you come back next month," Jett says as he flips the page of one of my notebooks and starts a fresh sheet.

"Next month?"

"Yeah. Didn't Ava tell you?"

"I'm not coming back next month. More like two or three months." More time away from you. *But a call to Ava is needed and an explanation as to why she hasn't told me any of this herself is required.*

"Not going to happen. I told Callum you'd be there for the next scheduled studio time. In fact, he demanded it. It's on the calendar so you better figure a way to get that cute ass of yours back to LA in time."

"I'll show up, but I'm not staying."

"Yes, you will."

"No, I won't," I groan. "Why is he so adamant I be there anyway?"

"He wants a progress report on what we have so far so they can direct us if they feel we're off track on the vibe."

"They what? Since when do they review the songs before they're finished?" I'm trying not to get my hackles up here, but in all the time I've been writing for Excel, I've never had a babysitting meeting.

"Since you weren't there and since I'm me." He chuckles unapologetically like it's funny when it's anything but. "I had to promise. You know they have a lot riding on this release. With the state of the industry and singles selling far better than whole albums, they're trying a new marketing scheme this time around. They want every song to be a hit."

I look at him like he's crazy. "Isn't that always the goal?"

"Yeah, but you know what I mean. It's a big—"

"You need anything, honey?" Grady asks as he walks onto the porch and presses a kiss to the top of my head. He leaves his lips there for a beat longer than the kiss lasts, and the warmth of his breath heating my scalp only serves to remind me of the heat of his body as he cuddled with me during the night.

Something neither of us discussed after meeting each other the way we did earlier. *With him almost naked and me horny.*

"What are you guys up to today?"

"Writing songs," Jett says as if Grady's a dumb shit. The muscle in

Grady's jaw pulses as he clenches back the smartass remark I can tell is on the tip of his tongue.

"Great idea. The sooner you get them done, the quicker you can head out. I'm sure you're dying to get back home to all of your adoring fans. I mean, you're so very generous to let them in your house and to sleep with you, too."

The two men have a silent pissing match through visual warfare while I sit between them.

"Do you have something to say, Grady?" Jett pops his neck to the side as if he's prepping for a fight.

"No, he doesn't," I interrupt, not wanting anything to happen between them because of me. The easier this is, the quicker the songs are done, and the sooner Jett leaves. Besides, I have enough bitterness for the lot of us.

"Yeah," Grady steps forward, ignoring my comment. "What's that saying? One man's fuck-up is another man's good fortune? Thanks for fucking up, Kroger."

"I don't have to put up with *this shit*."

"You're right. You don't." Grady's fuck-you smile is in full effect. "There's a Best Western down the street if you'd prefer to stay there *shit*-free."

Jett shakes his head, starts to walk away then stops, and turns back around with a smarmy look on his face. "Tell me something, Grady," Jett says as he narrows his eyes. "You two sure seemed to get cozy awfully quick. So much so I'm wondering if you weren't stealing my girl before she broke things off with me."

Oh. Shit.

Why didn't I think of this before? Because I didn't have to. Spending most of my days holed up writing had allowed me to fly under the radar in Sunnyville. No one had connected the dots with who I was and how I was associated with Jett. *I'd been free.*

How stupid could I have been?

I stare at Jett, wide-eyed and flat-footed, and just as I'm about to open my mouth and say something, *anything*, Grady steps in without skipping a beat.

"I'm a friend of Damon's. Dyl and I had met several times before, flirted, kissed." He shrugs as if it's a fact. "But we were always in different places, different paths . . . so thanks to your fuck-up, now we're right where we need to be."

Grady completely disregards whatever reaction Jett gives next, lifts my mug from my hands, and takes a sip. He fights the grimace at my blacker than black coffee, which is a far cry from the sugar-and-creamer-loaded mess he normally drinks.

"What are your plans today?" I ask him.

"Gotta help my dad with a few things. Then maybe go shoot the shit with my brothers, have a few drinks. You're welcome to come." He leans forward and presses a soft kiss to my lips, which throws me off guard. I know this is all for show, but damn, it doesn't seem to matter how Grady kisses—a peck, a brush, tongue, all in—because he makes my stomach flutter each and every time.

Even though I know it's fake.

Because it is fake.

Someone just needs to tell my body that.

And my heart.

SEVENTEEN

Grady

"WHY ARE YOU IN SUCH A SOUR-ASS MOOD?"

My middle finger is up to Grayson and his comment before I turn to look his way.

"Because *her* ex is in town," Grant fills in.

"Jett fucking Kroger is in Sunnyville?" Grayson asks, voice rising in pitch with each word while simultaneously grating on my every last nerve.

"Don't remind me," I groan as I look into my beer and wish for another before this one is even finished. I'm going to need it. "And no, Gray, you're not going to the house to get an autograph. Don't give the fucker the satisfaction of thinking he matters, you got that?"

Grayson narrows his eyes at me, and I realize I just proved his point that I am in fact in a shitty mood. "So what gives?"

I'm not even sure who says it, and I'm too busy thinking of Jett's phone conversation I overheard this morning while Dylan was in the shower to care. How he wasn't done winning her over. How he could tell she was caving and was planning to set up a romantic dinner to win her back.

The fucker.

"He isn't answering," Grant says with a chuckle. "That means he now has the hots for the woman he didn't have the hots for last time we asked him."

I don't even argue. "Playing house for a day or two does that to you." I sigh and look up to meet their puzzled looks. When I finish explaining our pretend couple-dom, I lift my finger to the waitress, silently ordering another round. "Do you know how hard it is to sleep in a bed with a woman and *not* be sleeping with her."

"*Hard* would be the operative word," Grant says and laughs.

"I don't find that amusing at all."

"Grumpy Grady," Grayson chimes in, using the nickname the two of them would call me when we were little and they wanted to push my buttons.

"The woman *can* kiss." It's the only input I give as I thank the waitress when she slides fresh drinks in front of us.

"And that's all you've done? Just kiss?" Grayson pries. "Nah, my bet is your dick's been in your hand more than once."

"You've seen her, Grant. Can you blame me if it has?"

Grant lifts his shoulder as if he's in agreement. "Then tell her you're interested."

"Easier said than done," I murmur.

"Why's that? Telling her you're interested doesn't mean you're gonna ball and chain it like this fucker," Grayson says as he hooks a thumb toward Grant.

"Yeah, but she isn't a Mallory," I explain and realize I haven't thought once about Mal since Dylan showed up. I haven't really thought about any woman but one.

"And what's that supposed to mean?" Grant asks.

"It means . . . nothing," I say but my thoughts keep running. About Shelby, now a widow, and how neither she nor Brody deserve that. About my promise to myself to never get attached to someone beyond the physical good time because I refuse to leave someone hollow and alone like Drew's death left them.

"Look, Grady," Grant says in his older-brother voice, which means a lecture is coming when I don't want a lecture. All I want to do is sit and drink my beer without interference or someone giving me advice. "I get you've sworn off meaningful relationships . . . so, for the life of me, I can't figure out why you're hesitating here. You have a gorgeous woman sleeping at your house—or rather, in your bed. She's staying here temporarily. She's on the rebound and probably isn't looking for anything permanent."

"She hates firefighters," I mumble and then shake my head when they both stare at me with confused looks on their faces. "Don't ask."

"She's on the rebound and you're not the type she likes . . . Not sure why you're balking taking the next step? Isn't this the perfect set-up for you? There's attraction but no want for more? Have some fun and then be done. I mean, she's probably confused as fuck. You're the king of flirting, but you aren't acting on any of it. How is she supposed to take that? You're treating her no better than Kroger has."

I hate that he's right. I hate that I've hesitated about this when the old me would have already been all over the opportunity living with her has presented. I hate that she has to be confused by how I can kiss her, distract her from delving too deep on me with my flirting, and not take another step to upgrade our roommate status.

"Are you naked when you and Mallory screw?"

I choke on my beer as I look over to Grayson and his stupid question.

"Of course he is," Grant says, but it dawns on me where Grayson is going with this. Always Mr. Intuitive, even when I've never broached the subject with anyone other than my own mind.

"How many people have you slept with since the accident," Grayson carries on.

I take a sip of my beer and glare at him. "Why? You need to live vicariously because you're going through a dry spell?"

"What? Five? Six? None?" he taunts as my jaw clenches. "And what? You keep your clothes on? You keep the room pitch-black?"

"Lay off, Gray," Grant warns when he realizes my temper is firing.

"No. He needs to hear this. We've been tiptoeing around this for months, and it isn't doing him any good." Grayson takes my beer out of my hand so I'm forced to pay attention to him. "Annie was a bitch. She didn't leave you because of the scars on your back or because she couldn't handle dating a firefighter. She left because she was a selfish wench who couldn't handle the limelight being focused on someone other than her. That's it. The twisted part is she was jealous of the attention you were getting when all you wanted was for Drew to still be here."

"That isn't—"

"I bet any of the other women you've slept with since her haven't given two fucks about your scars. Whether you fuck them in the dark, with a shirt on, without a shirt on . . . it isn't your back they're thinking of. And if it is, you're not doing it right."

"That's enough, Gray," Grant warns again, shifting in his seat as if he's worried I'll swing. I won't, but I do continue to glare at him, not wanting to hear what he's saying but unable to keep the words from echoing in my head.

"This Dylan chick," Grayson carries on as if Grant never spoke. "She's seen your scars. She hasn't run. She still lives with your ugly ass for some godawful reason when she's more than welcome to rent a room in my place if you get my drift. So get over it. What happened was horrible. To Shelby and Brody. To you. But Christ, Grady, to go through something like that and not want to live life to the fullest is a shame. Sleep with Dylan. Don't sleep with her. But for fuck's sake, don't use the excuse of your burns as your way out. You're a bigger man than that."

I shove back from the table, my stool scraping against the concrete floor of Hooligan's, and glare at my brother before I grab my beer and head toward the bar.

Fucking Grayson. He's the quiet one of all of us, so when he says shit like that, I know he means it. And I hate that my head's so fucked up I can't even screw a good-looking woman without overthinking all this bullshit.

I grab an open stool at the bar and take a seat. I don't want to deal with Grant and his fairy-tale wife or Grayson and his I-only-want-the-best-for-you bullshit. They mean well, but I still don't want to hear it.

But every goddamn word he spoke is the truth.

Fuck me.

"Another one, Dan," I say as I keep my head down and my eyes focused on the stack of cardboard coasters in front of me. I don't want to talk to anyone right now, especially since I'm on a first name basis with half the people in here.

A fresh beer slides in front of me while I feel the weight of my brothers' stares on my back. I'm sure they're chattering on like a bunch of cackling hens. I push the thought away. I try to shove all thoughts away actually, yet Dylan stays front and fucking center, preventing me from enjoying my beer.

I don't know how long I nurse my bottle—and the whiskey chaser Dan puts beside it, compliments of the house—before the chatter of the bar around me slowly fades to a white noise so I can relax.

It's Wes Winters' distinct laugh that breaks through my thoughts. He's the last person I want to see right now, considering he's slept with Dylan while I'm sitting here trying to figure out why I haven't.

Ignore him.

I do at first, but every time he laughs, the sound of it grates over my nerves and irritates me further.

"C'mon. It doesn't even count," Wes says.

"You've gotten more action than the rest of us," another voice says. I slip a glance over to see it's Mikey Peckham, a kid I used to play baseball with back in little league.

"Action? That doesn't count in the least." There is something about the tone in Wes's voice that has me listening more intently.

"*That*? How about *she*, you chauvinist bastard." There's a round of laughter that I don't find amusing at all.

Wes says something I can't hear, and I think the conversation is over until Mikey pipes up again. "So, you're telling me that you went to her place—"

"Malone's place," Wes corrects, and the hairs on the back of my neck stand on end. *He's talking about Dylan.* I grip the beer tighter in my hand and fight the urge to walk over there.

"Right. Malone's place. That ought to have been interesting."

"He wasn't there," Wes corrects.

Like hell I wasn't.

"That's beside the point. You're telling me you went to her place and got busy, but you aren't counting it as sex? Am I missing something?"

There's more laughter as I stand from my seat, head still down, anger firing anew.

"You're not missing shit. Nothing happened. We fooled around. We started to get to it and, dude, I couldn't get fucking hard."

"Good ol' whiskey dick," Mikey says through his laugh.

"It wasn't that. It was . . . Christ, I feel like an ass for saying it."

"Just say it."

"She had a pretty face but when the clothes came off . . ." Wes says something else I can't hear over the scrape of the stool beside me, and Mikey's laugh rings out again. "I've never been into the chubby-chasing thing before and . . . shit, that was all I could focus on when we got down to brass tacks."

"That's fucking cruel," Mikey says but continues to laugh. Still making fun of Dylan.

Every part of me riots. Chubby chasing? Is he fucking kidding? Dylan McCoy is a roadmap of curves and sexiness any man would be lucky to take for a ride, and he's calling her fat?

Walk to your brothers, Malone.

Walk.

Back.

Now.

I take one step toward Grant and Grayson, and the next thing I know, I hear myself calling Wes's name. It's followed by the bite of pain when my fist connects with his cheek as he turns to face me.

After that, everything moves in fast forward. The two of us falling and crashing against a row of barstools. The clatter of one of them hitting the ground—metal to concrete. The grunt as my fist connects again. The shuffle of patrons scattering, and the sudden stop as we land on the hard floor.

"You son of a bitch," I manage to get out right before his fist connects with my solar plexus. I grunt again.

Rage owns me.

Every part of me.

Each punch I land.

Every curse I spew.

Each thought of Dylan and the fucked-up shit he said about her.

I buck off the hands grabbing at my shoulders but come right back.

"Grady." It's Grayson.

"Grady, bro. Enough!" *Grant.*

Well, fuck.

Seconds clip by in still frames, and then Grant is pushing me out of the bar. The cold air outside clears the remaining fog of anger the fight didn't.

My fist throbs.

"Your ass should be in jail, Grady," he mutters as Grayson opens the car door for Grant to shove me in.

My cheek hurts like a bitch.

"The fucker deserved it."

EIGHTEEN

Dylan

THE SILENCE IS GOLDEN.

Jett left for the night on a jaunt a few hours north to Napa. He said something about meeting up with an old friend from his days pushing his demo tapes to record labels. I would put money on Sunnyville being too tame for him and he needed to go cause some trouble to keep his rock-star street cred.

But he said he'd be back in the morning when all I wish he'd do is head back home. *Not home. To Los Angeles. To his home.*

Then there is Grady, who is God only knows where.

I've checked on my mom, checked in with my brother, and even replied to an email from Ava despite still being mad at her for telling Jett where I am among other things.

That leaves Petunia and me to enjoy a nice glass of wine in the silence around us. Well, the quiet less her grunts.

And just as I lift my Kindle and start the first paragraph on the page, the back door slams open.

"He's all yours," Grant says with a chuckle as Grady comes in after him with Malone sandwich number three, Grayson, right behind him.

Just when I'm about to laugh and ask what he did, Grady looks my way, and the angry red mark on his right cheek says it all. "What happened? Are you okay?" I'm up and rounding the couch before the words finish passing over my lips.

"Just a little fight," Grayson says and shakes his head.

I reach up to touch Grady's face in reflex and then pull back. "That looks like it hurts like a bitch."

"You should see the other guy," Grady mutters and locks his eyes to mine. There's an intensity to them I can't decipher, making it hard to look away.

"You good, man?" Grant asks from the doorway.

"Yeah. I'm . . ." Grady lowers his eyes for a second before looking back at his brothers. "Thanks, guys."

"Yep. Later, Grady."

The door shuts behind them as I'm searching the freezer for a bag of frozen vegetables to put on his cheek. Sadly, I know from my experience with Jett that this is what works best. I finally find one, and when I turn around, Grady is still staring at me with that look.

"What happened?" I ask again as he hisses when I bring the bag to his cheek.

"It was nothing." He takes the frozen vegetables from me and walks to the other side of the kitchen. I swear he says something under his breath, but I can't make it out.

"It was nothing? That's all you're going to give me?"

"Yep." He drops the makeshift icepack on the counter and heads to get a beer out of the refrigerator. I push down the irritation that bubbles up at how cavalier he's being toward me when I've done nothing wrong.

"Seriously, Grady? You waltz in here with what looks like the start of an impressive black eye, bruised knuckles, and blood on your shirt, and all you're going to tell me is *it was nothing*?"

"Blood?" he asks, disregarding everything else I said and pulling on his shirt to look at the back of it where the blood is smeared in a few spots. "Fucking Christ." He mutters and grits his teeth for a moment before tilting up his beer and downing the entire bottle in long swallows.

There's tension building between us, and I can't help but feel like he's mad at me for some reason. Although, I have no idea what it could be for other than Jett. But Jett isn't here so . . .

Grady throws his empty bottle in the sink and then, in one swift move, pulls his T-shirt over his head. When he goes to toss it in the trash, I wince. Some of that blood is from him. I don't get a good look because the shadows of the kitchen fall over him, but it looks like there are slight cuts in a few spots on his back.

How the hell did his back get cut?

"How's Jett?" he asks with a bite as he turns around, and I mentally cringe when he catches me staring at his back. He doesn't realize it's because he's bleeding and not because of his scars, but he doesn't comment.

"I don't know. He isn't here."

There's a slight hitch in his movement as he leans his hips back against the counter and stares at me.

"Ah, the wonder boy decided to let you out of his sight for more than five minutes?"

"It doesn't matter if he does or doesn't," I say, suddenly feeling like there is an unspoken and testosterone-laced competition being waged that I have no knowledge of. "I'm not interested."

"Hmm." He folds his arms across his chest, angles his head to the side and studies me as if he's trying to figure out whether to believe me or not. "Where is he, then?"

"Napa."

"Why?"

What is this, twenty questions?

"To see an old friend."

"Huh."

He continues to glare at me without saying anything else, and I'm more confused now than ever. What happened to the man who kissed me on the head this morning as if we were husband and wife? I want that guy back. Not this version who's treating me as if we're a married couple on the verge of splitting up.

"Grady? Why do you seem pissed at me?"

"Because I am." The way he says it—void of all emotion—knocks me on my heels for a second.

"But why?"

His aqua eyes are impenetrable, and that muscle in his jaw tics as he clenches and unclenches it. Without a word, he pushes off the counter to leave. Aghast that he would just walk out like that, I go to say something, but he stops right in front of me and crushes his mouth to mine.

It takes a second for my mind to catch up to what my body is already reacting to—the onslaught of everything that is Grady Malone.

Because this isn't a let's-play-house kiss.

Oh no.

This is a take-no-prisoners, no-holds-barred kiss.

His hands are everywhere. On my waist. On my breasts. Sliding up my back beneath my shirt.

His lips are on my lips. On my neck. On the slopes of my shoulder. His tongue waging an all-out war against my senses.

There's so much greed. So much need. So many pent-up emotions that I feel each and every time our bodies connect.

My fingers thread through his hair. My palm runs over the coarseness of his five o'clock shadow. My body presses against his in the most delicious of ways as he pins me with his hips against the kitchen counter.

I don't have time to think. I don't *want* time to think, because Grady is intoxicating in his finesse and demand for more.

His hands frame my face and direct my head back as he breaks from our kiss. The same intensity as before is in his eyes as his chest heaves against mine.

"Thank fuck he isn't here because I'm going to fuck you, Dylan. It's all I've been thinking about. I shouldn't do it. I shouldn't pull you into this, but hell if I'll be able to stop myself until I'm buried in that hot, wet pussy of yours. You got that?"

My head dizzies with his explicit promises. He waits for my answer, his gaze fused to mine, and I know there is no way I will deny him. Not that I want to. The thought has crossed my mind more times than I care to count, and I'd be five shades of foolish to turn him down. And my body will disown me if I let the feel of him hard and ready pressed against me go to waste.

But can I do this? Can I sleep with him and then live with him without getting involved? Without letting my emotions get involved?

Yes.

His eyes darken and hands tense on my bicep.

Christ, don't make this complicated. It's one time. It's what I need. Grady said so himself. The best way to get over someone is to sleep with someone else.

Yes.

He waits with muscles so taut that his body vibrates from the restraint.

There's only ever been one answer when it's come to thinking about this question.

Yes.

I keep my eyes on his as I slowly run my hands down his ribcage and scrape my fingernails ever so slightly over those incredible abs of his to the button of his jeans.

I love hearing his quick intake of air. I revel in seeing his eyes widen in surprise before they darken with lust. "Dyl . . ." My name is the sexiest of groans on his lips as I tug his zipper down and slide my hand inside his boxer briefs.

He's hard already, and his dick pulses when I cup him as best as I can within the confines of his denim.

"Don't tease me, Dylan." I scrape my fingernails against the bottom of his balls. "Tell me you want this. I need to hear you say it before we continue because once we start, we won't be stopping for consent."

The fact that he's asking me again when I am so blatantly telling him yes only adds to the seduction.

I lean forward, my lips a whisper away from his. "*Yes.*"

And no sooner do I say the word than his lips are on mine again. His tongue commanding mine to give and take and want and need just as his hands are doing the same to my body.

Every touch is a splash of gasoline on a smolder. Every kiss is the match being lit. Every groan a lick of flame searing both my skin and my soul.

I'm not sure who starts the movement, but we slowly make our way down the hall. My back bumps against the wall. We stumble over the rug. When we enter his room, we become a frenzied mess of removing clothes. Each item one less barrier between us.

There's a brief moment when our clothes are strewn around us, and we stand completely naked, staring at each other. I expect his gaze to dip, to check out my body, but it doesn't. It stays fixed on my eyes, telling me he sees me without ever looking at my nakedness.

It's incredibly intimate. The look in his eyes. The way he steps forward and tucks a strand of hair behind my ear. The unspoken way he has of knowing this quiet moment is exactly what I need to prevent the nerves and insecurity from suddenly buzzing inside me like it typically would.

He takes a deep breath, and this time when he leans into me, the kiss is slow and mesmerizing. It's as if he's kissing every single ounce of oxygen from my lungs and holding it hostage until he can kiss me the next time.

"I want you." His words are soft, but they reverberate loudly in every part of my body.

And then the tenderness is gone. The next kiss is one of hungry desperation. How much can he take from me and how fast can he take it. We move backward until we tumble onto the bed, our laughter turning into my drawn-out moan and his libidinous groan as he sucks on my nipple.

"Grady." His name is the sound of unrequited need.

Impatient and greedy.

My hands are in his hair. Fisting. Tugging. Keeping his head right where it is so his mouth can continue to tease me with the sweet torture of his tongue and teeth against my nipples.

Not only does he *not* stop, but his hands part my thighs, finding me wet and ready for him. My breath hitches as he slides his finger up and down my slit, his thumb rubbing over my clit, his fingers toying with my entrance so I buck my hips, begging for more.

He doesn't give it to me. Instead, he leaves his fingers right there, just barely entering me so the heel of his hand can rub and press against my clit. I squirm. I writhe. I groan. I beg. All I want is something of him in me. Right. Now. The pressure is building, and I need that cock of his to fill me, to grate over those nerves and ignite the wildfire of bliss starting to brim beneath the surface.

"Grady." I moan his name again, letting him know I need him. That my body is succumbing to his touch.

"Condom," he murmurs against my chest as the weight of his body eases off me so he can reach in the drawer of his nightstand.

I can't wait, so as he sits back on his knees to open the condom and roll it over the delicious girth of his shaft, I let my fingers travel their way between my thighs. I'm a mess of arousal, so my fingers slide easily into me before coming back out.

He groans as he watches me. Teeth biting into his bottom lip. Hand working ever so slowly over his jacketed dick. Eyelids heavy and drugged with desire.

Watching him watch me is erotic, and while I'm typically shy when it comes to my body, the way he's looking at me pleasuring myself—the pads of my fingers on my clit, the way I slide between my lips to find more arousal before tripping back up to build my orgasm again—is empowering in a way I've never experienced before.

My breath grows shallow, and it becomes hard to keep my eyes open as the pleasure builds, one wave after another, and just when I'm about to come—back arching, legs tensing—Grady locks his hand over my wrist.

"Let me."

Those are two of the sexiest words I've ever heard.

My eyes flash open to watch as Grady moves between my thighs. He grabs the underside of my knees and pulls me closer. His thick head teases my entrance. He pushes in just enough for me to feel the slow, sweet burn of my flesh giving way to his invasion before he pulls back out. Wicked, delicious torture.

"You like that?" he murmurs as he watches where he teases.

He does it a few more times, and just as I'm about to grab his hips myself to prevent him from pulling back out, he enters me fully in one dizzying thrust so he's sheathed, root to tip.

We both moan from the onslaught of pleasure. From the restraint tested. From the frenzy of our bodies begging for more.

Our eyes meet. Our hands connect and fingers link. And then he moves again. Slowly at first, giving me time to adjust to him. When I have, I clench my muscles around him to tell him I'm good, and I love the way his eyes close partially from the sensation.

And then he picks up the pace.

He leans forward so our joined hands are pinned on either side of my head and adds to his pleasurable assault by kissing me again. His tongue moves in sync with his hips, and I writhe and buck, trying to draw out every ounce of bliss from our connection.

It's one bruising thrust after another. Every nerve of mine thrums and pulses as he rubs and grinds against them, until all I can concentrate on is him and the climax bearing down on me without mercy.

My body is a confusing combination of pleasure building to pain, want bending to need, and desperation feeding gluttony.

Seconds turn to minutes. Each one that passes a badge of honor for holding out, but I know it won't be for much longer. There's too much sensory overload, and I welcome every single moment of it.

The sound of our bodies connecting. The slap of flesh against flesh with each drive.

The feel of him. The girth of his cock. The way my fingers spread to fit his between mine.

The taste of him. His kiss on my lips. The hunger in it laced with desire and edged with the beer he had in the kitchen.

The smell of him. Soap and shampoo and fabric softener. *And sex.*

The look of him. Visual porn in every way imaginable. Muscles rippling. Sweat misting. Body aware.

And then the surge comes—every part of my body attuned to

him, every nerve touched, every erogenous zone satisfied. I cry out when I come. At first, it's a tidal wave of sensations—pushing me up, pulling me under, stealing my breath—then just when I'm about to drown in the pleasure of it all, another wave hits. One after another until I'm floating in a sea of ecstasy.

My hips lift to meet his. My nipples become ultra-sensitive to the feel of his chest grazing them. The muscles pulse around his dick and milk his own orgasm out of him.

It's my name on his lips now. It's my hands he crushes as the haze engulfs him. It's my body he uses until he's spent and lying on top of me, breath labored and lips pressed against the underside of my jaw as our heartbeats struggle to calm.

Eventually, our fingers loosen from each other's and the gravity of the moment settles over me.

"Well, that's one way to avoid talking about your fight."

"Look at it this way," he murmurs, his lips moving against my skin and sending chills over me. "We just had make-up sex and we haven't even had a proper fight yet."

"Next time I'll throw a plate at you first."

"Good idea." He chuckles.

Next time?

Next time.

If this is what make-up sex is like with Grady Malone, then I sure as hell can't wait to see what regular sex is like.

NINETEEN

Dylan

I wake with a start. My mind is scrambled from the dream that started out with Jett kissing me. Then, when he leaned back, it was no longer Jett but Grady whose lips were mesmerizing mine.

But now it's no one's. Now it's only the muted light of the predawn and the chill of the morning air against my nakedness. Trying to snuggle back under the covers, I roll to my side and am met with Grady's back.

My breath catches at the sight of it up close. Scars are layered one upon another in a plane of destruction. Some areas look tight to the touch, the scar tissue constricting the skin. Others look like a sea of lava slid its way down his back and left different grooves from spot to spot. There is red and pink and every shade in between, every texture from smooth to puckered, every indication of the hell he endured.

Add to that, there are tiny lacerations in various spots of his scars where his skin has cracked open some and bled.

The fight. The blood on his shirt. It wasn't the other guy's. It was Grady's.

So many thoughts race through my mind. Are the small tears painful? And if so, will it ever get any better so he doesn't hurt? *Add to that, does it hurt when I touch him*?

"We were in a three-alarm fire on the edge of town in an industrial park," he begins in a whisper, but the pain is just as raw and real as the scars on his skin. He keeps his back to me but continues on, somehow knowing I'm awake and studying them. "Drew . . . God, Drew. He wouldn't fucking listen. We were trying to knock down some debris in a room that was fueling the fire when he swore he heard someone calling for help. I couldn't hear shit besides the crackle and pop of the flames. We'd been told the building was cleared, but he swore he kept hearing it."

"Grady." I don't know what to say. "You don't have to explain anything."

"Well, it seems kind of pertinent since we are dating and all that." I hear the smile in his voice, and for a brief second, I wonder if he's being serious since we're both in bed—naked. Then I realize he's referring to the Jett situation.

I chuckle and give in to the urge to reach out and touch his arm in a show of silent support. He jerks when my fingers connect, but I keep them where they rest. Away from his myriad of scars but close enough for him to know they don't disgust me.

After a few seconds, he exhales a shaky breath and relaxes.

Baby steps.

"It seemed like it happened so fast and took forever all at the same time. I knocked a window out, and when I turned around, he was heading into the next room when we should have been getting the hell out because the fire was too damn hot. But that was Drew . . . selfless. Wanting to take care of others before he took care of himself. We got separated when a ceiling beam fell. Then another. And another. I couldn't get to him, and he was trapped somehow. Then I heard his PASS alarm. He'd stopped moving. I went crazy trying to get to him, but then the roof collapsed on me."

"Jesus, Grady."

"There was no Jesus there that day. If there had been, he wouldn't have taken Drew."

There's an understandable anger in his voice. The silence settles around us as I try to imagine the horror he endured. The fear. The helplessness. And I know that no matter what I imagine, the reality was a hundred times worse.

"The other day at the farmers' market," he continues, "that was his widow and their son. Shelby and Brody. I'm sorry I didn't tell you . . . I just—sometimes it's hard for me to talk about it. I think about it twenty-four seven, and we were having a nice time. I didn't want to ruin it."

"It's okay."

"Drew's last words to me were to take care of Brody since he knew his son was going to lose his father." I squeeze my hand where it is, words failing me as my eyes well with tears. "Do you know how hard it was hearing him say that and knowing he knew?"

"I'm so sorry."

"Not more than I am." I rub my thumb back and forth on his arm, accepting his comment for what it is—him and his guilt instead of a poor-me statement. "There are days I suit up and go to work . . . and, Christ, I don't want to. But being a firefighter . . ."

"It's not something you do, it's something you are," I murmur, knowing full well the commitment, the sacrifice, the selflessness, and selfishness that comes with the occupation.

"I was going to say something else, but that is definitely more accurate." He sighs heavily. "The playroom? I couldn't care less about the damn playroom, but I'm building it for Brody. So he has a place to go when he needs to remember his dad and hear stories about him from those who were his friends."

My heart swells in my chest. And he calls Drew selfless? It sounds like he's cut from the same cloth as his friend. There's no use in pointing it out though, because he'll just reject it anyway.

"I'm sure he'll appreciate it as he grows older. It will help keep Drew's memory alive."

"Yeah, well . . . it's the least I can do for him." He runs a hand through his hair, my hand on his bicep shifting with the movement. "Everything is just fucked up, Dylan. All of it. In every sense of the word. I should have been able to save him. I should have been able to get to him."

"You did everything you could. I wasn't there, but I know you did."

"It doesn't matter because it wasn't good enough. I didn't fulfill my promise to him. There was no two-in, two-out."

More silence smothers the room, but I give him a moment because I sense he needs it right now. I leave my hand where it is and close my eyes, freeing a tear that I'm sure he would hate that I've shed.

"There are cuts . . ." I say and cringe.

"The skin in some parts is thin. Some of the grafts aren't as thick as my natural skin is. Other parts are stretched so tight that when I do something that isn't typical—"

"Like punching someone."

"Like punching someone." He chuckles. "The skin tears. I don't always notice it. I don't always feel it. But it happens like it did last night."

"Do they hurt?" I ask while he's talking.

"Some spots always hurt. Others have no feeling at all. Supposedly, there will come a time when the pigment will lighten or I'll gain some elasticity . . . but there's no determining what scar tissue will or won't do, so only time will tell."

"I mean this in the nicest of ways, but they are fascinating to look at."

He laughs. "That's a first."

"No, I'm serious." I shake my head while mentally kicking myself for speaking my thoughts aloud. "I mean, of course, they look painful, but they're also a roadmap of where you've been and where you're going."

"Dylan—"

"No. Hear me out. We all have scars. Some are visible. Some aren't. In the end, they represent the fact that you're stronger now than whatever tried to hurt you. For you, it just means that you're stronger than the fire."

There's a weight to his silence, making me feel as if maybe I've overstepped.

"You're the first person I've met who isn't repulsed by them." His voice is solemn, and I wish he'd turn so I can see his eyes. So he can see mine.

"I find that hard to believe, Grady."

"It's true."

"Are you telling me that your brothers and your parents are disgusted by them? Of you? What about Mallory?"

His laugh is unexpected and confusing. "Christ. Is it embarrassing to say I've always left a shirt on with her? Either that or made damn sure the room was dark."

His insecurities hit a chord with me. One I know all too well but am not exactly sure how to give a voice to . . . so I remain quiet.

"You're the first person I've been with since and not kept a shirt on. I was pent-up on adrenaline—"

"Alcohol," I correct because that's surely why he slept with me.

"No. I wasn't drunk. You don't get to hide behind the alcohol to explain why we're here right now."

"And you don't get to hide behind your shirt and scars to ignore me at other times, either," I counter, hating that he has seen straight through my thought process.

"Not wearing a shirt was an oversight I've never made with others," he says, ignoring my comment. "One I didn't realize until I woke up."

"I'm not sure if I should be offended that you're mentioning the many *others* you've been with or I should take it as a compliment that you feel comfortable enough with me that you forgot," I say to try to ease the discord he feels.

"Or option C: the sex was so good that I fell into a coma afterward and didn't think twice about it."

"Option C could have been a definite possibility," I murmur and acknowledge to myself his knack for falling back on humor when he's uncomfortable.

"There haven't been that many women since, you know."

"Wild-child, Grady Malone? I highly doubt that."

He chuckles, but then it fades and falls flat. "You'd be amazed by how much all of this has put people off."

My heart hurts for him and the disgrace that taints every word he speaks. "I'm not scared, Grady. I'm not put off." The words are barely audible, but by the slight nod of his head, I know he heard me. "You don't have to wear a shirt around me. Hell, I have mermaid thighs and hips for days and one ab to your eight for God's sake."

"I don't have a single complaint about any of those traits of yours. In fact, I seem to like your thighs and hips and—"

"Ha. You like what's between them is what you're saying."

"This is true," he muses.

"Let me tell you, those traits of mine are all much worse than the badge of honor you wear on your back."

The muscle beneath my hand tenses as he physically rejects what I'm saying. "Christ, Dylan—"

"Don't." I stop him from arguing with me because it's my turn to make him feel better about himself—even if it's at my own expense. "I'm well aware I'm not svelte, so no need to try to stroke my ego."

"You're beautiful."

"And so are you," I whisper, leaning my head forward and pressing my lips ever so softly to the top of his shoulder in an effort to reinforce the words. His body flinches and his breath hitches as I make him uncomfortable but for all the right reasons.

"I'll be the first to admit I'm a vain son of a bitch. If you knew how many hours I spent in the gym before the fire, you would probably laugh. I was obsessed with adding definition to this muscle group or that one, and then I'd walk around shirtless to show them off. To be admired. My ego didn't need any stroking, that's for sure."

"You were proud of your body. That's something I'll never be, so I'm sure I'd be the same."

"I felt like the fire was fate's way of telling me it didn't matter how damn perfect I was because there were other things that were way more important. It's like I was marked for being self-centered."

"I disagree with you."

"Yeah, well, I used to work out because it was the way to feed my ego. Now I work out to save my soul." His words strike me to the core. A fresh round of tears well, and I fight them back, trying not to think about him alone in the gym, struggling against some unforeseen beast in his mind. "Most nights I go late because there is no one there to watch me. I go late because when my skin tears like it did last night, it bleeds through my shirt . . . and that's the last thing I need people to see, to gossip about, or pity me for."

"Do you really think anyone cares what your back looks like? You're a hero, Grady. You tried to save him."

His chuckle isn't convincing. "Tell that to my ex-girlfriend who broke up with me because she couldn't handle this. The scars. The nightmares. My fucked-up head. I mean, I'm sure I wasn't a peach after everything happened. But when I overheard her on the phone telling a friend how nasty my scars were and how there was no way she could look at them every day without cringing. How she couldn't fake being okay with them . . . well, that tells me people do care."

"She's a shallow bitch." The words are out, and I don't care that they are because she is one. I can picture him—a man struggling to heal physically and mentally and what comments like those did to him and his psyche.

"Perhaps she is, but she isn't the only one. This is a small town, Dylan. Everyone knows everyone, and they're all curious about what happened to pretty-boy Malone. They all want to see how bad he looks. They all want to know if the scars are really that horrible, and then, of course, there are the assholes who question if I was selfish and tried to save myself instead of trying to save Drew."

"No one thinks that."

"I bet Shelby does. How could she not? Every time I look her in the eyes, I know I didn't do enough. I know she looks at me and wonders how I couldn't save him but I could sure as shit save myself."

There are so many things I want to say to him. That he was trying to get to Drew to save him. That he wasn't being selfish. So many truths I could tell him that would negate what he just said, but I know they'll fall on deaf ears. He feels how he feels, and no one is going to change that. Least of all me.

"Will you turn around?" I ask him finally, hoping that we're both lying here naked is enough for him not to feel like he's the only vulnerable one.

He doesn't respond.

There's a momentary hesitation of indecision before he abruptly scoots to the edge of the bed. "I've gotta get to work on the playroom. I'm behind schedule."

And with that, I'm left alone in Grady's bed with the scent of him still on my skin, the desire for more of him still aching in my lower belly, and the sight of his bare ass walking to the bathroom door before he shuts it behind him.

TWENTY

Dylan

You walked away.
You left me there.
You made me feel as if you didn't care.
How can this be?
How can we love?
How can we . . .

"Grrr," I growl in frustration and stare at the last line I've jotted on the page in front of me. I can't get it right and it's driving me crazy.

I squeeze my eyes shut as the pounding outside begins yet again.

He's been swinging his hammer for over two hours. It's an oddly soothing rhythm in the background to my work, which is as comforting as it is harsh.

But it does nothing to combat the sudden conflict roiling around within me. The overthinking that is messing up my creative process. Sure, what happened last night was pleasurable in so many ways I lost count. After being with Jett, who I thought rocked my world in bed, he doesn't hold a candle to the unexpectedness of the man I was with last night. It's enough to throw a girl for a loop.

No, not a loop—a tangled mess of rope with frayed ends that are twisted and gnarled together.

I watch him hammer another nail in place. Hating the confusion

I have and wondering if he feels it, too. Is he as uncertain about where we go from here or is he already done and over it like most guys would be?

Was last night a one-off moment for him?

Am I the new Mallory to him? Stop in when I come in from out of town for a no-strings-attached lay?

I'm more than aware that Grady Malone does not do strings-attached. Or rather that's what the locals have said the few times I've gone into town. Even though I've tried to keep to myself, curiosity goes a long way in a small town. Innocent introductions in the grocery store or post office turn into subtle probing about what I'm doing in Sunnyville and why I'm living with Grady Malone. *The* Grady Malone who used to be wild but now is tame and most definitely doesn't stick with one woman for more than a few dates. Where does that leave me other than in the middle of an awkward situation I never should have gotten myself into?

My God. I'm sitting here thinking that last night meant something when I'm sure it was nothing more than a sudden urge on both our parts to release the tension having Jett around has created.

Didn't I say *yes* to him knowing that was the situation? Didn't I agree to sex because getting involved with someone is the last thing I need right now?

All I can do is laugh at myself though because while I may have convinced myself I could separate sex and emotion last night, is it too soon to admit to myself that I might be developing teeny, tiny feelings for him?

I'm sure those feelings were helped along when he unexpectedly opened up to me this morning and let me in a little. When he dropped his playful demeanor and was honest with me about the fire.

And then he shut me out and hasn't said another word since. Shouldn't his total indifference be my clue that he thinks sleeping together was a mistake?

Did I make an error in judgment as well?

Stop staring.

Stop thinking.

Start writing.

There's a big difference between one night of sex and emotions. The two can be separated.

I can separate them.

Then why do I keep trying to make myself believe that?

There's an odd ache in my chest when I look at him one last time before moving from the window.

I have at least two months here before I return to Los Angeles. Not for a recording session but to go back home for good. If last night was a mistake, that's a long time to avoid someone when you're sharing the same space. If it wasn't, that's a super long time to keep emotions and sex in separate corners.

TWENTY-ONE

Dylan

"C'MON, JETT."

"Don't you want to know about my time in Napa?" he asks as he points to the case of wine he set on the counter. I'm pretty sure he thinks booze will earn him brownie points with me. I don't think he realizes we're sitting in a house surrounded by grape vineyards, so wine is in abundance around here.

And I'm certain he has no clue what I'd really like to do with the bottles is empty their contents in his lap to prove to him that a case of wine isn't going to win me back.

Doesn't he get that nothing will?

"Not really."

"Well, at least let me take you to dinner?"

"No, I—"

"Let's get out of this house and go out and have a nice meal. Alone. We can bring the wine with us and—"

"Jett, I just want to get this song finished." The one he started writing about winning the love of your life back. The one that is currently grating on every one of my last nerves because now it all makes sense. His roundabout way to tell me how he feels in the lyrics he wrote followed by the promise of a dinner that I can presume will be romantic.

"And I just want you back."

I grit my teeth as I look at him across the family room and glare.

"Just play the damn chords again."

"You always were sexy when you were pissed at me," he murmurs, eyes alive and charisma in full force. Compliments won't win him points, either.

"And you always tried to charm me when you did something wrong. Too bad charming me—or wining and dining me—won't work this time."

I think of Grady last night. The anger. The tension. The kiss that knocked me off my feet and landed me on my back in his bed.

Such a total contrast to the man sitting across from me, and it's so much more noticeable than before. Almost as if being with someone else has woken me so I can see clearly.

He finally plays the chords. I sing the newest lines I'm trying out.

"I was yours to lose.

You tested the waters.

I tested her lips.

And then your claim on me began to slip."

Jett groans. "You're making him sound like a pussy."

"*A pussy*?" I ask with a laugh, slightly offended. "How about you write your own damn songs then?"

Jett stands and runs a hand through his hair in frustration. "I think we need to skip this one and move to the next," he says.

"How about you go back and leave me here to finish them. I was working fine by myself before you came."

His eyes flash over to mine, and there's surprise in them. "We always worked best when we were together."

"Apparently, not anymore."

"Dyl—"

"Good afternoon," Grady interrupts as he waltzes into the family room in the all-blue pants and shirt that make up the Class A's uniform he wears at the station and heads straight toward me as if Jett isn't even in the room. Grady flashes me an unabashed grin, telling me he knows exactly what game he's playing, before he frames my cheeks and levels me with a kiss to rival all kisses.

For a moment after his lips meet mine, I forget this is pretend. I forget that Grady is putting on a show for Jett and that last night was something that now feels like a hasty yet equally pleasurable lapse in judgment since neither of us has addressed it yet.

And even with all that, I still sink into the kiss and deflate when his lips leave mine.

I was wrong. Dead wrong. It's impossible to separate sex and emotions. Not when a man kisses like that and looks at you as if he can't wait to do it again.

"I'm in the room," Jett says, annoyance singing in his voice.

"But you're in *my* room, so . . ." Grady shrugs and pats me on the ass as he makes his way to the kitchen. "Everything okay? Things feel a bit tense between you two."

He walks to the fridge, pulls out a water, and leans against the appliance as he looks from me to Jett and then back to me.

I stare at him for a moment, so clean cut and preppy compared to Jett's all black clothes and colorful tattoos. Such a contrast, and yet it's Grady who makes my breath catch when it used to be Jett.

"Just peachy," Jett says and gives Grady a condescending smirk as their dislike for each other manifests in their expressions.

"You have a good time in . . . Napa, was it?"

Jett nods as he narrows his eyes and studies Grady, trying to figure out where he's going with this line of questioning.

Grady part laughs, part says, "Good," as he makes his way back toward me and wraps an arm around my waist, his hand possessive on my side. "Because we sure had a good time, didn't we, babe?" He smirks at me with so much suggestion that my panties might possibly catch fire.

Grady's being such a cocky bastard, and I'm enjoying every single moment of it.

"Dylan was telling me you're up to speed on what you came here to accomplish. Should I assume you'll be leaving us soon? Three's a crowd and all."

Jett chews the inside of his cheek as he glares at Grady. "My flight's booked for tonight. Dylan and I have reservations for dinner at La Blanc's, and I'll have her drop me off at the airport on the way home."

I snap my head to look at Jett. "I didn't—"

"Nice try," Grady says and shakes his head as he takes a few steps toward Jett, "but you're going about it all wrong. It takes a lot more to impress a woman like Dylan than a high-dollar restaurant. In fact it's way simpler than that. All it takes is a little respect, some undivided attention, and a whole lot of laughter to make a woman feel how she should. But then again, I wouldn't expect you to know that since you think cheating is the way you treat a lady."

"You're an asshole, you know that?" Jett says as he steps toward Grady.

"And you're an ungrateful prick who thinks just because he can sing he has a ticket to do whatever he wants to whomever he wants. Not this time. Not this woman. Not *my* woman." Grady chuckles, and it's so loaded with derision and spite that it's palpable. Jett bristles at the sound of it as the tension thickens between the two of them. "The door's that way, Kroger, and the airport's in the same place you found it. Dylan won't be driving you anywhere."

"We have to—"

"We have to head out because we have an appointment to get to so we'll wait while you gather your things."

"An appointment?" Jett and I both ask in unison. I don't recall having any appointment with Grady. And he's dressed and ready for work. *What's he up to now? And why is it I want to burst out laughing at his audacity to get one final dig in on Jett?*

"Yep." Grady's grin could light up a room. "Time to say goodbye, Kroger."

TWENTY-TWO

Dylan

"OUR APPOINTMENT IS AT THE FIRE STATION?" I ASK WHEN he parks his truck beside the building.

"Yep."

"All you had to do was ask me to come with you."

"And miss out on the satisfaction of messing with that fucker? No way," he says with a grin.

"Enjoying playing the game a little too much?"

"Of course I am. I've got the girl, don't I?" He hops out of the truck without another word and slams the door shut.

His words surprise me so much it takes me a few seconds to realize he probably didn't mean them how I took them. I need to get a grip. On my heart, my thoughts, and my libido.

As we walk up the pathway, I stare at the brick building for a moment, so many memories rushing back. A stark reminder of the disdain I've been conditioned to have for this profession and all the baggage that comes with it. I'm reminded of how I used to get so excited when my mom took Damon and me to the station to pick our dad up from a three-day shift because we'd missed him so much. The car ride would be a flurry of cut-off sentences as we tried to fill him in on everything he'd missed.

Then goosebumps prickle my skin as I remember how fiercely we'd avoid that very same firehouse after he left us. How we'd drive the long way around the block so we didn't have to pass the one thing my dad loved more than us. His job. His fire family. The attention from other women his uniform brought him.

"You okay?" Grady asks, pulling me from the memories and back to reality.

"Yeah. I'm fine. Ready to show me your fire pole, Malone?"

"I already pet your kitty, so I guess my pole is the next best place to start."

"You're sick." I laugh.

"And you love it."

Yes, I do. And that may be a problem.

"So that's everything." He shrugs as he enters the bay where two engines wait in limbo. There's a smile on his face and an ease to him I haven't seen before.

"You really love what you do, don't you?"

There's a brief flash of something in his eyes that passes before I can catch it, but he nods. "It's the only thing I've ever wanted to be." He says it with such conviction that I believe it. "A wise person once told me, it isn't something you do, it's something you are."

I smile. "Whoever said that must be brilliant." I reach for his arm on reflex and then pull back, uncertain of his status with the guys here and how my being here might reflect on him.

"And pretty." *Sigh.* And now he turns on the charm. "The other day, you took the time to show me what you do. I thought I'd show you what I do before my shift starts."

"Thank you." The gesture touches me unexpectedly. Maybe it's the fact he cares. Maybe it's just because it's the first time I've stepped into a station since my dad left, and it hasn't been as traumatic as I expected. Actually, it's been quite the opposite.

"Hey, Malone? You ready to pose for the camera, pretty boy?" a voice calls out from the other side of the bay, and Grady's demeanor changes so swiftly it's as if someone flipped a switch.

"I told you, Veego. I'm not doing it. Get off my case, will ya?"

"We can't do it without you, man. Then why is she—oh, sorry. You're not Marcy," Veego says when I turn to face him as he walks into view and does a double take.

"Not Marcy," I say with a chuckle, although I'm suddenly wondering who Marcy is and why she would be with Grady.

"She's a photographer," Grady mutters under his breath as if he already knew where my thoughts went.

Veego bears down on us. He's short and broad and has a smile that would light up a room. "Sorry, Grady. I didn't realize you had company."

"Dylan McCoy." I reach my hand out and shake his while he stares at me for a beat longer than normal.

"Ah, the roommate."

"Yes, the roommate."

"Are you going to convince him to do the calendar?" he asks, which earns him a glare from Grady.

"What calendar?" I glance from Veego to Grady and then back to Veego, ignoring Grady's warning look.

"We're doing a—"

"Drop it," Grady says, but Veego keeps going.

"—Sunnyville fireman calendar shoot. The beefcake kind," he says with a wink, and the flush to his cheeks makes me smile. Marcy's relevance to the conversation suddenly makes sense. "It's to raise money for the fireman's widow fund. Pretty-boy Malone here refuses to be the month of August when he's the best looking of the ugly lot of us. Too bad that shiner will be gone by the time we shoot the photos though or else I'm sure that would just add to his bad-boy vibe the ladies will get all wet over—"

"It's a dead issue," Grady says again, cutting me off when I begin to speak. "Is that what Bowie called me in early for? To have a meeting on this bullshit?"

I may be confused as to what he's referring to, but I see the panic flicker through Veego's eyes just as easily as Grady does. Whatever Grady is referring to has nothing to do with the calendar and everything to do with something that's brought an unwelcome chill to the conversation.

"Fuck this," Grady says as he shakes his head. "Not now. Of all times, *not now*."

I'm in the dark as to what's going on, but the emotion that flows in the look the two men share is overwhelming. One defiant, and the other resolute.

"Grady . . ."

"C'mon, Dylan."

"You can't hide forever, Malone." Veego's voice is full of compassion, and a part of me feels like I should shrink into the shadows and give them privacy.

"I'm not hiding from shit. I'm walking Dylan to my truck. Figure out how not to make this happen or else I'm heading home with her."

They glare at each other again.

"See you in a few," Veego says, grief I don't understand heavy in his voice. He turns to me. "Nice to meet you, Dylan."

Grady is silent as we head out of the bay and toward the parking lot. I'm not sure what to say, I'm not even sure what just transpired, and yet, I feel on edge as I figure out how to handle this.

"I might be overstepping . . . but why are you so upset about the calendar?" I realize the answer the minute the question passes over my lips—*his burns.*

"There's no way I'm going to stand there and let people stare at me. The calendar idea is crap."

"Crap?" I push, not caring that I have no right to. "It's for the widows' fund. I'd think you'd be willing to help. When is the last time a firefighter died in the line of duty before Drew?"

"Christ, I don't know."

"Then wouldn't the majority of the proceeds go to Shelby and Brody? Why won't you participate?"

If looks could kill, I'd be dead right now. "Stay out of it, Dylan."

"What's the big deal? You said it yourself. You're vain. Let them take a picture of all your hard work. You have an incredible body. Sell some calendars. Help Shelby and Brody. I don't know what your hang up is," I say, knowing very well what it is but not caring as I shamelessly use his guilt to help him get over his own insecurities.

"No one wants to look at me, I can assure you of that."

"I do."

"Save it."

"Save what?" I scoff. "Do you know how often I sit in the house when you're out working on the playroom and stare at you?" I love the shocked look on his face and laugh. "What? A girl needs inspiration while she's writing songs."

"Don't do this . . ." He shakes his head, confusion welling in his eyes.

"Do what? Tell you that the camera is going to love you? That it's going to be looking at your front and not your back, so what's the big deal? And if it were snapping a picture of your back, you know what it would show? A man who went to hell and back to try to save his friend. I don't know a single person who would think otherwise."

"First the guys, and now you? You were the one person I didn't have to worry about piling on with the bullshit."

I can see the bluster in his bravado and know he's afraid to see himself as he looks now. He's afraid to document it for everyone else to see.

"The guys just want what's best for you, like I do."

"Like you do?" His voice rises in pitch as he takes a step toward me, shoulders squared. "What do you think this is? We screwed so that gives you the right to tell me what to do?

His words are sharp, but the fear in his eyes is sharper. There's something more here. There's something he isn't talking about.

"Don't be an asshole."

"That's who I am, Dylan. An asshole. If you've got a problem, feel free to stay with someone else. I'm sure Jett's ready to whisk you back home and start right where you left off." The minute the words are out, he hangs his head and scrunches his face. He groans before looking up and meeting my eyes. "Look, I'm sorry. I didn't mean that. There's just . . . there are other things going on here besides the calendar."

The phone call from the other night when I was making the cannoli comes to mind. The one about a meeting on Thursday, which is apparently a lot more important than it sounded.

I scramble with what to say. With how to dissipate his anger, his fear, his irritation, all of which I helped cause.

Humor. Humor always works best.

"Is this our first fight as a couple?" I ask, a ghost of a smile on my lips and a plea for forgiveness in my eyes.

He struggles with the shift in gears before saying, "Yep. Jett's leaving, and we're already breaking up." His smile is half-hearted, but his expression says he's still upset.

I wish I knew about what.

"Well, shit." I put my hands on my hips. "I think we've got this all backward."

A little more sincerity edges his smile now. "Mmm. We had make-up sex before the fight."

"We did." Is it weird that he understands where I'm going with this conversation without any further explanation? *Is it weird that it gives me hope?*

We stare at each other, smiles soft and apologies unspoken but accepted.

"You should get going. My shift's about to start." I'm taken by surprise when he holds his keys out to me. A man and his truck are a sacred thing. "I'll call you tomorrow to pick me up if that's okay. If not, I'll have one of the guys drop me home."

"I'll come get you. No biggie." I open the driver's side door, climb behind the wheel, and then look at him. He still seems unsettled, and I wish I could help with whatever is bothering him. "You know I'm here for you if you need me, right?"

"Yeah." He nods ever so slightly and looks at his boots for a second before looking up to me. His aqua eyes a sea of discord. "I do. Thanks."

And with that, Grady walks into the fire station with what looks like the weight of the world on his shoulders and a tiny piece of my heart in his pocket.

TWENTY-THREE

Grady

"WHAT'S THE DEAL?" I ASK WITH MAJOR ATTITUDE THE minute I walk into the common area.

Veego, Bowie, Dixon, and Mack are all sitting around the table with somber expressions on their faces. Their eyes all flicker to each other while they wait for Bowie, the highest in command, to speak first.

"Take a seat," Bowie says and kicks a chair out for me. I grit my teeth and refuse to sit when he motions to it. I'm pretty sure I need to remain standing for this one.

"Please tell me this isn't about the goddamn calendar." Dylan's words outside resonate in my head. Make me feel even guiltier that I'm not willing to strip my shirt off to help Brody and Shelby.

Shit.

I don't have a choice, do I?

"Because if it is, I'll do the fucking thing. You happy?" I throw my hands up. "Can I go now? Class dismissed?"

I know I'm being an asshole, but a confrontation is the last thing I need right now. I have the memory of Dylan in my bed and the reality of Shelby's request in my head. The one she called me about earlier that I can't quite wrap my head around how I'm going to be able to do it and not lose it myself. Talk about the highest high to a heartbreaking low.

"The calendar's a good start, but it's the least important of what we need to talk about," Veego says and looks toward Bowie to continue.

"We're worried about you, Malone," Bowie says matter-of-factly.

"What? Am I not pulling my weight around here? The rig's clean. The grocery shopping is done. The—"

"When's the last time you were active on a call?" Mack speaks up and gets to the heart of the matter.

"I'm active on all calls."

"Let me rephrase, when was the last time you were engaged on a call, Malone?" It's Dixon's calm voice that grates on my nerves and ignites my temper. "You know, walked into the fire beside us instead of stood there and watched us go at it alone."

"Fucking Christ."

"You were out six months. On desk duty for what? A year?" Bowie asks.

"Uh-huh," I say void of all emotion and recall how miserable it was being a desk jockey while I waited for the medical doctors and the department psychologist to deem me physically and mentally fit to return. "And on active duty for six months. Your point is what exactly?"

"How many fires have you been engaged on?"

"There haven't been many fires in Sunnyville since I've been off desk duty, so I couldn't tell you."

"Don't be a smartass."

"Okay then, I'll be a dumbass and ask the question you all seem to know but aren't letting me in on. What the fuck is going on?"

"Can we trust you to be there?" Mack asks, and I can tell that having to ask that question makes all the guys uncomfortable.

"Can you trust me?" I blink as if it's going to help me understand what they're asking.

Trust is knowing your brother is there even when you can't see him. Two-in. Two-out. No matter the cost.

I think of Drew saying those words to me. Of the two of us reciting them as we sat at a beach bonfire and polished off a six-pack. The tap of our beer bottles against one another's. The promise made to always look out for each other.

And with the memory comes the anger at the rest of the guys looking at me. The disbelief that they're questioning me.

"Oh, I get it. This isn't you worrying about my well being. This is you worrying about me having your back on a call. This is you worrying if my head's straight enough to save you if you get in trouble . . . or if I'm going to let you die like I did Drew? Right? That's what this is?" Mack tries to talk, and I cut him off. "Well, *fuck you*. Fuck all of you." My fists clench, and it's hard to draw in air as I turn my back to them and pace the room. Fury and hurt and distrust eat at every part of me . . . just like the guilt does.

"Grady."

"Stop Grady-ing me! Just stop! You don't know what it was like. You don't live with what happened in your head. His voice asking for help. His screams begging. Having to hear his PASS alarm going off and not knowing how to save him. You don't close your eyes every goddamn night and worry about how bad the nightmare is going to be this time, do you? You don't get called to a scene where a fire is hot and worry about whether it's going to happen again. So you're fucking right, I'm messed up. But you can bet your ass that when I walk into a fire, it'll be because I'm ready and know without a shadow of a doubt I'd do it again to save one of your sorry asses. If you don't like that, or don't believe I'm capable of doing my job, take it up with command. Kick me out of the department. But don't you *ever*"—I slam my hand down on the kitchen counter so hard it stings—"tell me you worry about me having your back."

Every part of my body vibrates with an anger I haven't felt since the day I woke in the hospital bed and was told that Drew didn't make it. Four sets of eyes stare at me with a shock and concern that's incomparable to anything I've seen before.

"We just want to help you in whatever way you need it," Mack says. "But you won't let us. You walk around like everything is fucking perfect when we know it isn't. It isn't for us, for fuck's sake so how can it be okay for you?"

"We're here for you. That's all we're saying," Dixon chimes in when I want to tune him out.

"We'll help you work through it on the next call, but we need you to tell us how to do it," Bowie says. And it's harder to ignore him when he knows more than any of them about the panic attack I get when I'm on scene. He's the one who trades places with me—goes into the fire while I take his command—so I don't lose it.

"There's nothing you can do," I whisper, embarrassed and unable to meet their eyes. I look at the pictures on the wall. Every member of the firehouse has their picture there . . . even Drew. It's still there with the chip in the corner of the frame. Seeing his goofy grin kills me more than any of their words do. He should be here instead of me. Shelby should have her husband, and Brody should have his dad. No one needs me. *Why was he the one who died?* "Just let me get through this week. Let me get through what we have to do on Monday. Then I'll wrap my head around all of this." I look up and meet each one of their eyes.

Do they still trust me?

Do they still think I am capable? Still believe *in* me?

I swallow my pride and anger and take a deep breath in an attempt to dial back the emotions eating me whole. "Thank you for your concern. Thank you for caring. Thank you for giving me time."

My eyes sting as I walk from the common area to the bunkroom. I don't know how to work in a place that holds all the incredible memories I never want to forget but can't bear to be reminded of.

How do I live a life that does exactly that?

How do I move forward when I'm terrified the past will repeat itself?

TWENTY-FOUR

Grady

"WHERE'S YOUR TRUCK?"

I climb into the passenger seat and glance over at my dad. "Dylan has it."

"Dylan? Why would you let that musician-creep drive it?"

I laugh harder than I should as he pulls away from the station. "Dylan is the girl staying with me. Remember Damon McCoy from that sleep-away football camp you sent me to when I was in high school? She's his sister."

"Oh."

"The musician-creep is Jett."

"Jett? As in like an airplane type of jet?"

"Exactly."

"It's easy to confuse your old man," he says with a laugh but then falls silent as he slides a look my way.

Christ. Not again.

"Who talked to you?" I sigh. First the guys at the start of shift yesterday and now him.

"No one." But his lack of explanation as to what I'm referring to is an answer in and of itself. "I heard you got in a fight the other night with the Winters kid."

The Winters kid. I feel like I'm back in grade school again the way he says it.

"The fucker deserved it."

"Grady—"

"He disrespected Dylan, so don't give me a lecture on how fists don't solve problems. I get it. I know better. I'm not twelve anymore, and I didn't pledge my life to upholding the law. But this time around, he deserved it. You don't brag about sleeping with a woman when you didn't and then say rude shit to disrespect her." There's more anger in my tone than there should be, but I'm so sick and tired of being pushed right now.

I look over to my dad to see his lips pursed. It's his tell when he has a shitload to say but is holding back.

"And this Dylan woman," he finally says, "what did she think of you protecting her honor?"

"She doesn't know."

"Hmm." He nods but gives nothing more on the subject. "You've missed the last couple of Sunday dinners. You know what that does to your mom. Maybe you should bring this Dylan around the house sometime since it seems you don't want to leave her."

"It's not that I don't want to leave her. It's that I've been on shift. And bringing Dylan to the house would only encourage Mom's matchmaking you-should-marry-this-girl-and-give-me-grandbabies frenzy. No thanks."

"She means well." After forty years, there is still affection in his voice every time he speaks of her.

"I know she does."

"So are you?"

I'm pretty sure I choke on the air I'm breathing. "Am I what?"

"Are you going to marry this girl and give us grandbabies?"

If whiplash were possible, I'd have it from the breakneck speed I turn to look at my dad. "We aren't even . . ."

Aren't what? We aren't dating but we're fucking?

Classy, especially after I was just talking about respect and women.

"Grandbabies aren't in the future."

"But you like her." It isn't a question. Just a statement.

I chew the answer on my tongue before nodding. "Yeah, she's pretty cool."

"You got in a fight for her, Grady. That means she's more than pretty cool in your eyes. In fact, it says you more than like her."

"Seriously?" I laugh, feeling like I'm on the playground bickering with a classmate.

"A songwriter, you say?" he asks, switching gears like the seasoned interrogator he used to be.

"I didn't say what she did." He has definitely been talking to my brothers. "But yes, she's a songwriter."

"Does she sing too?"

I think of her voice. How it's throaty and sexy with that hint of rasp to it when she sings. "Yeah. She has a great voice."

"So is she going to transition to singing for herself instead of hiding behind the scenes?"

Let the cross-examination begin.

I know my dad, and right now he's angling at something. "No," I respond as we turn down my street. "I keep telling her she has a hell of a talent, and it's too bad she isn't putting it to use."

My dad pulls up to the curb in front of my house and looks at me for a beat. "Kind of like you."

"*What*?" My fingers tense on the door handle.

"You have a hell of a firefighting talent." He shrugs. "Too bad you aren't putting it to use."

Trigger pulled. Point made.

I stare at him, wanting to lash out but knowing it will do no good. Being the ex-chief of police, his ties run deep in this community. Someone at the fire department talked to him. Someone voiced his concern. Without me saying a word, he knows I haven't been back into a fire since the accident.

"I know. It's a rough time of year for me." I slide from the car, wanting this conversation to be over and done with.

"Hey, Grady?"

I lean down and meet his eyes. "Yeah, Dad?"

"It's okay to forget what hurt you, but just remember to never forget what it taught you."

"What did it teach me, other than to fear the one thing I love?"

"Fear has two meanings, son. Forget everything and run. Or face everything and rise." He gives me a soft smile as I try to process what he just said. "You've been doing the first for a while. That's understandable. It's been a long road, and a part of me wants to tell you to run forever and not look back, because I almost lost you once. That's the safe bet. But that isn't you. That isn't the son I know. You'd die without being able to do your first love, fighting fires. So now? Now you take it day by day, call by call, nightmare by nightmare . . . but you face everything about it and rise."

I nod as he starts the car and drives off without another word. I watch his car until I can't see the taillights and then stare after it a bit more.

Face everything and rise.

My dad's words ring in my head as I walk in the house, their poignancy hitting closer to home than I want to admit. It's too much for me to think about.

So I don't.

Instead, I grab a beer from the refrigerator and flip through the mail sitting on the counter as Dylan's voice comes strong and focused through her closed bedroom door.

She's working. Figures.

Jett's gone. That's a bonus.

I move to the hallway, Petunia beside me, and listen to her sing. Every part of me wants to open the door and sit on her bed to listen to her while she works. Watch that little crease she gets in her forehead when she's concentrating. Study the way her fingers work with skill over the strings of the guitar. Listen to how she varies the same line over and over with one word changed, an inflection altered, to try to see what sounds better.

But I don't do any of those things because I've been thinking about her way too much and thinking about a woman when it isn't only how I'm going to get her back in bed is not something I can rationally afford. I mean, hell yes, I've thought about how I want her back in my bed, but I've also thought about so many other things. Things that make me think of Shelby and Brody and the fact that they'll live the rest of their lives without Drew. Things that tell me I need to stop playing house with her and go back to being roommates.

I run a hand through my hair and force myself to retreat from her door and the comfort her voice brings. It's when I walk into my bedroom and find the T-shirt and boxers I lent her washed and folded and set on the corner of my bed that it hits me.

In order to be roommates, we'll no longer sleep in the same bed.

And without her in the same bed, my dreams will return. My nightmares.

With her beside me, they didn't haunt me. It may have been only three nights, but they were the most peaceful three nights I've had in a long time. Not to mention one night of incredible sex.

I stare at the bed for a few moments before shaking my head.

Quit being such a pussy, Malone. Suck it up.

But instead of taking a shower like I planned to, I drop my bag right inside the door, shuck my shirt, and head out back to work on the playroom.

I need something to do with my hands that doesn't involve them being on her skin.

So I begin to work. Nail after nail. Board after board. But it's my dad's words that keep ringing in my ears.

"It's okay to forget what hurt you, but just remember to never forget what it taught you." It taught me I'm not infallible. It's taught me I can't let someone close to me, because one day, I may be the one who doesn't come home.

TWENTY-FIVE

Dylan

"I should have seen that coming a mile away," Grady says to no one, followed by an exasperated laugh that pulls me out of my bedroom to see what he's talking about.

He's standing at the back door, looking out at the yard, and I hate the little flip-flop that my belly does seeing him there.

"Seen what coming?" I ask.

He turns, his smile crooked and hair disheveled from sleeping. "Good morning, sleepyhead."

"It isn't that late—oh it is," I say when I look at the clock to see that it's past ten. "I worked late. I was on a roll and didn't want it to stop. You worked late though, too. I mean in the backyard. Not at the station. But you never called for me to pick you up. So I was surprised when I heard the hammer. I should have come out and said hi. I should have . . ."

Am I rambling? Stop rambling. When did these nerves start around him? And are they why I stood in the kitchen and watched him but was too chicken shit to go out and talk to him? Add to that it felt awkward not heading to sleep in the same room as him.

"I know you did. You were still going at it when I went to bed."

"Sorry if I was too loud and kept you up. I lost track of time."

"No. Don't apologize. I like listening to you sing." I blush, suddenly self-conscious knowing he was listening. "It's Sunday."

I nod my head." And . . .?"

"My family has a Sunday tradition of having dinner together." I narrow my eyes as I try to see where he's going with this. "Do you have plans today?"

"No, why?"

"Do you want to go to dinner with me?"

"But it's not dinner time." I smile.

"You're right. It isn't. Let me start over." His grin widens. "Good morning, Dylan."

I laugh. "Good morning, Grady."

"I'm going to apologize in advance for this, but I'd like to know if you have any plans today."

"If I didn't, your approach is telling me I should pretend I do," I play along.

"No, it isn't that bad." He chuckles. "It's just my mother scheming to meet the girl who's staying at my house and make an excuse for me to show up to a family Sunday dinner. When my dad drove me home last night, he was asking about you . . . so I should have expected an invitation from my mom like the one I just received." He holds up his cell as if I can read the text or email from where I stand.

"For what?"

"They're having a barbecue at the lake house. They invited a bunch of people, so don't worry, it won't just be you and me and them trying to figure out what's going on between us . . . but you were invited."

Invited. As a friend or as . . .?

"To Sunday dinner during the day?"

"Yes. Something like that." His dimples deepen and every part of me wants to melt at the little-boy appeal they give to such a virile man's body.

"The lake house?" I ask, my first thought is that there's water, which means wearing a bathing suit, and bathing suits and I don't get along in the least. Or rather, we do get along but the mirror and me wearing a bathing suit aren't exactly the best of friends.

And my second thought is I'm still trying to figure out what's going on between us, so it isn't fair for his family to know before I do.

"Yes, the lake house. Sunshine. A rope swing over the water. Good food." He shrugs and smiles. "You can't stay locked away writing forever, can you?"

"Actually, I can." I laugh, thinking of how many days I've felt like a vampire because I'm knee-deep in an album and hardly see the sun.

"But I won't let you." He grins. "Grab your suit and sunscreen. I'm not letting you say no."

Bathing suit.

The two words I dread more than many others.

And looking around at the perfect bodies on display, my insecurities are justified and then some. There's Grant and his wife, Emerson. A shirtless Grant is a perfect example of why the Malone boys seem to have the reputation for being unfairly gifted in the looks department. And then there's Emerson, who even at a few months pregnant, looks stunning with her little baby bump.

Next up is Grayson and his mini-me son, Luke. The two are more than adorable together, but I shouldn't expect anything less, considering I'm convinced that there isn't a rogue gene in this family.

There's a myriad of other friends, too, some from Grady's fire station, I believe, but they are floating out on the water on inner tubes, so I've yet to meet them beyond a wave across the distance.

"You have a lovely place here. The scenery is incredible." And it is. Pine trees line the water's edge, and the sun glistens off the lake. It looks like a postcard.

"It is, isn't it?" Betsy Malone, Grady's mother, stares at me with a soft smile on her lips and excitement in her eyes. "So, Grady tells me you're a songwriter?"

"Yes."

"And he met your brother at football camp? Do I have that right?"

I smile. "Yes."

"And your parents live in Los Angeles too?"

I hope she doesn't notice the stiffening of my smile. It's not always the most comfortable to admit I have no clue where my dad is and the only reason I know my mom's whereabouts is because the address of her latest rehab facility is on the bill sitting in my inbox. "Yes, in the Los Angeles area," I lie with ease to hide my discomfort.

"And are you staying in Sunnyville long?"

"Leave her alone, Mom. You're going to scare the poor woman off before Grady has a chance to," Grayson says as he leans over to steal a piece of watermelon off the table where we're sitting.

"Shush. I'm just trying to get to know her better, and be nice to your brother."

"She wants to see how long you're going to be in town," he says and lifts his eyebrows. "She's plotting out when she can expect her next grandchild to be born."

I sputter out a laugh as Betsy reaches her hand out to pat my arm. "No, I'm not, dear. I just wanted to know more about you."

"Famous last words." He laughs. "I bet if you ask Emerson, she'll tell you that she got asked the same questions, and look what happened. Now she's pregnant."

I can't help but smile at his ribbing and the annoyed look on Betsy's face as she shoos him away before turning her attention back to me. "So will you be here for very long?"

I bite back my laugh because Grayson nailed her intentions on the head. And I'm not the least bit fazed, either. Grady warned me that she'll try to corner me and figure out when the next Malone is coming.

Is she forward? Yes. Is she also adorable and madly in love with her sons and her family? Absolutely, and no one can fault her for that.

"Four or five more weeks," I answer, and her smile falls a moment before she refortifies it.

"But you'll be back, right? I mean you like Grady enough to come back?"

"Yes, I like Grady," I say, my voice softening as I look at him throwing the football to Grayson's son, Luke. And for a moment, I watch the two of them, and when I realize I am, I snap my eyes over to see Betsy staring at me with a knowing look on her face.

"Uh-huh." That's all she says.

"Leave poor Dylan alone, Betsy," Grady's dad says as he sits on the picnic bench beside me and nudges my elbow. "Just ignore her. She's been known to run off some of the women the boys have brought home in the past." He winks as she swats at his arm and laughs. There is a brief exchange of a look between the two of them, and their love for each other can be felt as if it were tangible.

Laughter erupts on the lawn when Grady tries to evade Grayson's tackle, but he gets his hands in Grady's shirt and pulls him down.

"He'd be better if he ditched the shirt," Chief Malone mutters under his breath. "It's just us, for Christ's sake." There's hurt there. The parental kind. It's hard to hear it and not feel for both parties.

"He's getting there," Betsy murmurs in response, but the chief's face is still full of concern as he watches his son.

I can't imagine what it must have been like to watch their son go through the horror of his accident and the long, dark time it took to recover. *Physically.* So often, we focus so intently on the injured person that we give zero thought to the family standing behind them, supporting them, loving them, and helping them heal. It's unfathomable to me. First they went through the fear of losing their son and then were forced to watch him struggle. Because they have to know what he's going through, and it has to be so hard to stand by in silent support as he figures it out on his own.

Hell, it's killing me, and I've only been here such a short time in the overall time of his recovery.

The scanner goes off behind me. Some call. Somewhere. I shake my head at the fact that the Malones seem to bring work with them everywhere.

"I know," Betsy says and laughs when she realizes what I'm shaking my head at. Thankfully, the chief is oblivious to my reaction since he's homing in on what dispatch is relaying. "That damn scanner is like an extra appendage for all of my boys, but you get used to it. What's worse is that when they're out on the line, you find comfort in hearing it because you know what they're doing. It's ten times better than the horrors you're imagining in your head."

I hold her eyes and nod. She's right . . . and yet, it's still funny that on this rare occasion when all three of her sons are off duty, they are still, in a sense, on-duty.

"What can we say? We're creatures of habit," Grady's dad says, surprising me when he reaches back and turns the scanner off. "Are you having a good time, interrogation notwithstanding?"

"I am, thank you. It's just what the doctor ordered."

Betsy and the chief look to where Grady has tackled Luke to the ground and is tickling him before looking back toward me. The smile, the joy, on his face causes a flutter in my chest I try to ignore, but can't. "It most definitely is," Betsy murmurs.

TWENTY-SIX

Dylan

"ARE YOU GLAD YOU CAME?" GRADY ASKS AND PULLS MY attention from where Luke and Grayson and a few others are taking bets on who can clear the longest distance by swinging from the rope into the water.

"Yes. You?" I murmur as Luke flies with a shriek through the air and lands with a huge splash into the water.

"Yes. I'm glad you came too." There's something about the way Grady says the words—suggestion riding shotgun with playfulness—that grabs my attention and doesn't let go. He sits beside me on the dock with a smirk on his lips as we let our toes dangle in the water, feet lazily kicking back and forth.

His comment may have suggestion written all over it, but there hasn't been a single moment during the course of the day where anyone who looked at us would have thought there was anything more between us than roommates.

I study him and wonder how this works. Are we just going to ignore the fact that we had sex two nights ago and never talk about it? Are we not going to acknowledge that every time we look at each other, I stare at his lips because I want him to kiss me and he undresses me with his eyes? Or do we sit here and ignore the sexual tension that increases with every accidental touch of a hand or brush of our bodies against each other's?

"What?" I ask after he never looks away and I've grown self-conscious under his silent observation.

"How come you haven't braved the lake yet?" he asks, making me cringe internally.

So much for doing a good job of hiding from the water, or more importantly, having to wear a bathing suit in front of everyone. Luckily, my eyes are hidden behind my tinted lenses or else he'd probably see right through every excuse on the tip of my tongue.

"No reason." I try an excuse anyway.

"He really did a number on you, didn't he, Dylan?" There's so much compassion laced with a hint of anger on my behalf that it opens the door to the hurt and lays down a welcome mat for it.

I sigh. Then start to speak. Stop myself. Then try to explain. "It wasn't so much Jett as it was every other woman who wanted to be with him."

"You mean every other woman who wished she were you so they'd tear you down with lies to justify why they couldn't hold a candle to you? You mean those women?"

It sounds stupid when he says it. It's even worse that despite it sounding stupid, the women were still successful in affecting how I saw myself. *See myself.* But at the same time, it isn't exactly hard to look at the proof—Jett screwing what's-her-ho—to reinforce the way I feel.

Add to that, I hate that Grady's observation means so much that a mixture of shame and wounded pride makes my eyes burn. "They're not lies when they're the truth."

His sigh is audible, and the shake of his head reads almost disappointed. "That's not how I see it."

"C'mon, Grady. I appreciate you trying to make me feel better about myself but . . . I'm not blind here. I know my body isn't like the Hollywood crowd. I'm well aware that when the media used to take pictures of Jett and me, he radiated on the page while most of them Photoshopped the hell out of me. The ones that didn't, told a nasty story to justify why rock-god Jett Kroger was with someone who didn't meet the public's ideal for him."

"The media doesn't know shit. That I can tell you. Heroine chic is the furthest thing from sexy. And it's women who do this. They're the ones telling the men what they should like when they don't know shit other than their own insecurities. You really want to know what a man likes?"

"I have a feeling you're about to tell me."

"Sure am. Men like women who eat. They like women they can take to dinner and won't push food around on a plate because they're afraid to be seen actually putting food in their mouths. You know, like we all have to do in order to survive. Men like women who are muscular and strong and don't look like they'll break if we toss them around in bed."

"Whatever," I say with a roll of my eyes, but the smile on my lips is genuine.

"Men like women who are confident, who know how to handle themselves, and who don't fucking care if their thighs touch or not, because it isn't when they're pressed together that men are thinking about. It's when they're spread apart that we're hoping for. Crude? Yes. True? Hell, yes." My laughter rings out at something I should probably find offensive, and yet the context in which he's saying it—to explain to me why I have a bad self-image—is endearing. "You have this confidence I can hear clear as day when you sing in your room and work through a song, but it disappears the minute you're asked to go to the lake because you might have to wear a bathing suit."

"Grady . . ."

"What? It's the truth. I saw you hesitate the minute I asked, and I thought it was because you didn't want to go with me. Then we got here and you avoided going anywhere near the water, and I figured out why." He looks to where Luke yells as he sails through the air again. "I hate the way you see yourself, Dylan."

"And I hate the way you see yourself, Grady." Maybe he needs to listen to his own words.

He brings his bottle of beer to his lips ever so slowly without looking my way. "I agreed to do the calendar. Happy?" There's no edge to his voice like I'd expect there to be, just a sad resignation.

"Not happy, no. I detest that it makes you uncomfortable, but at the same time, I think if you don't participate, you'll regret it later."

"Mmm." That's all he says, and I hate that he still hasn't looked my way.

"I can be there during the photo shoot if you want," I offer then feel like an idiot who has overstepped the minute the words are out. "I mean . . . if you need silent support."

"Thanks."

He doesn't say yes or no, so I fall quiet, suddenly uncomfortable with this conversation. We sit like this for a bit while I swing my legs, run my toes through the water, and lift my face to the sun to welcome the warmth.

"Tell me about your dad."

Every part of me tenses at the mention of the man who abandoned us, so I keep my eyes closed momentarily and concentrate on the sun's heat on my cheeks. I know it's my turn to offer up a part of myself, so I grow a pair, and let out a deep breath while I try to find the words.

"What is there to say other than he loved his job more than he loved us." Grady grimaces at my explanation. "One day, he was there, a part of everything we did. The glue that held us all together. And then the next, he was telling my mom that having a family—*damn responsibilities,* is I think what he called us—wasn't part of life for a firefighter. That he needed to be able to chase the next flame when it came without worrying."

"That's a euphemism if ever I've heard one." I can hear the disgust in his voice, and it makes me feel better if at all possible.

"Pretty much. There were four of us, the McCoys on Mistress Court . . . and yes, the irony of our street name is not lost on me. One day we had the white picket fence in suburbia, and the next there was nothing. My mom was a shell of herself. Damon was angry all the time. My dad participated from afar for a while. Then less and less with each subsequent year until there was nothing left. Not even a card on Christmas. The white picket fence became faded and fell down. Weeds grew where the grass used to be green."

"And what happened to little Dylan?"

"Little Dylan grew up with a distrust of firefighters—*and* men in general. As you can see with Jett, she had every right to feel that way." I hate that my voice swells with emotion I can't hide. Grady notices, and it has him slowly swinging his eyes my way.

"Your brother is obviously good now, married and happy with the twins. I know how you are. What about your mom?"

I focus on my fingers where they pick at the paint on the dock. I feel embarrassment all these years later when I have to talk about my mom. "She's on her who-knows-what-number stint in rehab." My voice is quiet, my disappointment in her always present.

"I'm sorry, Dylan. I didn't know."

"How could you? It's not something I'm proud of or like to admit. And it's definitely something I'm sick and tired of footing the bill for . . . but it's my mom. What am I supposed to do, walk away?" I shake my head and try to push the emotion from my voice.

He makes a noncommittal sound. "Just another reason why you can't walk away from this album, right?"

"Mm-hmm," I murmur, grateful he connected the dots between the money and my need to stay beyond making a name for myself.

The two of us slip into a comfortable silence as the others frolic in the distance, their laughter reaching our ears and making me feel even sadder for some reason when I should be anything but.

"I'm sorry for what your family went through, but not all guys are assholes."

"True." The word is measured, and yet anyone hearing it will know I don't truly believe it.

"And not all firefighters abandon their families. Plenty of guys have a good solid relationship and are successful at it."

"And where do you fall?" I ask, desperate to turn the conversation off me and onto him.

Now it's his turn to flinch, his feet hesitating mid-swing. I've hit a nerve. "I'm a different situation altogether."

"What's that supposed to mean? Are you going to be the forever bachelor?"

"Yes, but not for the reasons you think."

"You lost me," I say with a laugh because he isn't making sense.

"I'm not afraid to settle down because I'll miss the single life. It definitely has its perks . . . as you can see, I come from a close-knit family. Don't tell my mom, but I'd love to be a dad and give her those grandkids she nags me for, but I can't . . ." His words are followed by a sigh that holds so much sadness and grief it's almost palpable. "After Drew's death, I watched Shelby lose every part of herself while trying to be strong for Brody. Having Brody ask me when I'm going to bring his dad home from the station. I just . . . I can't knowingly be with someone, have a child with someone, and then continue to risk myself every time I get a call."

"But they'll know it's a possibility too. They'll walk into a relationship with you knowing your job is what you love. It's who you are. They'll understand and take the chance because they love you."

I know he hears me because he nods as he looks at his feet splashing in the water, but he doesn't respond. I don't expect him to either. He's been so emotionally scarred by the events of the fire and the aftermath.

"Grady! Don't be such a pansy. Get your ass over here and let me beat you!" Grayson yells, pointing to the rope swing where he is across the shore.

Grady finally looks at me. "So, Dylan? Are you going to be confident and take that cover-up off and show off those curves of yours? Or am I going to have to carry you into the water in your clothes so you have nothing to wear home that's dry except your suit?"

"You wouldn't dare?" I say as I push myself up from my spot on the dock as he does the same.

"Either way, I win . . . so try me."

"It goes both ways, Malone."

"It does, does it?" he asks, a smile slowly curling up the corners of his lips, sensing a challenge.

"Yes. If I have to wear my bathing suit, you have to take your shirt off."

His smile falters momentarily as he angles his head and stares at me from behind his lenses. And then without saying a word, he pulls his T-shirt over his head and walks off down the dock.

"You better not chicken out on your end, McCoy. I know where you sleep at night," he calls over his shoulder before jumping from the wooden slats to the shore and heading toward his brother.

I catch the glance his mother gives his father and the one Grayson gives to Grant right before all four sets of eyes turn in my direction.

Knowing I did that for Grady makes me stand a little taller as I follow in his footsteps on the sandy shore. They love him despite what he considers imperfections.

Now, let's hope they can turn a blind eye to mine.

"Your family is incredible." My grin hasn't faded since we pulled away from the lake house and started our trip home. Neither have my thoughts. After watching Grady play with Luke and seeing how good he was with him, all I keep thinking about is how much Grady is going to miss by not being a father.

And of course, I've thought of every way imaginable to broach the subject again with him, but for what? He's been through hell and back. He has concrete reasons for his opinions. There's no way anything I say will change his way of thinking.

"You and Luke get along really well."

"He's a good kid," Grady says. "I don't know how Grayson made a kid that cool, but he definitely must have gotten those genes from me."

"Oh, please. It's obvious you're good with children. I hope I'm not overstepping when I—"

"Don't go there," Grady warns, and before I can respond—*apologize*—for doing what I told myself I wasn't going to do, the scanner interrupts me.

I wait for Grady to turn the sound down as he typically does, but this time, when his fingers are on the button, they don't move. Codes are being given left and right and despite the dispatcher's calm demeanor, I can tell she's unsettled.

"Everything okay?" I ask when his arm tenses.

"Yeah. Sure. Fine." His answer is distracted at best, and the easy-going banter we've enjoyed the entire drive home dissipates.

He pulls into the driveway and stares at me. His jaw is set. His shoulders are square. His hands keep flexing on the wheel.

"Hop out. I've gotta take a drive."

"Is everything okay?" I ask for a second time, knowing in my gut it isn't.

"Feed Petunia for me. I'm not sure when I'll be back."

I climb out of the truck and turn back to stare at him through the open window, but he only looks behind him as he reverses and drives off without another glance.

TWENTY-SEVEN

Dylan

"He forgot his phone." Grant is standing in the doorway to the house with his hand extended and Grady's cell in it.

"Thanks. He isn't here, but I'll give it to him when he gets back."

"Where'd he go? You guys couldn't have left five minutes before us."

"I don't know. There was a call on the scanner, and Grady said he had to take a drive." Grant swears under his breath and sighs. His reaction makes me uneasy. "What is it?"

"The one time Emerson convinces me to turn it off." He laughs, starts to speak, and then stops. He runs a hand through his hair with the same mannerism that his brother does and it makes me smile. "He's having a rough go of it." I can tell it pains him to tell me, almost as if he's betraying his brother by talking about it with me.

"You're the second or third person who has used that phrasing." Damon, Desi at the grocery store, and now Grant. "What exactly does a rough go of it mean? What am I missing?"

He twists his lips and then continues. "The guys at the station are worried about him. We're all worried about him, in fact."

"But he told me he agreed to do the calendar. It's a step in the right direction, isn't it? It shows he's coming to terms with his burns?"

"It is, a big one for him personally, but it's the scars we can't see that are worrying me. One of his crew, Bowie, called me a few weeks back. He said Grady isn't engaging on the job. If there's a fire, he can't bring himself to breach the building." My heart falls. "Bowie said he's fine on medical calls but show up at a hot scene, and he freezes."

"Which doesn't instill any confidence in the guys," I conclude and then think back to Grady's rejection of whatever meeting was going on at the station yesterday. The exchange with Veego. I thought Grady's unexpected request to take me to the station was to get back at Jett . . . and now I wonder if it was to prevent them from pulling him into a confrontation he didn't want to have. It all makes sense now, and I grieve for Grady. "I was there the other day. I thought it was just about the calendar."

"He's too proud to let anyone know he's having trouble." Grant's concern for his brother is so real. It's almost as if he's trying to wear the burden to carry it *for* his brother.

"Is there anything I can do to help?"

"I wish I knew, but all I can think of is that he needs more time. I don't know. None of us have been through this before. I wish there was a way to help ease the survivor's guilt or else when he actually gets the nerve to walk back in the fire, I fear he's going to be looking for punishment."

"He's punished himself enough."

"He has. And he'll always blame himself so there's no use trying to tell him different. I know from experience."

"Then what do we do?" I all but plead.

"We have patience. And we find a way to show him every day that if he doesn't start to live again, he's wasting his second chance at life."

The front door shutting startles me awake. My guitar falls off my lap and onto the floor with a musical thud as I scramble up and look toward the kitchen.

Grady stands there, shoulders sagging, eyes wary, and every part of him on edge. Our eyes meet for the briefest of seconds, his more like a glare of contempt before he throws his keys on the counter and walks back out without a word.

It's the first time I've ever felt uncomfortable in his home, and frankly, I'm not sure what I should do or what is going on.

And then I hear it.

The pound of the hammer. The deep, resonating *thud, thud, thud* of his aggression being taken out on wood and metal in what appears to be the only way he knows how to cope. I stand at the window and watch him, the scanner's steady, controlled chaos the background to my thoughts.

I'm not sure how long I stand there and watch Grady move here and there beneath the spotlight illuminating the small part of the backyard where he works, but the tension in his movements never seems to diminish.

My feet move without thought, the need to comfort more important than the awkwardness of intruding on his private moment. Outside I wait, not saying anything but knowing he is aware I'm there.

And still he doesn't say a word.

"Is everything okay?" I finally bite the bullet and ask.

He grunts in response.

"Do you want me to go to a hotel for the night so that you can have the house to yourself?"

"No. It's fine. I'm fine."

Uh-huh. Like I believe that for a second.

So, I sit on the steps of the porch and watch him work. Time passes, measured by the number of mosquitos I swat away.

"There was a fire tonight," he finally says, but he doesn't stop marking a piece of wood and lining it up.

"Are all the guys okay?"

He grunts again, which I take as an affirmative.

"You want to talk about whatever is bugging you? Tonight's fire? The guys?" I take a deep breath and go there. "*Your fire*?"

"Jesus fucking Christ. *Again*? Which one of them called you or stopped by and set you up to pretend you're my goddamn shrink?"

I exhale an unsteady breath. "None of them. I figured something was bugging you. I'm a smart girl, Grady. Most of those around you who care about you are smart too. I assume they all want to help you with whatever it is you need help with."

"I don't need help with anything." He spits the words out despite their untruth.

I don't push further. The cadence of the hammer becomes a metronome to his anger until it slowly eases with each and every stroke.

And then there is silence. Nothing but the silhouette of a man in conflict against the blinding light. His head hangs down, his hands fall lax, his shoulders sag.

"Today is the anniversary. *Of my fire*."

"Oh."

"Yeah. It was convenient timing for my parents to have a barbecue at the lake." He chuckles but shakes his head. "There was a fire tonight in the same set of warehouses where our fire happened. When I heard the call, my first thought was arson. The point of origin in our fire was never determined, and it's always been easier for me to blame someone for everything that happened instead of faulty wires or some shit like that. So, I heard dispatch on the scanner, and all I could think about was if it was arson, the son of a bitch wanted to come back and take a trip down memory lane. Get a thrill from watching firefighters run in that building and get off if one of them didn't make it back out."

"Was it?"

He pauses momentarily and then moves toward me, taking a seat beside me unexpectedly. "Nah. It was just one of those things. A perfect storm of mishaps in an old building."

"Well, that's good, right? Not the fire part, obviously."

"Mm-hmm."

"Did you wish you were there?"

"I was there. I watched it from afar." His voice is distant and cold, but his body is warm beside mine. It seems like such a weird dichotomy to me.

"No, I mean, did you wish you were fighting it?" I ask despite Grant's comments earlier.

"Are you going to push me on this too, Dylan?" He doesn't look my way, just stares at the hammer in his hand.

"I wasn't aware I was pushing. I just wondered if being back there made you want to get your firefighting fix."

His laugh is long and low with a hint of self-deprecation. "My firefighting fix? I think I got plenty of that. I think the question you're asking is why I'm being such a pussy and not grabbing my turnouts and laying down pipe like a probie running into his first fire. Am I right?"

Proceed with caution, Dylan.

"That isn't what I said."

"It may not be what you said, but it's what you meant."

I start to skirt around the issue but figure it isn't going to do either of us any good if I do. So, I dive right in. "You're right. It is what I meant."

His body jars beside me. "At least you're honest when everyone else tries to beat around the fucking bush."

"So?"

"I wanted to go in. Fires are few and far between in Sunnyville, so it isn't like there's a fire every week to test me . . . but when there is, it screws with my head. Every part of me wants to run in and do my job, and then I hear Drew screaming, feel the flames as they try to eat me alive, and I have a full-blown panic attack."

I'm shocked by his honesty, so I give him some right back. "Having a panic attack would seem like a completely logical reaction, Grady."

He hangs his head for a beat. "My dad used to say that bravery was being scared to death and suiting up anyway."

The correlation he's drawing is instantaneous to me. He doesn't feel like he's brave anymore. And yet, I will not refute him. Such a thing will fall on deaf ears, so I try another angle.

"Does this have anything to do with why you insisted I go to the station the other day?"

He crosses his arms on his knees and rests his forehead on them. I give him the time he needs and stare at the many moths flying through the light while I wait. "It was a company meeting. A we're-not-sure-if-you'd-have-our-backs-in-a-fire meeting." There's hurt in his voice, but more importantly, there's fight left too.

"They don't blame you, you know," I say when every part of me knows he thinks they do.

"I know they don't," he lies.

"No one does, Grady."

He grunts as his shoulders heave up and down, but he doesn't look up, and he doesn't speak.

"Is there anything anyone can do to make the transition easier for you? This is what you love, it has to be crippling you not to participate in what you live for."

"Stop talking about it. There's a start. Stop whispering behind my back. Stop staring at me like I'm going to fucking break. I'm already broken, Dylan. That's what they don't get."

"Grady . . . there has to be something—"

"How about this? I'll step into the fire when you decide you're going to sing your own songs yourself instead of wasting all your talent and ability on people who take you for granted like Jett does."

It's my turn to have my feathers ruffled, and they definitely are.

"What's wrong, Dylan?" he asks. "You don't like having ultimatums thrown at you? Aren't you the one who told me you'd take off your cover-up if I took off my shirt? Well, guess what? I took off my shirt. Now, I've upped the ante."

I stare at him through the dim light and hate that we are both letting our fear get in the way but have no idea how to get past it. Neither of us do.

"Don't turn this on me, Grady."

"It's a complicated fucking mess, isn't it?" he says as he finally turns his head to face me.

"It is." My voice is barely a whisper because in the split second of time, we're face to face, our lips inches apart.

My breath hitches as the air around us shifts and changes, charges with the instantaneous chemistry between us. His eyes flicker to my lips and then back to my eyes as he leans forward.

And then he kisses me.

It's a tender brush of lips, but it's one of those kisses I can feel so deep in my bones that my body wants to sigh with satisfaction. And when it ends, he leans his forehead against mine and we sit like that, neither of us moving away nor denying the connection we share.

"What are we doing here, Grady?" It isn't exactly the best time to ask the question, and yet, I can't help but ask it. Because when his lips are on mine, it feels like whatever this is, is real. Then, when they're not and he's acting like we're roomies, it's confusing as hell. I've had enough confusion.

"We're sitting in the dark on the porch," he says.

Another brush of his lips to mine. A lift of his hand to cup my neck and deepen the kiss, his tongue licking against mine and then gently retreating. Our foreheads resting against each other's, his hand still on my neck.

"I mean what is *this*? What are we doing here?"

"We're kissing." He chuckles and then kisses me again.

"Funny," I murmur as my body sags against his in contentment. "But . . ."

"We're enjoying each other."

A brush of his lips against mine, and then he pulls my bottom lip gently with his teeth, kissing me fully again. His free hand drops the hammer—which lands with a soft *thud*—and then slowly slides up my thigh.

"But . . ."

"I'm getting lost in you, Dylan. It's so damn easy. When I'm with you, I forget the bad. I forget the fire. I forget the bad dreams. The three nights you were in my bed were the first nights in forever I didn't have nightmares. So, I'm kissing you because when I'm with you, my mind stops, and the world starts turning again."

His name is a sigh on my lips, and my heart stops and then starts again at words more seductive than have ever been spoken to me before.

"But what about when I have to leave—"

"We're enjoying each other. We're getting lost in each other. And that's enough for right now. That's what both of us need. You're getting over someone, and I'll never be in a position to commit . . . and that's okay."

The desperation in his kiss and the conviction in his words drown out the questions and concerns I know I should be thinking to guard my heart.

It's my turn to lean forward and initiate. And while my lips kiss his to tell him his words are enough, my hands slip beneath the hem of his shirt and pull it over his head. I need to feel his skin. I need to give him the same unspoken reassurances he's given me in the only way I know how to.

"I thought you didn't like firefighters." He laughs, his lips moving against mine, and his hand coming up to cup my breast and ignite the frenzy of nerves in my hardened nipple.

My mouth spreads into a smile I know he can feel. "I'm making an exception this one time."

"One time?" He leans forward and steals another kiss. "Baby, I plan on making it a hell of a lot more than one time."

"Promise?" I chuckle.

"You say I need to get used to firefighting again, you know what the first step in training is?"

"What's that?" My breath hitches as he rolls my nipple between his thumb and forefinger, sending a lightning rod of sensation straight down to the apex of my thighs.

"Knowing how to use my hose."

My laugh turns into a moan as his hand slides down my torso and dips beneath the waistband of my shorts. "Mm, I don't think you can put this fire out, Malone."

"You bet your ass I'm going to try."

With that, our lips crash against each other's as his hands go to both of my hips and shift me so I sit astride his lap. I can feel him hard and ready against his board shorts, and as I deepen the kiss, I slide my hands ever so gently over his flank and onto the ridged skin of his lower back.

I swallow his gasp, refusing to let him pull away. Not allowing him to think about his back or his scars or be self-conscious. If he's getting lost in me, I want all of him to be able to. His doubts. His insecurities. His everything.

And so I let my lips and my hands do the talking as they continue to slide over his scarred skin until they hook under his arms and pull him against me. Just like any normal couple would.

Without thinking about our pasts.

Without thinking about our future.

And I ride him under the glow of moonlight, on the steps of the back porch, and we get lost in each other once again.

TWENTY-EIGHT

Dylan

"EVERYTHING GOING GOOD FOR YOU?" MY AGENT ASKS.

"Yeah. Sure," I reply, distracted as I hold the phone to my ear, balance the box the delivery man just handed me in the other, and close the door with my hip.

"Are you sure?"

"Besides the fact I'm still pissed at you for telling Jett where I was? Other than that, yes, everything is fine."

"You know I meant no harm by it."

"Uh-huh." I set the box down and grab a scissors to cut the tape on its edges.

"Callum was antsy. Jett was freaking because of it. I tried to fix the situation."

"And picking up the phone was not an option, why?"

I lift the top of the box up and hold back a cry of surprise to find what looks like two dozen pale pink roses. I stare at them for a beat as memories flood back—memories I don't want—before picking up the card resting atop them and turn it over in my hands.

"Dylan? Are you there?"

"Yes? What? Sorry. I was distracted."

"Apparently."

"I'm still mad at you." I stare at the flowers and feel . . . unsettled.

"You'll forgive me."

"Ha." I shake my head and turn my back to the flowers so I can concentrate for a moment. "Is there a reason you called or is this a social call?"

"How are the songs coming along?"

"Over half are completed, but you already know this because I'm sure you spoke to Jett already, right? So what's going on?"

"Callum is getting a little nervous that you're not around."

"I'm sending him songs, about one a week. He can't be unhappy with that." I'm irritated and frustrated. I'm ahead of schedule and still being questioned.

"Yeah, but—"

"Christ. What did he do this time?" The hesitation has dread dropping into the pit of my stomach.

"Would anything surprise you at this point?"

"No."

"He had some time with Kai in the studio. He wanted to work on some tracks and there was a bit of a tantrum and some storming out."

Fuck.

I pinch the bridge of my nose and sigh audibly. "So what are you telling me?"

"Kai and Callum want you present at the next scheduled studio time."

"When?" She can hear my anger, but she knows it's not directed at her.

"I don't know but I'll get an answer and let you know."

"Gee. Thanks."

"I know, Dylan. I know."

I end the call, toss my cell on the counter, and then stare at the card for a minute before tearing it open.

I miss you.

Do you miss me yet?

Come back home and let's start over.

I love you.

—Jett

I look at the roses over the top of the card and shake my head. He's clueless. And to further prove the fact, he sent me roses. How, after being together for two years, does he not know I hate roses?

When I look at them again, all I see is the last gift my dad gave me on my tenth birthday. I remember the empty words and watching his back as he retreated down the steps through my tear-blurred vision.

As if on cue, the scanner goes off, reinforcing the tinged memories of my dad and the feeling of abandonment.

After dropping the card into the trash, I pick up the bouquet and head to the front door. I may as well take them to the sweet widow who lives a few houses down. I'd rather them brighten her day than let them go to waste.

TWENTY-NINE

Dylan

It's like scoring the perfect Michael Kors bag on sale.

At least that's the best way to describe the feeling when I complete a song and know it has the *it factor* that will make it a hit.

When I walk out of my room, Petunia is staring at me as if she isn't too impressed with the cheer I sent up when I saved the finalized lyrics on my Mac.

Now I feel restless. Like I need to go celebrate but have nowhere to go. Add to that, when I look at the clock, I realize that it's only seven thirty in the morning. I awoke with a start at five o'clock, the lyrics I've been struggling with suddenly coming to me, demanding I write them down. Since Grady was on shift, I got up and decided to have a go at them.

I don't care how early it is, though, I want to commemorate this small victory. Going to a bar before breakfast and ordering a celebratory drink isn't exactly something most would approve of. I grin, picturing Petunia and me sitting at a high-top table together, and shake my head. Pigs probably aren't allowed in bars.

Meaning the four-legged kind at least.

I have thirty minutes before Grady is off shift. Maybe I'll drive into town and see if he wants to meet up for Bertha's pancakes to celebrate. Syrup may not be wine, but at least it's something.

Once cleaned up and with a quick dash of makeup on, I text Grady.

Me: Heading to Mama Bertha's to celebrate with pancakes. Want to meet me there after your shift?

But when I reach Bertha's café and still don't have a response, I decide to head to the fire station in case he's tied up on a call and ran over on his shift. I take the meandering route through the tree-lined neighborhoods of Sunnyville toward the firehouse.

I get a little lost, but right as I find my bearings at the stop sign on Cherry Blossom Drive and Willow Bend Street, a truck parked on the opposite side of the intersection grabs my attention.

It's silver and has the firefighter emblem in the back rear window on the left-hand side. It's either Grady's truck or someone else in town has the identical truck complete with decal placement. It's a possibility, but right when I've dismissed the idea, I see Grady on the porch of the house across the street.

I'm not sure why something calls on me to go through the intersection and park against the curb so I can watch, but I do. There's something about Grady's posture, about him dressed in his Class A's, about him standing in a random front yard that demands my undivided attention.

I feel like I'm part stalker, part crazy ex-girlfriend and know I'm invading his privacy and should drive away, but I don't. I sit there on the side of Willow Bend and watch as the little boy—Brody—from the farmers' market comes running out and jumps into Grady's arms.

My breath catches. The way Grady hugs him, as if he never wants to let him go, causes a huge lump to form in my throat. The way he buries his head in that place where little kids smell like little kids—the crook where his neck meets his shoulder—and breathes him in has my vision blurring with tears.

The two stay like that until Brody tries to wiggle away. Grady sets him down, and Brody pulls on his hand and leads him toward the front door where Shelby stands with one arm crossed over her stomach and the other elbow bent so her fingertips are touching her lips. The moment her son's attention is focused on her, her face transforms with the smile that lights it up, but it's as if a switch is flipped, erasing the grief there moments before.

A car door slams. Then another. Another truck has parked in front of Grady's. Four more firefighters in their Class A's climb out and shout animatedly at Brody as they cross the street. Each one high-fives Brody and then swallows him in a huge hug before setting him down and ruffling his hair. They then all walk over to Shelby and give her a kiss on the cheek or a hug in greeting.

Every part of me sighs seeing these gruff men being so sweet to this little boy and widow. To their extended family.

And before I know it, there are several more guys climbing out of their vehicles walking toward the house. My eyes swivel from the men to Brody and back again.

The yellow school bus lumbers down the street ever so slowly. The Star Wars backpack Shelby is holding in her hands looks way too big for Brody. The eight adults walking Brody down the driveway and waiting at its edge. I finally get it.

It's Brody's first day of school.

I bring my hand to my mouth as the school bus pulls up to the curb in front of Brody's house. Each firefighter lines the sidewalk so Brody has to give them a high five as he makes his way to the opened school bus door. Some do a spin and make him guess where to hit their hands. Others kneel down and give him an easy target. Bowie stands there with a camera, taking photo after photo as Brody interacts with each one of them. They all have reassuring smiles on their faces as he passes them. And when he gets to the end of the line, Grady is standing there, grin huge, hug even bigger, before he helps Brody slip his backpack on his shoulders. He then kneels down and gives him what looks like a man-to-man chat that simultaneously breaks my heart and fills it.

Then Shelby steps in and gives her own pep talk to Brody before she takes his hand and walks him to the door of the waiting bus. The guys erupt in a roar of cheers and excited waves as they wait for him to take his seat at the window. At their second wave of cheers, I assume

Brody waves back, and it keeps going until the doors shut and the bus slowly makes its way to the intersection.

Shelby watches the bus make the turn, and from the time it passes between us, blocking my view of the firefighters on the driveway, to when it clears, Grady has stepped forward and now has his hand on her shoulder in a show of silent support.

But then her shoulders shake.

And her hand comes up to cover her mouth as the bittersweet feelings the day has evoked barrel through her. Grady tries to pull her into him for a hug, and she fights him at first, determined to stay strong. But he wins out. The minute he envelops her in his arms, her shoulders sag as her arms wrap around him and hold on for dear life.

It's then that my heart breaks. If I thought I was emotional before, dear God, I was wrong. The tears don't stop. The small taste of the personal torment Grady lives day in and day out has hit me squarely in the solar plexus so hard I wonder how he breathes most days.

And yes, I've peeked long enough into this life that is not mine, but this moment seems so much more personal than watching them high-five Brody.

I can't take my eyes off them. I can't stop my mind from spinning and turning. I can't look at Grady anymore—or at the group of men who made time to see a little boy off for his first day of school—and lay the sins of my father at their feet.

How I ever thought Grady was anything like my father is beyond me . . . because after what I just witnessed—after every bit of heartfelt kindness he's shown me—they are nothing alike. Not even close.

It takes me a few seconds to accept the revelation. To reverse years of conditioned thinking. But it's really not that hard because firefighter or no firefighter, Grady Malone just proved to me he's in a class all his own. He's a man worth so much more than I pegged him for.

And after a few minutes more of watching them, I put my car in drive and pull away from the curb as Grady and Shelby stand there, finding a solace in each other from a pain that may never be cured.

THIRTY

Grady

I DRIVE.

In an endless loop through town.

Off to Miner's Airfield, where I sit on the side of the highway and watch the parachutes exploding against the blue of the sky. I'm sure my sister-in-law, Emerson, is up there somewhere, directing the jumpers in her skydiving class.

Then again, maybe she isn't.

Maybe Grant has put his foot down since she's pregnant and is not allowing her to do it anymore.

How do I not know if that's happened when I typically know everything about my brothers? Am I that out of touch? Have I really cut myself off from my life? Have I really been so damn focused on myself, *on the guilt*, that it's all I've been able to see for the past however long?

"Christ," I mutter and lean my head back against the headrest and close my eyes. All I see is Brody and his infectious smile. All I hear is his whispered words in my ear, asking me if I thought his daddy knew it was his first day of school. All I know is how fucking hard it was to hold back the tears and pretend everything was perfectly normal when inside I was dying.

And is it sadder than fuck that right now I'm out here at Miner's when every part of me wants to text Dylan back and say screw the damn pancakes, I only want her.

But I didn't. Not even I'm that much of an asshole.

If I went home and did what I wanted to do to her to ease my own fucked-up head, I'd be using her. Using her to make it through the next day. The next night. The next everything.

The kicker? We both know she'd give it to me. It's the kind of beautiful she is. But then what? She leaves and feels more used than Jett made her feel, and I'm left needing more, still broken, still spiraling.

I start the truck and pull out of the airfield, telling myself I'm going to hit the gym and work out until Brody's first day is over so I can check on him and see how it went. But for some reason, my truck doesn't head there. Instead, my hands take the familiar turns back to my house. Left on Hollister. Right on Danville. Left on Prosperity. And then the long drive to my house.

I sit in the truck and stare at it for the longest of time. What would it be like to come home every day to the same woman? *To Dylan?*

To have a family. A little boy like Brody with inquisitive eyes and a quiet smile. Or one like Luke, who's loud and rowdy and likes to cause trouble but has a good heart. What would it be like to come home every day after shift and have them run and jump in my arms like we used to with my dad?

Christ. What the fuck am I thinking?

I shift in my seat and feel the stretch of my scarred skin on my back and know that's the crazy talking. The crazy that will never be. Can't be.

Could I really put a wife and kids through what Shelby and Brody go through every day?

No.

Does lightning strike twice? What are the odds of walking into a fire and being hurt twice?

Slim.

Christ. I repeat what seems to be my word of the day and sigh.

Then I get out of the truck and head inside. I have every intention of walking in, heading for the shower, and crashing. While we didn't have any fires last night, we did keep busy with non-stop medical calls, and I'm exhausted.

But when I open the door, Dylan's standing in the middle of the kitchen, eyes wide, smile soft.

"Hey."

"Hey." I take a seat on one of the kitchen chairs and without another word, pull her into me. I rest my forehead against her abdomen and squeeze my hands on her hips.

She doesn't speak. She doesn't ask. She just threads her fingers through my hair and rubs my scalp as I take whatever it is I need from her without her needing to know why.

We remain like this for some time, with me breathing her in, and Dylan selflessly giving me the comfort I need.

"It was Brody's first day of school."

"Hmm."

"I played the part of dad." My voice is barely audible, but the kiss she presses to the top of my head says she heard me.

"I saw you," she murmurs, and her confession surprises the hell out of me. "I was wandering, wasting time until you texted me back . . . I saw you guys. You broke my heart and made it whole all in one fell swoop. I owe you an apology. You're nothing like my dad. You're a good man, Grady Malone. A damn good man."

"Not hardly."

"Maybe if I say it enough times, you'll start to believe it."

That means you'll have to stick around.

The thought ghosts through my mind, and I realize I want her to stay. For so many reasons.

But all of those reasons are overshadowed by what I had to do today.

By the constant reminder of why I can't have more.

Why I can't want more.

Why she can't stay.

Why she needs to forget everything and run.

THIRTY-ONE

Dylan

"I KNOW THAT LOOK."

I glance over to Emerson. "What look?"

Desi laughs that cackle of hers. "The *I've fallen for a Malone man and I can't get back up* look . . . although, I'm not sure why you'd want to if one of them have fallen on top of you."

"I have not fallen for a Malone man. I'm with Jett—"

"Such bullshit." Desi laughs. "You so have and your secret is safe with me."

"You two have had too much to drink and are now hallucinating." I laugh and try to play off the raised eyebrows she's giving me—the ones that are saying she knows the truth but won't tell—as another round slides in front of us.

"Pregnant woman here," Emerson says and points to herself. "Not drinking."

"Then pregnancy brain," I reassert.

"You are such a liar," Desi scoffs. "You've seen Grady, right? All ripples and perfection and—"

"I've seen him, all right," I murmur as I take a sip and think about yesterday. Grady coming home from *being dad* on Brody's first day of school. The silent desperation in his every movement and expression. The way he held me, pulled me in, and didn't take his hands off me until a long time later when we were naked beside each other in his bed and his breathing evened out.

"She's fucked him."

I'm not sure what else was said while I was thinking of all things Grady, but those three words definitely catch my attention. "Excuse me?" I sputter out a laugh.

"It's written all over that face of yours," Emerson says.

"Dreamy eyes," chimes in Desi. "Check."

"Squirming in your seat because . . . just damn." Emerson sighs and then winks. "Check."

"You guys are incorrigible." I shake my head.

"We might be, but you know it's true."

"Double check," I finally confess, garnering a holler from Desi.

"I have a million does-he-know-how-to-use-his-hose jokes I can throw at you, but I'll spare you," Desi says as she taps her wine glass to mine. "Just tell me one thing . . ."

"Oh God." Emerson puts her hands over her eyes, worried about what comes next.

"Does he find you hot and leave you wet?" Desi throws her head back and laughs as I roll my eyes. She slaps a hand on the table. "I've always wanted to ask that."

"Hey, Desi," I say as I crook my finger for her to come closer. "You know what they say about firefighting, right? It's all about the size, the equipment, and the technique . . . I'll vouch that Grady's the total package."

"Well, hot damn. At least there's one Malone man left. I still have hope."

"Grayson is so not your type," Emerson says.

"For the night he could be." She lifts her eyebrows and laughs.

"Who's gotta go pee? This prego," Emerson says and raises her hand.

"C'mon," Desi says as she slides off her own stool. "I've gotta go, too."

I watch the two of them weave through the bar toward the bathroom as I play with the stem of my wine glass. This is just what I needed.

"Management says you're not allowed in here for another week," the bartender at my back says.

"I didn't start shit," a voice says, and I hate that every part of me hunches over to hide. It's Wes Winters. The last time we saw each other, he was making an excuse as to why he couldn't get hard and rabbiting out of Grady's house. The night of reckless sex Grady said I needed to have in order to get over Jett ended up an embarrassing catastrophe.

But at least I got the good end of the stick. I smile and straighten my shoulders. I've got Grady Malone. Does Wes really even matter anymore?

Desi and Emerson come back and are getting seated when something is said that gets all of our attention.

"Why are you not allowed in here?" a male voice asks.

"Because of that asshole, Grady Malone. The fucker took a shot at me a few weeks back," Wes says, and I can see Emerson slide a glance over to her side to see who is speaking.

"Malone? He's usually chill. Why'd he have a beef with you?"

"He didn't like the truth."

The three of us look at each other, and suddenly, there is a pit of dread dropping into the bottom of my stomach. Like I want to turn this show off but can't stop watching it, either. Because the only tie that connects Wes to Grady is me.

"The truth?" the friend says and laughs. "You're worse than an old lady, Winters. Quit beating around the bush. What the hell happened?"

"Malone got all fired up because he overheard me talking about his roommate. Shit, I had beer goggles on when she asked me over to her place, and once I got there, I couldn't fucking follow through. I'm all about getting laid, but even a drunk man has standards, and she . . . dude, you know me. I like 'em petite, and she's definitely not petite, if you know what I mean."

My cheeks grow red and heat flushes my entire body as Emerson and Desi give me the dreaded look of sympathy. Every part of me wants to crawl under the table and die from humiliation.

"That's cruel," the friend says.

"But it's the truth," Wes jokes in a boisterous voice. "So he threw a few punches to defend her honor and then probably went home and gave her a good pity fuck until someone better-looking comes along."

I lower my eyes and stand slowly.

"Don't listen to him."

"He's a prick," they both say in unison, but I lift my eyes and meet both of theirs. "It's okay. Please stay. I'm gonna go."

And with that, I slink quietly out of the bar, mortification skewing my every thought and self-loathing at an all-time high.

I walk the streets of downtown Sunnyville. Each step another thought I shove away. Each street crossed another attempt to hide the heat of the tears coursing down my cheeks. Each house I pass, a way to evade the mortification that I'm slowly drowning in.

And each foot up Grady's driveway is another stick prodding my shame to morph into anger and irrationality.

I haven't thought of what I'm going to say to Grady, but the minute I walk in the door, I freeze. He's sitting at the barstool bringing a spoonful of Cheerios to his mouth, and it stops mid-motion when he sees me.

"Where've you been?"

I know Emerson has called him by now. I know he knows what Wes said. The insults repeated for another person to know my shame.

"Is it true?" *Was I just a pity fuck?*

"Dylan?" He part laughs, part rejects the question with a shake of his head as he drops his spoon into the bowl.

"Yes. Or. No. That's all I want to know, Grady."

"What the ever-loving fuck are you talking about? Is what true?"

"Didn't Emerson call you? Fill you in?" His blank stare tells me she didn't, and for that, I owe her one for saving my dignity—or what little is left of it. "Your fight. Wes Winters. How he couldn't fuck me because I wasn't pretty enough or skinny enough or some shit like that. Ring a bell?"

Grady runs a hand over his jaw, the chafe of his stubble the only sound filling the room. "He's an asshole."

"And you punched him, but then when you came home, you couldn't tell me who you hit or why you did it. Did you not want me to know? Did you not think I'd find out?"

"You weren't exactly up front about telling me you two didn't actually sleep together, either."

I glare at him. His point is valid if who I did or didn't sleep with is any of his fucking business. The hurt riots inside as I stare at Grady, so goddamn handsome, and I question myself. How did I think there was actually something between us when right now I feel like it was all started on a ruse? Because knowing I was a pity fuck isn't exactly the best way to boost my ego.

"Would you have come home that night and slept with me without hearing what Wes said? Or did you walk in so pissed at him for being an asshole that you felt sorry for me? First Jett and then Wes . . . poor Dylan, right? So what? You knew I was self-conscious so you thought you'd step into the role—*lower your standards*—to help me feel a little better about myself for a week or two. Then make sure I'm gone when an *attractive* woman comes along to twist up your sheets."

He stands where he is, angles his head to the side, and just stares at me, eyes pinning me motionless. There is so much conflict in his expression, but it has nothing on how I feel.

"You're actually questioning me on this?" Anger colors his voice and disbelief weighs on his posture. "You actually think it was that bastard's bullshit comment that made me want to sleep with you? You really think I'm that weak that I need another man to help determine who I fuck? Glad you think so highly of me, McCoy." He rounds the counter and stands a few feet from me, his spine stiff, the muscle pulsing in his jaw as he glares at me.

"I know what I heard. I know what you did. And since you haven't told me a fucking thing, I'll believe what I assume."

"Fuck you and your assumptions."

"Considering you haven't answered me yet, I guess I can say fuck you too." I grit the words out as my tears burn paths down my cheeks.

"Sorry you slummed it with me for a bit. I'll make sure to be scarce so you can tune into your regularly scheduled program of *beautiful* women."

"You're wrong, Dylan. So fucking wrong."

"I saw the look on your face when glitter-dress girl left that first morning. No one's ever looked at me like that. So why should I believe you?"

"I haven't slept with anyone since you showed up."

I raise an eyebrow at him. "Um . . . glitter-dress girl?"

"Correction." He sighs. "*Since* I actually met you. Don't you think that says something? A lot of somethings?"

"Where I come from in Hollywood, all we say are somethings, and none of them hold any value."

"Well, in my job, sometimes your only value is your word. When I say I'm going to be there for someone, their fucking life depends on it . . . so when I speak, I mean it." He rolls his shoulders, and I can see his frustration.

"You still haven't answered my question." And I don't care how many words he speaks or if he's worth his weight in words because it's the ones he's not speaking now that scream the loudest.

"You don't get it, do you? You don't see what I see." He steps forward and reaches out to me, but I yank my arm away. I'm too hurt, too ashamed, too irrational to be touched. I don't trust myself, and if I don't trust myself, then I sure as hell don't trust what my reaction to even the tiniest ounce of comfort would be.

"Christ," he mutters and paces from one end of the kitchen and back before turning to face me. "You want your words? Here they are. You're fucking gorgeous. There, I said it, and I know you're going to reject the compliment so I'll say it again. You, Dylan McCoy, are the things wet dreams are made of. You and those thighs of yours you hate but I love."

"Grad—"

"No." He holds his hand up to stop me, and he just stares at me with such intensity I can't remember what I wanted to say. "You weren't a pity fuck, Dyl. You were far fucking from it. You're the woman I keep thinking about, keep wanting more from, but can't bring myself to ask you for it because I can't give you shit. I can't give you what you deserve because every time I think I can, I see Brody and Shelby. So, how can I ask you for more when I can't give you a relationship? That isn't fair to you . . . so I'm using you. Yep, I am. Using you because you're the only thing I can get lost in when nothing else has made a dent in my pain. Using you because it's what I need when I haven't asked you what you need. Call me an asshole. Call me a fucker. But don't you ever tell me this started with a pity fuck. Far from it."

"Grady. Please don't."

"*Please don't*? Screw that, Dylan. You wanted to know until I started telling you the truth . . . until I started telling you good things about yourself and made you uncomfortable, so hold tight, sweetheart, because I'm not even close to done." He takes a step toward me as I shake my head, conditioned to mentally reject the things he's yet to say. "*This* started the minute I saw you standing over there in a white fluffy robe held close at your neck, judging me like you had every right to. *This* started when you walked up to me in the kitchen and kissed the ever-loving life out of me to prove to Jett he couldn't have you. And guess what? That night, the taste of your kiss seared into my goddamn mind, making sure no one else's kiss could ever come close. *This* started when I walked in the kitchen the night of the fight so amped up on adrenaline wondering how in the world a man couldn't get hard by just looking at you since that's all I'd been doing since you showed up. You were standing right there"—he points to where I was sitting the night of the fight—"looking so beautiful, and I couldn't help myself anymore. Sure, I was livid at Wes for what he said, but I was also so fucking thankful he didn't get to do the things to you I was about to. I jerked off imagining you on *my* cock the night the bastard brought you home from the bar. Your moans. Imagining your body. Your taste. Your hot fucking pussy. That was all I needed to fucking come, and I hadn't even tasted you or had you at that point."

I look at him slack-jawed and stunned, his every word spoken with such conviction that they hit my ears and reverberate through my body so I can't deny them.

He stares back, teeth gritted, eyes intense. He reaches out, pulls his hand back, and then reaches again without a hint of hesitation.

His lips meet mine. There's anger on his tongue. There's frustration in his touch. There's passion in every movement of his mouth against mine.

I fight him at first. The mixture of his words and my anger and Wes's shame spin in a storm of uncertainty, making my head dizzy and my heart ache, but *his lips* . . . his lips steal its thunder with each and every second they claim mine.

He takes without asking. He claims and seduces and demands without a single word. But the one thing that is constant is his anger. And just when I think I'm drowning in the swell of emotion his kiss evokes, he ends it abruptly. He shoves away from me as if he's been burned.

He stands before me, my lipstick smeared on his lips, his shoulders heaving, his hands flexing at his sides, and his eyes piercing. "If that's pity, Dylan, take pity on me, because I'm the asshole who would do it all over again without a second thought. So blame me. Hate me. But don't you ever fucking blame yourself again."

Grady heaves in a deep breath and then throws his hands my way as if to say he's so angry with me and this conversation that he has nothing else to add. Then he slams out the back door, leaving me standing there staring after him with my fingertips touching my lips. Lips that are still buzzing from his kisses. My head is a bigger mess than when I walked in here, but for a very different reason.

Tears well in my eyes, and a contradictory laugh falls from my lips.

"You were standing right there looking so beautiful, and I couldn't help myself anymore." Talk about the unexpected. Now what the hell am I supposed to do?

Find 'em hot and leave 'em wet just got a whole new meaning.

THIRTY-TWO

Grady

"If I was living with your ugly ass, I'd run for the hills too."

I lift my middle finger up for Grayson to see as he's hanging the drywall.

"Momma said you're not allowed to let your bird fly that way."

Fuck.

I lower my finger and look to where Brody sits, hands under his chin, green eyes wide like I'm in trouble. "She does, does she?"

"Yep. She says that birds should only flap when you're really angry, and I don't think you're really angry."

I shake my head. Shelby's doing a damn good job with him. "Does your mom ever let her bird fly?"

"Only when she's driving." He fights a smile. "She also says you shouldn't use the word A-S-S, but I'm a big kid so don't worry about me. I've heard it before."

I laugh loudly and press a kiss to the top of his head. "Grab a beer, we need to have a man-to-man."

He giggles without a care in the world like every little boy should and grabs his bottle of root beer, looks at it like it's the coolest thing, and then scoots closer to me.

"Cheers," I say as I tap my bottle of beer against the top of his root beer.

"Cheers." His smile is beaming.

"So . . . now that we're getting closer to getting this done," I say, pointing to the almost completely drywalled playroom, "we need to start discussing what type of things we should fill it with. Foosball. Air hockey. PS4. Nintendo Switch. Darts."

"Darts?" he asks. "I don't think my momma would like me playing with those. She's always talking about eyes getting poked out and stuff."

"Well, that's the best part about being here. We're men, and men don't worry about that stuff. Besides, we have to have our own secrets. That's why we have the Boys' Club here. Right, Gray?"

"Yep." He takes a seat and taps his beer against Brody's. "Boys' Club rules. You can always come here and be a man. Burp. Fart."

Another giggle sounds off. "I'm not allowed to say that word at home," he says with a roll of his eyes.

"What word? Fart?"

He nods.

"You're not?"

"Nope. I have to say toot. It's so lame. I sound like a girl."

"I'll have to have a talk with your mom about that one, Brody. That's where I draw the line. A man's gotta be able to say the word 'fart' or he won't get any playground cred. Especially now that you're a kindergartener." Grayson just looks at me and shakes his head. "What? Don't tell me that Luke can't say it, either."

"He can. In fact, I'm sure when he comes home from his play date later I'll be hearing all about farts."

A horn honking interrupts us. "Your mom's here."

"Ah, man," he says and grabs one last handful of M&M's that he knows his mom isn't going to let him have.

"None of that," I say as I ruffle the top of his hair. "Finish your beer and go grab your stuff. I'm gonna talk to your mom."

He says a garbled okay around the M&M's he's chewing while he hugs Petunia and takes off for the house.

"How was Boys' Club?" Shelby asks as she walks up, hand

shielding her eyes from the sun.

"It was good. But, Shelb, *toot*? You've gotta let a boy say fart or he's going to get made fun of at school."

She starts laughing, and it's such a good sound to hear after so much sadness. "This is what you're teaching him?"

"What happens in Boys' Club, stays in Boys' Club." I wink. "Did you have a good time?"

"Yeah. It was nice to relax and feel girly for a bit. They tried to talk me into going out with them next weekend, but I'm not ready for that yet." Her voice falls.

"You should. You deserve some non-mommy time out with your friends. Drew wouldn't want you to be lonely forever." The words pain me to say. It's as if saying them aloud means he's really never coming back. But she needs to hear it. She needs to believe it, even if the blanch in her expression when she does mirrors how I feel inside.

"Grady . . ." Her eyes meet mine, and the look in them fucking kills me. "Hey, sweetie. You have fun? You ready to go?" Her face transforms into a mask of happiness the minute Brody comes jogging our way.

"Yeah. It was rad. We talked about playing darts and . . .," His words drift off when Shelby's eyes widen. "Never mind." He looks at me and tries to wink but both eyes close instead. "Just man stuff, mom. No big deal."

"Man stuff," I repeat and stifle a laugh.

"Thanks again," Shelby says, and her eyes light up with humor.

"Any time." I watch them climb in her car and stare after them while they drive off.

"You going to tell me what the hell's going on?" Grayson asks as he walks up beside me and hands me a fresh beer.

"What do you mean?"

"Ha. Nice try, baby bro, but you don't have Brody here anymore to protect you from me asking where the heck Dylan is. Did you scare her off already?"

Maybe.

I think back to last night. To the hurt in her eyes when she walked in the back door. To the shock that made her jaw go slack when I told her how I really felt. To the wince in her posture when I told her I was using her. And to the taste of her kiss that fucking killed me to walk away from. If I hadn't, I would have used her again—right there.

"Not sure," I confess. "I woke up to an empty bed and—"

"An empty bed implies it was occupied."

"Knock the grin off your face."

"So was it?"

"Occupied? *Yes*. But for strictly platonic reasons."

"Bullshit." He coughs out the word.

But he's wrong. My bed has been empty since Jett the fuck face left. Empty so the nightmares returned.

Except for last night it wasn't.

For some reason, when I came in from working out here, she wasn't hidden away in her room. No, she was asleep on her side of my bed. *Her side*? I've already given her a side? And I selfishly opted not to wake her because with her next to me, my nightmares wouldn't come.

That *and* I wanted her there.

Had she gone in there to wait for me to cool off and accidentally fallen asleep? Was she still upset and needed some company?

I don't know. I can't ask her because she fucking left without waking me to say goodbye.

"I woke up to a note," I say, the sting still there. "It said she had to head to L.A. for a couple days to work on a few of the songs in the studio."

"And you buy that?"

The way he stares at me says he knows there is so much more going on, but he doesn't outright ask it. If it was Grant, he would. But Gray is the peacekeeper and will let me explain if I want to or leave it be if I don't.

"I knew she had to go and had been waiting to know when it was scheduled. Otherwise she'd risk violating the terms of her contract."

He looks at me like he doesn't believe me, and I don't know if I even believe myself. I know it's what I want to believe. I know it's easier to think she left because of work instead of fleeing because she still thinks she was my pity fuck. "Honestly, dude, I'm not sure what I believe when it comes to why she left."

"Ask yourself this, were you disappointed she was gone or were you breathing a sigh of relief. The answer will tell you all you need to know."

THIRTY-THREE

Dylan

"YOU ARE MY SHOT IN THE DARK.
The flame I can't put out.
The nightmare I need to walk away from.
The dream I constantly doubt.
But you're under my skin.
You've stolen my heart.
How am I ever going to be able to walk away from this?"

"Nope. Start over," I interrupt Jett mid-bridge and hold up my hands. "That line still isn't right." Frustrated, I shake my head and look to Kai and then Jett.

Groans fill the room.

"It sounded good to me," Jett says as he picks up his glass of whiskey and takes a sip.

"Good isn't good enough. I want perfect," I say, scribbling down a possible fix and tucking my pencil behind my ear. "I need to hear it one more time without the mix. I only want the acoustic track."

"You sing it," Jett says. "You always hear it better when you sing." I look at him and know he's right but hate the idea of having the audience.

"No." I shake my head to reject the idea.

"We'll sing it together then." Jett lifts his eyebrows as if he's asking if that will work.

"Fine. Sure. Let's go."

Kai sighs. "What the lady wants, the lady gets. For the thousandth time, let's try it again, folks. Cue the track," he says and directs the tech in the booth.

I press my hands to my eyes and try to concentrate, but I'm tired. Too little sleep after waking up from a bad dream to find I'd fallen asleep in Grady's bed while I waited for him to come back in so I could talk to him. Make things right with him? I don't know what with him.

Then finding the text I'd missed after the chaos of the bar when I'd gotten up to get a drink of water. The one that said there had been a cancellation at the studio and the label had taken the spot for Jett. That I was required to be there.

Add to that too much driving. Too much thinking about Grady.

And that's why this song isn't working. Because every time I sing the lyrics, I think of him.

Of the confusion I feel.

Of wanting more with a man when I'm in no place emotionally to want more.

Of wanting more with a man who will never be able to give it to me.

The chords play again, and I lift my eyes to meet Jett's. They used to hold so much for me, but now I look at him and feel nothing.

So I close my eyes and think of Grady and feel *everything*.

"You are my shot in the dark.
The flame I can't put out.
The dream I need to walk away from.
Because it's myself I constantly doubt.
But you're under my skin.
You've tattooed my soul.
The fate of my heart yours to control."

The gravel of Jett's voice fades, but I hum the ending again. Tears sting my eyes so I keep them closed past the last chord played and the room falls silent. It's Grady I'm singing to, but when I open my eyes, it's Jett's eyes I meet. He's staring so intensely that a lump forms in my throat, and I'm not sure why.

"Can you give us a minute?" Jett asks, not shifting his gaze as chairs scrape across the floor, instruments are put down, and the sound booth switch is turned off. When the door shuts behind the last person, he asks, "You okay?"

I nod, not trusting my voice.

"It's weird being back in here, isn't it?" His voice is soft, warm.

"It hasn't been that long." And mine is barely audible.

"He's hurt you, hasn't he?"

I keep my face impassive, at least I try to, and lower my eyes from his, aware enough to know Jett is the king of taking advantage of my emotions. "No. There's nothing really to hurt. I'm getting over you, and he's dealing with his own issues." I tighten the strings on the neck of my guitar to busy myself. "We're at the right place and the right time for each other."

"Dylan, I don't believe that for a second. I miss you. I miss *us*. Didn't it feel weird walking into your house without me there? My stuff. The smell of my cologne. The music I always have on? I mean, look at us. Look at the music we're making right now. You can't do that if you don't have a special connection with someone."

It was weird walking into my house without Jett's presence, but it was even more so when I realized it didn't feel like a home the way Grady's does.

"Jett, can we just get this song—?" And when I turn to look up, Jett is right there, in my space. His hand is on my cheek. His face is tilting forward. His breath is on my lips.

I close my eyes out of habit, and the minute his lips touch mine, I stand abruptly and shove my chair back with a clatter. "No," is off my tongue as my chest heaves and heart twists and insides riot.

"Dylan. Babe . . ."

I stand in the empty studio—a place symbolic to us—and look at Jett. I see everything that is familiar to me. The everyday norm I used to have. I know what life is like with him—unpredictability and spontaneous chaos. A life-long party of insecurity and self-doubt.

And then I picture Grady. Shirt off. Eyes wary. Smile cocky.

You're my shot in the dark.

He's everything that is outside my box.

The flame I can't put out.

He's everything I want, and I know exactly what to expect.

The dream I need to walk away from.

The outcome is predetermined.

But you're under my skin.

The emotions are under lockdown.

You've tattooed my soul.

The future is nonexistent.

The fate of my heart yours to control.

And yet, he's the one I'm thinking of right now, not Jett. It's his kiss I want to taste, not Jett's. It's his bed I want to crawl into, his scent I want to smell on the pillowcase when I'm tired and an emotional wreck.

Not Jett's.

"He's a rebound, Dylan. I'm the real thing, standing here in front of you. Wanting you."

His words strike my ears, but it's Grady's from the other night that still ring true. His honesty. His anger. His truths.

"No. You aren't what *I* want anymore. I used to wait for you. Want you. Need you. But after what you did to me, and the things that Grady has taught me about myself, it no longer holds true." I look around the room, needing an escape, a moment, anything to gain physical distance from him. "We're over, Jett. We're done."

I look at him one last time before I leave the studio, feeling strength when I never had it before. I'm not going to be a victim, someone whose worth is determined by what a man feels about me.

Then I think of Grady and know I'm not *quite* there in terms of confidence. I think it will take me a while to believe the things he said about me. *Beautiful. Wanted. The things wet dreams are made of. The woman I keep thinking about, keep wanting more from.* I feel a different form of vulnerable.

The first is a welcome change; the second scares the shit out of me. If Jett is right about anything, it's that Grady is a rebound and rebounds never last. I lean against the wall outside the studio and rest my head against it.

It's fine. *I'm fine.* Grady being a rebound is perfectly okay because I'm going to be back here full-time in a few weeks anyway. It's probably best this way. I can enjoy what I have with Grady while it lasts and then walk away better for it and thankful he helped me get over Jett.

"The fact that you're out here eating dinner should worry me, right?" Kai asks through a laugh. I look up from where I sit, my back against the building's brick wall, and my senses soaking up everything so perfectly Los Angeles around us. The distinct sounds of people getting to where they need to be in horns and sirens and laughter. The warm night air that's stifling, when in Sunnyville it always seemed refreshing.

"Am I that bad?"

"Nah. You are a perfectionist. There's nothing wrong with that. And you're exceptional at what you do, so you're forgiven for being a pain in the ass."

"Thanks a lot."

"Your version of pain in the ass is nothing compared to *that* pain in the ass," Kai says as he lifts his chin to the studio where Jett is.

"Talent never overrides tact, huh?" I say when I've turned a blind eye to Jett's stunts for so long.

"Never." He shoves his hands in his pockets. "Thanks for coming out on such short notice."

"I promised I'd be here."

"Yeah, I'm pretty sure Callum and the other execs weren't feeling confident after Jett pulled *a Jett* last time we were here."

"What was his temper tantrum over?

His laugh says it all. "The whiskey was wrong. The room was too hot. The light was too bright—same old prima donna bullshit. So much so that he waltzed out in a tizzy saying he didn't have the right atmosphere to make music in."

"Christ." *Will he ever grow up?* How did I put up with this for so long? Why did I enable him? Because I was blinded by what I thought was love.

"They weren't too happy when no tracks were laid down or recorded."

"I'm sure they weren't, but I did my part, Kai. Jett had lyrics to put vocals to. Not all of them, but a good portion, so he should be a lot further along than he is."

"He should be . . . but he isn't the same unless you're here."

I'm sick of hearing this.

"He's a big boy, who's going to have to figure out how to deal next go round. Or rather, I should say the label is going to have to figure out how to manage him. My handholding is done after this album."

"The Jett whisperer."

"If I don't ever hear that again, it won't be soon enough."

He lifts his eyebrows and sighs, knowing exactly what I'm referring to. "You doing okay? I'm sure this can't be easy on you after, you know, everything he did to you . . ."

"You know?" I ask, voice incredulous, eyes darting around to see if anyone is around to hear him.

"Yeah." He shrugs like it's no big deal. "I overheard him on the phone with the other chick. He was blaming her one minute for you finding out about them, then telling her you meant nothing to him the next."

"I-uh—"

"Don't worry, your secret is safe with me." His smile is sincere and his eyes are full of compassion. Relief surges through me knowing I don't have to hide from *every* person what's going on. "This can't be easy for you."

"I'm good." I force a smile I'm sure he doesn't believe. "The time away has been good for me."

"Time away is always good for the soul. *And the heart.*"

"That remains to be seen," I murmur to myself as I collect my trash and stand. "You ready for me to be more of a pain in your ass?"

"Bring on the pain."

We laugh as we enter the studio. The humor lasts us for the first two hours and then slowly begins to dissipate with each repeated take. With every lyric I ask Jett to sing again. With each one of my requests to start over.

"Dude, I'm done for," Jett says as he dives headfirst into the couch in the studio.

The night has turned to early morning, time unknown since the soundproof booth is windowless.

"You're such a pussy, Kroger. What's it been? A whole month since you were in here last? Everything is exactly how you want it—the light, the thermostat, the whiskey—and you still can't hang? Dude, we're going to have to revoke your rock-star status."

Jett lifts his middle finger into the air but keeps his head buried in the pillows.

"Uh-oh," Kai says. "McCoy has that look on her face that says she isn't satisfied yet."

Henry groans and slumps where he sits at the soundboard. "Seriously? We're going on, what? Ten? Eleven? *Forty* hours now?"

"I know, but our time with Dylan is limited. Surely by now you understand *her* level of perfectionism."

Jett lifts an eye up from where his face is buried in his crossed arms. "I'm not liking this already."

"Definitely revoking your status," Kai jokes and then smiles when he meets my eyes before looking to Henry. "Hang in there. I know it's a long day, but stay focused because this is when songs typically are made into hits."

"If you two little old ladies are done complaining, I'd like to get started." I lift my eyebrows as if impatient.

"Yes, ma'am," Kai says and offers up a salute. "Where do you want to start?"

"I'm not completely sold on 'No Matter the Cost' yet," I say, referring to the song title. "I need to work it through a couple more times and hear the playback. Something isn't sitting right with me, and I'll know it when I hear it."

"Jett?" Kai prompts.

"Let Dylan run through it. I need a fucking break."

Kai looks over to me, and I nod, telling him I'm good singing the song myself. There is a short instruction given to Henry about where he needs to cue the music as Jett rolls over on his side and starts scrolling through something on his phone.

"You ready, McCoy?"

"Start from the top."

I put the headphones back on and enjoy the absolute quiet before the music floats through them. I imagine the hard edge of a guitar and the strident beat of the drum that will accompany the current piano background paired with my acoustic guitar.

I close my eyes and feel the music, my fingers on the strings, the emotion of the past few days flowing through me, and wait for my mark.

And then I begin to sing.

THIRTY-FOUR

Grady

"There's a Santa Ana moving in."

Bowie, who's joined me in the apparatus bay, nods. The warm Santa Ana winds are never welcome in this heat. "I know. You can feel a fire in the air."

"Lotta dry brush after a long summer without rain."

"Spells trouble."

"It spells overtime," he says with a laugh, and I shake my head even though he's right. "You're gonna show up, right?"

He's the fourth guy to ask me this question, just in a different way. It seems to be a coordinated effort to make sure I'm not going to bail on the calendar shoot.

"I told you I'd be there. Satisfied?"

"Baby, I'm never satisfied," he teases, "but I'll take what I can get."

"If you're looking my way for your satisfaction, you need serious help."

"I always need help, but I'm glad to hear you're going to show us all up."

"Like I said, I'll be there," I grumble, already regretting agreeing to this.

"You want to head out and grab a beer after shift? Try to put a little fat on that belly of yours so we don't look so out of shape in comparison in the pictures? That is, of course, if you don't have other plans *with Dylan*."

I know a fishing expedition when I see one. "She isn't around."

"She head back to L.A. already? I thought she was here for a few more weeks."

"So did I," I murmur as I double-check my gear in my riding spot on the engine. Anything to occupy myself and avoid this conversation.

"She coming back?"

"Your guess is as good as mine."

"Well, is her shit still at your place?" he continues.

"Bowie, why don't you just come straight out and ask me whatever you're trying to ask me." I slide a glance his way and wait for him to acknowledge my question.

"Are you hitting it, or what?"

I tuck my tongue in my cheek and place my gear in the grab rail. "And that's your business why?"

"Because I'm trying to figure out why you're in a shitty mood when you've been Mr. Happy for the past month or so."

"Mr. Happy?" I chuckle. "That sounds like a bad nickname for my johnson."

"So?"

"You know, if you worked out as much as you ran your mouth, you'd be in killer shape."

"This is easier. And you're changing the topic."

"*Yes*. Her stuff is still in her room," I say, not realizing until now how important that is.

"Thank fuck, because you need that hose of yours serviced before your next shift so I don't have to deal with your grumpy ass."

"At least I have someone to service mine," I call over my shoulder as I walk out of the bay.

THIRTY-FIVE

Dylan

I TAKE A DEEP BREATH AND STARE AT THE FRONT DOOR. NOTHING has changed in the few days since I've been gone, and yet, nothing feels the same.

The time away. The time with Jett. The clarity I gained with distance. I'm in *more than like* with Grady Malone.

It's a confession I've refused to acknowledge, but now I'm standing at his front door, summoning the courage to open it, I can't refute it.

How did I not see this coming? How have I lived here with him, shared his space, and convinced myself that roomies with romp time would be okay?

The worst part about recognizing it is knowing it can't go anywhere. *We* can't go anywhere. If I let myself fall for him, the love won't be returned and I'll be left brokenhearted again. Although, I suspect it will take my heart longer to recover from Grady Malone.

So I lie, and tell myself the here and now is exactly what I need. Grady is in fact a rebound and that is all it will be. I'm about to walk into this house and pretend as if we are still *enjoying* each other and that's enough for me.

I take a deep, fortifying breath, shove my heart down as deep as it can go beneath the scarred layers of hurt, and enter the house.

The television's on, and I can hear Petunia rooting around. I find

Grady passed out on the couch, uniform on, belt unbuckled, arm hanging over the edge.

Every part of me that said I needed to keep my emotions at bay falls completely and utterly silent when I see him. I want to reach out and touch him. I want to curl up beside him. I just want to be with him.

Instead, I walk to the side of the couch with my bag in my hand and my heart in my throat and acknowledge this is going to be so much harder than I thought it was going to be. Uncertain of why I'm doing it, but doing it nonetheless, I sit on the edge of the cushion and reach out to touch his cheek, the urge too hard to fight.

"Hey, you," he murmurs in his sleep-drugged voice, a lopsided smile on his lips. "Long shift." His eyes flutter open briefly and then close at the same time he reaches out and pulls me into him. I'm part on his chest, part on the cushions, and when his arms wrap around me and he presses my face to nestle in the crook of his neck, all resistance leaves me.

Before I can sink into the feel of him—the warmth of his body, the scent of his cologne—his soft snore fills the room. I snuggle against him, breathe him in, and realize how much I missed him in the short time I was gone.

Sure, I used to miss Jett when he was touring. Of course I enjoyed the crazy, frantic sex we'd have the minute we'd see each other again. Hell, I even loved the way we'd rip our clothes off, as if we would die if we weren't skin to skin, but this *feels different*. This isn't only about the physical. This is about comfort, about feeling wanted here. About feeling like I belong here in this life. *With him.*

Grady mumbles something in his sleep and presses a kiss to the top of my head as if it's the most normal thing to him.

And as I lie there with him and slowly drift off to sleep, one thought is heavy in my mind: how will I walk away from this?

Grady's kissing me.

We're on the shoreline at the lake house, the sand is beneath my back, the sun's heat is on my skin, and Grady's lips are on mine.

It's a dizzying, mind-numbing kiss that feels as if it could go on forever without me tiring of it.

Grady.

He's my only thought. The only thing I want. The only thing I need.

His hand slides up my torso and over my arms and then cups the side of my neck. He deepens the soft sigh of a kiss. It's lazy but thorough. It's passive but desperate. It's greedy but generous.

And then I startle awake. The room is dark, the scanner is faint in the background, but Grady's lips are on mine. Still kissing me. Still letting me dream even now that I'm fully awake.

I sink into the kiss, the possessive feel of his hand on my neck, and the hard and ready length of him against my thigh. Into the simmering ache I've had since I left that he's now throwing kerosene on.

"Grady." His name is a moan on my lips as his other hand slips beneath the waist of my shorts and cups me. I hitch my leg up and crook it over his hips to grant him better access. He wastes no time parting me and slipping a finger into the well of my body.

His hand on my neck tightens, and he groans when he finds me already wet for him. He begins to work me over. One finger. Out and up and over the top of my slit and then back down. Two fingers in and out, rubbing my nerves within and drawing every sensation out of me before sliding back up and using my own arousal to rub circles over my clit.

His lips tease and taunt me just as thoroughly as his fingers do. There is no need to draw this out. There is no need to suspend the pleasure that is a forgone conclusion based on how responsive my body is to his touch.

Is it the few days apart that has made me this way? Or are my emotions telling me they can no longer separate enjoying each other from feeling for him? Either way, I know I'm going to come, and I'm going to come fast.

I grind my pelvis against his hand, which has my leg shifting, rubbing against his dick and eliciting a groan from him that I swallow. His fingers continue their torment of building me up and then letting me fall back down so I don't hit my peak. I start the one-handed process of unzipping his pants. Of wrapping my hand around his cock and pulling it free. Of stroking it until Grady's fingers tense within me because I'm returning the pleasurable favor.

And as if choreographed without words, the next few seconds are a clumsy dance of intimacy as I stand and discard my clothes while he shoves his pants down to his knees and protects us.

I climb back onto the couch and sit astride his hips. His hand slides between my thighs and holds his dick in place as I position myself over him and slide inch by pleasurable inch onto him.

Our collective moan fills the room as he stretches me, fills me completely. My head rolls back as his hands find their way to dig into my hips and hold me there so he's sheathed fully inside me. Every part of his body tenses as he tries to hold on to his own control. "*Oh my God*," falls from his lips in a long, drawn-out groan that sounds just like how I feel—desperate.

I hold his gaze through the dimly lit room as I begin to move, grinding circles at first that cause his head to fall back and the tendons in his neck to strain. Then on to rocking back and forth over his cock so his crest hits my G-spot as I slide one hand between my thighs to try to help it along.

A moan falls from my lips as the combination hits every zone it needs to and Grady's patience snaps. His hands guide my hips up, and he thrusts at the same time as he pulls me back down. There's no other name for the sound I make than pure pleasure.

And it is.

As Grady pistons his hips up and I grind my hips down, the heat within me builds to a fire. The ache starts to burn. And then, every nerve combusts in an array of sensations I couldn't describe if I tried.

All I can do is feel.

All I want to do is succumb to every ounce of bliss they evoke and allow Grady to take me there and then some.

Because it seems like no matter how much he gives me, I still want more.

And he does. He gives me more until my head grows light and my muscles turn tense. I'm so spent by the time he climaxes that my only option is to collapse on top of him. So I do. I press my lips to the underside of his jaw and rest my hand over his heart so I can feel it jumping against his ribcage.

I try to find solace in the now. In appreciating the moment.

Eventually, when he catches his breath and his fingertips dance up and down the line of my spine, he murmurs, "Welcome home."

THIRTY-SIX

Grady

THE NIGHTMARES WERE RELENTLESS LAST NIGHT. EVEN WITH Dylan beside me, and the scent of her shampoo in my nose, they never let up.

It happened because of what I'm doing against my will. But I gave my word, and my word seems to be all I have these days.

But the panic attack still tries to take hold when I walk into the studio. I hate knowing I'll be standing in front of a camera, documenting the body I can't look at in the mirror most days. *Mine. Physically strong. Horrifically imperfect.*

I'm ready to walk out of the studio not two seconds after I walk in. Two fucking seconds, but what I see when I throw open the curtain in the studio breaks my fucking heart.

And solidifies why I'm here.

Brody, standing in front of a black backdrop. His little legs are drowning in Drew's turnout pants, his dad's helmet is huge on his head, and his eyes are looking straight at the camera with the same mixture of grief and pride that I feel every time I look at him.

My feet are rooted in place. My eyes lock on the little boy who has so much courage that there is no way I can walk out of here. There's no way I can run from showing my scars when he has invisible scars he lives with every single goddamn day. *And he's five.*

I watch with tears burning in my eyes and an ache in my gut that makes me feel physically ill.

You promised, Malone.

You promised Drew you'd take care of them. The calendar helps with that.

You promised the guys you'd do the shoot. That proves they can depend on me.

You promised Dylan you'd follow through. That proves that she means more to me than I'm willing to admit.

THIRTY-SEVEN

Dylan

I WISH HE'D TOLD ME.

Our phone conversation replays in my mind as I turn into the parking lot, going a little faster than I should.

"I didn't want to bug you because I know you're busy trying to get the songs finished, but . . . would you mind coming here for a little bit," he asked.

"What's wrong? Are you okay? Always interrupt me."

"I'm at the calendar shoot."

"I'm on my way."

The sound of his voice, the uncertainty, rings in my ears as I all but jog across the parking lot to the address Grady texted me.

Why didn't he tell me ahead of time so I could be here for him?

Because I'm not his girlfriend.

I'm not anything to him.

I'm his enjoyment for the time being—that's why.

And even though the stinging thoughts are in my head, the minute I push open the door to the studio and see Grady, I know why I'm here. *For him. To help him heal.* He's pacing back and forth on the side of the room. His hand keeps going to his head and then stopping when he realizes he can't mess up his hair.

Another firefighter—Dixon, I think—is in front of the camera. His shoulders are square, his chest is bare, and he has his turnout jacket hooked by one finger over his shoulder. His nervous chuckle and his awkward and forced positioning reflect how uncomfortable he is.

There's a catcall from a side of the room I can't see, and I'm sure it's another one of the guys giving him shit.

"Romeo, Romeo, get your hose out to save me, Romeo."

There are snickers and laughter, and I realize there is a whole crew of guys in the corner razzing him. Dixon lifts a finger and flips them off.

"Now, now. We can't be doing that on film." The photographer laughs as she clicks a candid picture of Dixon laughing. "Okay, you're all done."

"Thank, Christ. This modeling shit is for the birds. Give me a hot fire any day over these hot lights."

"Pussy," one of the guys says.

"Don't worry, GQ *won't* be knocking down your door," another says.

Everyone in the room is laughing and relaxed except Grady. He's standing in the corner, staring out the window, shoulders a wall of tension.

"Grady."

He turns when I say his name, a mixture of relief and unease fleeting through his expression.

"You're up next, Malone," the photographer says, an encouraging smile on her lips and an upbeat tone to her voice.

The crew in the corner whistles and catcalls.

"Take it off."

"C'mon, you sexy beast."

"Put us all to shame."

Grady laughs, but it's his eyes as they meet mine that communicate how he really feels. He may proclaim that he's vain, but right now his insecurity owns him.

Does he not change in front of the guys at the station? Does he not realize they don't care what his scars look like just as I don't? Or is it that he's afraid to be the reminder of what can happen in their job? Does he fear they'll shun him so they don't have to see the consequences?

I'm not sure which one it is, or if it's a combination of all of them, but my heart breaks seeing him try to put on such a strong front when he's struggling internally with something none of us clearly understands.

"So, what am I going to do with you?" the photographer asks as she looks at him shift on his feet and radiate discomfort. She angles her head to the side. "Turnout pants, suspenders, helmet." She nods for emphasis as the rest of the guys whoop it up.

They can't be oblivious to what he's going through, so I can only think they're being boisterous intentionally. But it isn't working. I can see it in his hesitation to walk to where his pile of gear is waiting on his chair, his helmet resting atop it.

His shoulders rise and fall as he stares at his gear in indecision.

"Hey, guys?" I ask as I walk over to them. "What would you say if I told you I wanted my own private show here?"

Bowie's eyebrows arch, and he nods to let me know he gets what I'm saying and will play along with my ruse. "You know this is a PG calendar, right, McCoy?" He chuckles and lifts his chin to the guys in an unspoken directive. If Grady has been keeping us sleeping together on the down-low, I just screwed that up for him.

"I'll take my chances, but you never know what might come over me when Malone puts on those turnouts. They've been known to make female hormones get a little hot and bothered."

"I think that's our cue to vacate the premises," Dixon says. "Are you going to be okay with her here, Malone? I mean, do you need backup in case she can't control herself and jumps you on the spot?"

"I assure you, this is one fire I know how to put out." Grady chuckles and picks up his gear to head to the changing room.

The guys gather their stuff and begin to file out of the studio. Bowie hangs back, waiting for the guys to clear before turning to me. "Thanks for coming. I was worried how he was going to do with this

. . . but I know he'll be fine now that you're here."

I open my mouth to speak, but he just shakes his head as if to tell me nothing more needs to be said before patting my shoulder and walking out.

"Marcy Holden." I look over to where the photographer has her hand outstretched and curiosity etched in the lines of her face.

"Dylan McCoy. Nice to meet you." I shake her hand.

"Is there something no one's telling me here?" she asks in a hushed tone.

I wage a mental war between giving away private information on Grady and then realize this is a small town. If Marcy is shooting photos for the calendar to benefit the widows' fund, she knows what happened. And if she knows what happened, I can draw the conclusion that she's aware another firefighter was injured, so I give enough information not to feel like I am betraying and emasculating Grady. "He's the one who was injured in the fire."

"Oh." Her eyes widen and the sound comes out in a gasp of shock. "How did I not put two and two together? That's what I get for being new in town. I'm sorry. Is there something I'm not supposed to do or—?"

"Where do you want me?"

I'm not sure how long Grady has been standing there, but we both turn to face him at the same time, worried he overheard us. I stare at him, my mouth waters, and the murmured hum of approval Marcy emits beneath her breath is equivalent to the sucker punch of lust that hits me when I see him in his turnouts.

His everyday service uniform is hot. His Class A's are sexy. But this, his yellow turnouts with reflective tape, red suspenders, and no shirt on underneath are everything and then some.

Perfection with a little bit of grit thrown in.

Any woman who says a firefighter in his gear isn't sexy is lying because *damn* . . . that's the only word I can form.

Grady's standing before us with his red suspenders on one shoulder, the other hooked but hanging down. The turnout pants hang low on his hips so every perfect ab is on display.

It takes me a second to snap out of the lust clouding my thoughts and realize we are both ogling him in a way that will either help his insecurities or exacerbate them.

"Right. Yes. How do I want you?" Marcy asks with a shake of her head as she walks toward him, recovered and suddenly all business. She places a hand on his shoulder to direct him. It's an innocent touch, but I see Grady steel himself for it and walk sideways to keep his back away from her line of vision. "Have you ever done anything like this before?"

"No." His voice is stunted and eyes flick to mine.

"Okay, so I'm thinking . . ." She steps back and angles her head to the side as she stares at him before walking over and grabbing a yellow turnout coat and then holding it out to him. "I'm thinking you hold this over your shoulder. We'll start there. Your definition is going to play well with this lighting."

"Sure. Yeah." Grady moves toward where she directs him in front of the backdrop. His body is stiff, his smile forced. The fluidity to his movements, which is usually so natural, is all but gone.

Over the next thirty minutes, Marcy photographs him while I sit silently in the corner. She struggles to get a photo that reflects the man we see the minute the camera is off him and his body is not being stared at.

Will this ever change for him? Will he ever grow comfortable in this new skin he's been given and this new chance at life?"

"Okay, shake your shoulders out, Grady. You're looking stiff."

Grady shoots her a look with a kind smile, but I see so much behind those eyes. I wish I could do anything to take his discord away. To take his insecurity away. To show him how gorgeous he is, even with his scars.

"I had Brody in here earlier," Marcy says quietly. "He's the sweetest little boy. He talked a lot about you, you know? I didn't put two and two together until you went to get changed."

Grady's shoulders fall some, but his head lifts. A genuine smile slides softly onto his lips despite the sadness in his eyes. “He’s a good kid.”

Marcy pushes the button in her hand that takes the photo without her having to look through the lens. There’s a constant whirring *click* as the shutter continues to snap pictures.

“He is. I took some incredible shots of him in his dad’s gear. I thought it was important for him to have them for his memories.”

“I’m sure it will mean a lot to him.”

Click. Click. Click.

“It’s a good thing you’re doing here. This calendar for him and Shelby and whoever else they appropriate the funds to.”

Click. Click. Click.

“It’s the least I can do since . . .” His voice fades off, but I know what he left unsaid. *Since I didn’t save him.*

“The calendar will make some women happy.” She laughs. *Click. Click. Click.* “A lot of women happy. In fact, I’d love to shoot you another time. You have an incredible body.”

“Thanks, but no thanks.” His voice is soft, his cheeks flushing as his movements remain still despite her efforts to relax him.

“The offer stands,” she murmurs.

She positions him a few more times, and yet even to a layman like me, it doesn’t matter how striking Grady’s body is, his expression reflects his disquiet. But he’s patient and never complains. He does what she asks, turning his body every time she moves around him to reposition her camera so that any hint of his scars are out of the frame.

“Okay, give me a few seconds to check my shots and make sure I have enough to choose from.”

Grady nods and stands in the middle of the studio. He doesn’t look my way. He doesn’t say a word. It’s like he’s on an island by himself without wanting anyone to save him. *Without believing anyone would want to.*

He looks so lonely and isolated and every part of me yearns to be able to provide the solace he needs, but deep down I know he’s the one who needs to find that. He’s the one who needs to accept that life moves on regardless of how hard that may be.

Marcy looks over the top of her computer to Grady and then back down, the clicker still in her hand. A line forms on her forehead as she furrows her brow in concentration. "I think I've got it. Thank you, Grady."

"I'm done?" There's a mixture of relief and gratitude in his voice as he stares at her.

"You're done." She offers up a smile to him as he walks over and sets down the borrowed turnout jacket he had in his hand. In my periphery I catch Marcy wince when she sees Grady's back for the first time as he relaxes, knowing the hard part is over.

Her reaction is natural and unintentional. I know it. But I also feel the need to protect Grady from it. From possibly turning around and seeing it for himself. So I move into her line of sight so I'm the only one who can see Grady in this vulnerable state.

Desperate for a connection with him, *anything*, so I can let him know how proud I am of him for following through with this, I call his name. "Grady." He looks back over his shoulder at me. *Good job.* I mouth the words across the space, and when he smiles at me, it's the truest smile I've seen since I walked in here.

And for the briefest of seconds, I let myself believe he feels the same way about me that I do about him.

THIRTY-EIGHT

Dylan

"Hey," Grady murmurs into my ear as I stir slowly from my sleep.

I feel the bed dip. The covers lift. The heat of his body as he slides up behind me. The feel of his hand on my abdomen pulling me against him.

"Good shift?" I ask, my mind trying to catch up to my body, which is already awake and alert to the feel of his.

"How come you're in here?" he asks and the heat of his breath hits the back of my neck.

"This is my room."

"But I have nightmares when you're not in mine." He says it so nonchalantly, I close my eyes and squeeze them tight as I try to control the emotion that swells into my voice.

"I don't feel right sleeping in there when you're not here."

"Don't be silly." He rests his forehead against the back of my head and falls silent. Just as I'm about to fall back asleep he murmurs, "We lost a kid tonight. Traffic accident. He wasn't buckled in his car seat properly. Grayson was called to the scene and they flew him to General but we lost him."

My heart breaks. "Grady, I'm so sorry."

"I can still hear his mom screaming when she saw us loading him in the chopper." He sniffles, and I shift immediately to turn over, but he holds me in place where I am. "Uh-uh. Can I just—I need this right now. Need you right now. Okay?"

"Yes."

"I could listen to you sing all day." Grady's sleep-drugged voice interrupts me from where he stands on the porch, hair a mess, and sweatpants hanging dangerously low on those strong hips of his. I blush at his compliment, and my cheeks heat with embarrassment. I can sing in a studio full of techs and musicians, but tell me Grady is listening, and I want to die of embarrassment. "It's late."

I look up from my guitar and over to the clock. "It's eleven. In my world that's early." I laugh. "It isn't late until you're waking up after lunchtime."

"Sounds similar to the station." He stares at me for a beat. I can tell he wants to say something but is unsure, so I wait him out. "How are the songs coming?"

"Good." That isn't what he wanted to ask, but I let it slide. "I have most of them started. About eighty-five percent finished to the point that I'm happy with them for now. They'll need some further tweaking once we hit the studio and I can hear them played back to me. And the other fifteen percent I'm hoping to wrap up in the next two weeks." The last three words are hard to get out. They put an expiration date on this. *On us*. And I'm having a difficult time accepting that.

"We'll have to celebrate when you finish."

I nod but swallow over the sudden lump in my throat. *Celebrate*? Does that mean he's happy I'm leaving?

"We should," I lie and then change the topic because leaving here is the last thing I want to think about. "I turned the scanner down so I could work and you could sleep, but it sounds like there is a pretty big fire up north."

"I heard. Bowie called and woke me up." Concern fills his eyes.

"Are you guys going to be called out to help?"

"Not sure," he says. "But I want to take you somewhere today. Do you have plans?"

THIRTY-NINE

Dylan

"Let's go hiking, he said. It will be fun, he promised."

Grady laughs as he strides ahead of me, barely out of breath while I huff and puff like a little old lady who smokes a carton of cigarettes a day.

"If I wasn't aware I was out of shape, I am now."

"You aren't out of shape," he says, stopping and putting a hand on my back to help me up a slide of rocks. "It's just the altitude that's getting to you."

"Is that all?" I laugh. "Didn't you know I'm allergic to exercise? How long have we been doing this? And if you say ten minutes I'm going to push you off that ledge over there."

"Nah. We've been going for well over an hour now." He ducks as I swat at him.

"And we're doing this, why?"

"Because I wanted to show you how beautiful wine country is."

"Couldn't we have done it while sitting in a winery drinking some of the libations that said wine country has produced?"

"We could have."

"Then why aren't we?" I ask and wheeze in a breath. This seriously is not what I thought we'd be doing when he said he wanted to take me somewhere.

But I have to admit the view isn't too shabby. Watching Grady's ass as he climbs the mountain is a sight I'm not complaining about in the least.

"How come I haven't seen anyone else on the trail?" I ask, looking behind me and growing slightly dizzy at how high we've ascended. "Should I be worried that Mallory called and wants to have some fun, and you aren't sure how to tell me so you've brought me up here to off me instead of hurting my feelings and telling me so?"

Grady's feet falter, and he turns back to stare at me from beneath the brim of his Sunnyville Fire Department baseball hat. The sexy-as-hell smirk on his lips makes me want to kiss him. "*Off you*?"

"Yeah." I shrug playfully, needing this banter to distract me from realizing how much exercise I'm actually getting. I bring both hands to my neck as if someone is choking me. "Off me."

He takes a step toward me. "For the record, Mallory has called, and I've told her not to bother calling again because my bed is otherwise occupied." He presses a chaste kiss to my lips, which have fallen lax from his comment, and then turns around and starts walking again.

I stare after him, the cavalier way he made that statement more striking than the confession itself. Almost as if he thinks I'm crazy for thinking otherwise.

My mind spins at breakneck speed as I wonder if this means Grady Malone has feelings for me like I do for him. Sure we're having sex. Yes, he cuddles up to me at night after a long day at work. Admittedly he just said he turned down his in-the-meantime-in-between-time girl, but that doesn't mean I can read into his words any more than I can let myself believe when my time is up here he might actually ask me to stay.

Because I know that isn't a possibility. He's made that more than clear.

"Wait up!" I shake my head and scramble after him, not wanting to get too far behind because that means I'll just have that much farther to walk in an accelerated speed.

"You have quite the imagination," Grady says when I catch up to him.

"It's an occupational hazard to make up stories."

"Well, lucky for you, Grant's a detective so if I did have some elaborate plan to *off you*, I'm sure he'd sniff out my lies and throw the book at me."

"So you aren't going to off me then?" I pant, needing the levity and our reflexive banter to prevent me from overthinking what Grady said moments ago.

"Nah. I'll at least let you enjoy the view first." He chuckles as I step beside him. My breath catches at the sight before us. The valley is laid out in greens, and the hillside is an array of row after row of lush vines. It's mesmerizing and utterly peaceful all at the same time.

"Oh, wow."

"Exactly," he murmurs.

"I feel like we're on top of the world."

"Not hardly, but it's close."

I take in the scenery as Grady removes his backpack and takes a seat on a large, pancake-shaped rock. When I look back at him, I'm startled to see him with a bottle of wine in one hand and a paper cup extended to me in his other.

"We have reached the wine portion of our program."

"Are you serious?" I laugh.

"Deadly."

"I knew I lov—" *I loved you.* My mind staggers over why the words falter. Normally, I'd say them because wine equals love and the person who provides it deserves my adoration, and yet for some reason, my saying the words to him seems like they will mean so much more. Either that or I want it to mean more. But Grady's sitting there, looking at me and probably wondering why I stopped midsentence, so I scramble to think of something to say. "I knew you'd reward me."

"Pain and suffering deserves some pleasure." A coy smile plays at the corner of his lips as he leans back on his hand and watches me.

I take a sip and meet his gaze over the lip of the cup. "So . . . you aren't trying to off me. You're not trying to get me drunk and push me off the edge of the cliff to shut up my complaining . . . then what exactly are you trying to do here, Grady?"

"Who says there has to be an ulterior motive besides needing fresh air?"

"You're a guy. Aren't ulterior motives part of your MO?"

"Ouch." He fakes a dagger to the heart and then grins as he takes a drink of his own wine. Then sighs. "Sometimes I just need to clear my head. This is where I come to do that."

"The accident last night?"

"Mostly." He nods, his voice softening. "It's been a long week. The photo shoot. Some shit at the station. Drew . . . but mostly last night."

And it always comes back to Drew. Full circle every time. Every trigger, every emotion is rooted in that one event for him.

I take a seat beside him but keep my eyes on the Northern California valley below. "Want to talk about it?"

Grady stares at the view and doesn't answer.

"It has to be hard. I often wondered how a first responder deals with the emotions and fallout of the things they see on a daily basis."

"Some days are easier than others. Some like last night, not so much. The upside for me is that I have my brothers to talk to about it. They see it all too, and they understand. And then there's my dad. I have a support network most others don't have, so I'm lucky. But I'm not going to lie and say it doesn't stick with me. The sights. The smells. It makes me react to things in my everyday life a little differently."

"Like how?" I ask, wanting him to maybe see the contradiction in his words and his actions since his accident.

He shrugs and takes a sip of his wine. "I appreciate every day. I realize I get to come home when others don't." His voice is soft, reflective with a hint of sorrow.

"Do you feel like you're doing that?" I'm not sure how he's going to respond, but I feel the need to ask the question.

He sighs and twists his lips as he thinks. "I know where you're going with this, and I'd rather not, okay? After the accident, I should want to live life to the fullest and all that jazz. Never miss another moment to make memories. I get it. *I do*. But you know what? I lived, and he didn't. I walked away, and he has a wife and son he never went home to." There is no anger in his voice, just solemnity.

"Do you think that by punishing yourself the rest of your life it's going to make his death count for something? Because the way I see it, it makes it count for less." Grady starts to stand, and I grab on to his hand and make him stay put. "No, hear me out then I'll drop it." He sits back down, but his muscles beneath my fingers don't relax. "You were given a second chance, Grady. You were given something most people don't get. Think about how you lived before the accident. Think about how you've lived since. Sometimes, life gives us a second chance at things. At realizing we should test ourselves and question ourselves . . . maybe you got a second chance because the first go round you weren't ready."

In my periphery, I can see him close his eyes briefly and try to rein in the emotion my words have conjured. "I tell myself every day I'm going to do better. I'm going to *be* better. I'm going to face everything and rise."

"Face everything and rise. I like that."

"It's one of my dad's favorite sayings." I get a tight smile from him and then he continues. "And then I feel the stretch of my scars. I see something that reminds me of Drew. I hear someone in town whisper as I walk by. And then I'm back to square one."

"You feel the stretch of your scars because you're alive, Grady. You see something that reminds you of Drew because he was like your third brother. I'd worry if you weren't reminded of him. And the townspeople whisper for several reasons. First, they point you out because you're the hero who tried to save your fallen brother. Second, they point you out because they think you're sexy and wonder how to approach you, and third, they whisper because I've staked my claim on you and they wonder why Grady Malone, son of Sunnyville, would dare be with an outsider of the town instead of with one of their own."

He slides a look to me as his smile widens on his lips and his eyes alight with humor. "Staked your claim on me, have you?"

"Damn straight," I say with a smile. "You know people are saying,

'She could have Jett Kroger and she's picking Grady Malone. His dick must be *huge*.'"

His laughter echoes around us, and I love the sound of it. "Is that so?"

"There's no complaints from me in that department." I lift an eyebrow and smile.

"There better not be." He part tackles, part hugs me until I lie back on the rock, my wine sloshing over the edge of the cup in the process. "I'd be happy to make you not complain again . . . right here, right now." He presses a kiss to my lips that stifles my laughter.

"I knew you had an ulterior motive for bringing me up here."

"Sex al fresco." His lips are on mine again in a languorous kiss that draws sensations from my toes all the way to my hair.

"Can't say I've had sex on a mountaintop before."

"You sure you want me to make you go weak in the knees before you have to walk back down?"

"Oh God." I laugh. Then sigh the words again as his lips find the underside of my neck and cause chills to chase over my skin. "So, you are trying to off me," I finally say when I can find words again.

"Mmm. Death due to being orgasmicly sexed," he whispers in my ear before running the tip of his tongue around the edge of my lobe. "I can think of worse ways to go."

FORTY

Grady

"YOU WATCHING THIS?"

I stare at the news on television and watch the destruction unfold. "Yeah," I say to my dad, who sits patiently on the other end of the phone. "We've already been given notice. If they can't contain it, we'll be called up."

The fire rages on the screen. It marches up the hill and eats the dry vegetation as if it's starving. Black clouds of smoke billow. Lines of yellow jackets from the strike team edge the top part of the screen as they try to cut a fire line into the hill to slow down its progress.

"It's already doubled in size in less than four hours."

"I'm aware," I murmur.

This used to be what I lived for. The thrill of the fire. The unexpected pull. That tingle in my belly, telling me I get to be a part of it.

"You gonna be able to handle it?"

And for the first time in almost two years, I feel the hum in my veins. It's welcome. It's scary. It may very well disappear if we get called up, but for now, I'll take what I can get.

"Yeah. I'll be able to handle it."

"It's the season. Long, dry summer. Santa Ana winds. If it isn't this one, it will be another one."

I nod even though he can't see it. He's planting the seed I need to prepare for facing the fire as if I haven't been already. "I know."

"I have faith in you, Grady. Face everything and rise."

"I know, Dad. I'm trying."

"You call me when you know."

"I will."

I end the call and watch the fire rage on. Petunia roots around, her grunts become background noise. The chords from Dylan's guitar as she works through one of her final songs push through her closed door.

The world keeps moving as the fire rages on and destroys someone else's property.

House.

Life.

World.

FORTY-ONE

Dylan

"I HOPE YOU DON'T MIND THAT I STOPPED OVER WITHOUT calling first." Emerson stands in the doorway and smiles, her strawberry-blonde hair pulled back in a ponytail and her little baby paunch finally showing.

"No. Please. Come in." I open the door wider and do a mental rundown of if I look presentable or not. Too many late nights working and a lot of Grady covering the station for the crews called up north to cover the wildfire slowly being contained means makeup and hair have been left by the wayside. "I could use the break. It feels like I've been working on the same lyrics for days without any progress."

"How's it going?"

"I'm down to finishing my final three songs."

"And then you'll be leaving us?" I notice her pursed lips and hate what my response has to be.

"Yes." I clear the emotion in my throat that the knowing look in her eyes causes.

"I'm sure you're excited to get back to your everyday life. The hustle and bustle of Los Angeles. Hell, now that Jett's out of the picture, I'm sure you'll have a blast living it up, playing the field, and meeting someone new."

"Hmm."

"He is out of the picture, right?" she asks with wide eyes and raised brows.

"Yes. He is. It's definitely over." This time my response has more resonance to it.

"Then *yay*, you get to go back home with a fresh start."

"Sure." There is nothing convincing in how I say the word. In fact, the thought of leaving here and playing the field is the farthest thing on my mind because there's one problem with each one of those suppositions. None of them include Grady.

Or the comfort of the scanner that convinces me he's okay and near, even though he isn't. *Like now.*

Emerson angles her head and studies me for a beat, but when she finally speaks, she leaves the topic alone and moves on. "I don't know how you do it," she murmurs as she sits in the chair across from me. "If I had to be that creative all the time, I think my brain would fry."

"And if I had to jump out of airplanes for a living, mine would fry." I laugh and then shrug. "There are many days the creativity isn't there. But when I feel a song and I'm on, I can write it in less than an hour. Other times, like now, it takes days."

"What's the song called you're working on now?"

"'Hard to Say Goodbye.'" Our eyes meet briefly, and I know she can see the truth in mine. That I'm writing a song about my imminent departure, but she just smiles softly and nods as I stand and move nervously into the kitchen. "Would you like some water? A soda?"

"What I'd really love is a glass of wine, but that's frowned upon since I'm pregnant and all." She laughs, and yet I can hear the adoration in her voice over her impending baby.

"Damn doctors." I roll my eyes and take a seat across from her again. "What can I do for you?"

"I have something for you, hot off the presses and I thought you might want to see."

"What are you talking about?"

There is a mischievous smile on her lips as she reaches into her monster-sized purse. "Did I mention to you one of my clients is Marcy Holden?" That gets my attention. "I stopped by her studio to book some pregnancy photos—that I'm sure Grant will bitch about having to take with me—and she happened to get her first shipment of these in. She thought that since I'm Grady's sister-in-law and everything that I might swing some by the station. So I did. But not before I grabbed an extra to bring to you."

She pulls the calendar out of her purse, and for some reason I'm hesitant to look at it. I'm nervous for Grady and how his photo turned out, considering how anxious he was.

"Have you looked at it?" I ask and then feel stupid when I see it wrapped in plastic.

"I figured I'd let you do the honors."

I glance at her as I take it from her hands and slowly peel the wrapping off. The front cover is a picture of all twelve guys with their turnouts on, their jackets unfastened to reveal their shirtless chests underneath. If I may say so, the Sunnyville Fire Department has some hot firefighters. Grady's smile is wide in the photo, and it's more than obvious they were all laughing about something.

When I flip to the first page, both of our breaths hitch. It's a picture of Brody in his dad's gear. The uniform almost swallows him whole, but it's the smile on his face and tears welling in his eyes that grabs my heart and doesn't let go. And beneath his photo is a thank-you note for supporting the fireman's widow fund.

Talk about a knife to the chest.

I lift the first page to January and laugh when I'm met with Bowie and his cheesy grin. He's attractive in his own right, but I can't get past picturing the silly antics of his. Dixon's up next, and I'm impressed with how much the camera likes him. Emerson and I go through each month, making small comments here and there, but it's when I hit August that the gasp falls from both of our mouths.

My first thought is Grady's going to lose his mind.

My second thought is *oh my God, that's the Grady I know.*

The image is in black and white. It isn't of Grady in his turnouts, flexing his muscles. It isn't him looking serious (and uncomfortably stiff) back at the camera. It's of Grady looking back over his shoulder when the shoot was complete, relief in his eyes, and a genuine smile on that handsome face of his.

It was when he was looking at me.

Marcy captured the moment perfectly. The authenticity of it. The emotion in Grady's eyes, and the pleasure in his smile.

And his burns.

They are part of the picture—like they're a part of him. Probably the only part of the picture he'll notice, but deep down, I know no one else will see them because they'll be too busy falling in love with Grady Malone.

Just as I have.

I inhale an unsteady breath as the reality of the thought hits me like a sucker punch to the solar plexus.

"Holy shit." It's Emerson who speaks. The words are drawn out and full of unexpected awe.

"That about sums it up." I laugh nervously.

"Don't tell Grant I said it, but his little brother is seriously hot."

My laugh turns more genuine as my hands clutching the calendar relax some, but my eyes never leave the photo. "I won't."

"This picture . . . it's everything."

"It is," I murmur.

"He's going to hate it," she says.

I love it. "I know."

"It shows his burns, but no one is going to notice them because they are going to be staring at—"

"The look in his eyes," I finish for her. We both fall silent for a moment as we take in the picture again. The dark contrast of his burns against the lighter parts of his skin. How they seem so muted when compared to the look on his face. In his eyes. The smile on his lips that lights his face.

"I'd love to know what he was looking at," she says.

Me.

I don't say it, though. I don't trust my own voice not to betray the emotion rioting through me from realizing that I love him. To betray the hope this picture brings—that he feels the same. But then comes the devastation in knowing that it doesn't matter whether I love him or not, because the calendar's prelude—the opening picture of Brody and the sadness it exudes—is exactly why Grady will never acknowledge or act on the feelings his eyes reflect.

"I'm not sure."

FORTY-TWO

Grady

"SPECIAL DELIVERY," DIXON SAYS AS HE WALKS INTO THE common room and tosses a pile of calendars on the table we're all sitting around.

"For fuck's sake. Do you have to ruin my appetite?" Bowie laughs. "I see these assholes shirtless all the time, and believe me, it's enough to make me gag if I have to eat and look at their hairy chests at the same time."

"Says the king of bear rugs on his back," Dixon fires back as everyone but me laughs.

I can't laugh. I'm too busy staring at the calendar. My palms coat with sweat and my pulse rages in my ears. For a man who used to stare at himself in the mirror every day to see which muscles were popping better, the fear of seeing what I look like through the eyes of someone else is terrifying.

Grabbing a calendar off the table, I head to the bay, needing a moment to come to grips with what I'm going to see and, at the same time, feeling like the biggest pussy on the face of the earth. I turn the calendar over in my hands, looking at the cover picture and thinking of the raunchy joke the probie Johnson said to make us all laugh.

With a deep breath, I flip it open. And there's Brody. Brave, funny-as-shit, and incredible. My heart sinks. That little boy is fucking everything to me, and I know Drew would be so damn proud of the little man he is becoming. I bite back the guilt—the voice that convinces me his loss is on my shoulders—and listen to Dylan's voice from our hike. I focus on her words; I have to live to the fullest or I'm letting Drew down. It's the same shit everyone else has said to me, and yet, her voice has replayed over and over in my head since then.

I smile at Brody's picture. He's the reason I agreed to do this calendar. No matter what I find when I come to August, I'll accept it. I'll deal with it. I'll move forward because it was done for him.

The guys look hilarious as I go through the months. Puffed-out chests and unsuccessful attempts at smoldering expressions. Things I laugh at only because I know the fuckers in real life, yet I know women will buy the calendar and appreciate them.

And then I get to August.

I close my eyes and flip up the page.

Then I open them.

It's my scars I see first. The black-and-white film mutes their harshness, and as much as I try to stare at them, find the disgust I feel daily, it's the expression on my face that draws my attention. My eyes. My smile.

This isn't the photo Marcy took for the calendar. This isn't the expression I gave her.

This is how I looked at Dylan.

This was the face of relief. The photo session was over, Marcy hadn't asked a thing about my scars, and most importantly, Dylan had been there patiently waiting in silent support. *I hadn't been alone.*

A part of me feels betrayed. Like Marcy took this photo—this side of me that I don't show anyone—and put *it* on display. The other part of me is a little shocked. Shocked that when I look at the picture, I don't feel revolted by the scarring on my back. In fact, they are the last things my eyes focus on when they should be the first. There is also this final part of me that is freaked out by what I see in my expression. Or rather, how I'm looking at Dylan. *I know that look.*

I've seen that look before. It's how Grant looks at Emerson. How my dad looks at my mom. And how Drew looked at Shelby.

I don't know how to feel. Everything inside me is a mess of contradictions because when this calendar goes out, everyone who buys it will see the one part of me I've kept hidden since the accident. Yet at the same time, they'll see the other side of me I've tried to keep hidden from even myself—my feelings for Dylan.

Well . . . *fuck*

"Dude, you are so fucking screwed."

I look up to see the guys all standing there with the calendar in their hands and huge grins on their faces. "What are you talking about?"

"You know we're doing an event to sell these, right?" Bowie says.

"An event where we all sit down and sign our month," Mack interjects.

"Yeah. So?" I'm not getting it.

"Your line is going to be so goddamn long with women with hearts in their eyes and cleavage on display. It's going to be sickening," Veego says while the rest of the guys make kissing noises. "Pretty-boy Malone kicking ass and taking names, er, phone numbers, without even having to try."

"Whatever." I laugh, the tension slowly easing from my shoulders.

"You're the only fucker who doesn't have a body shot in this whole calendar, and yet you're the one who looks the hottest," Dixon says with a roll of his eyes.

"You checking me out now, Dix?" I ask and climb down from my spot on the rig where I went for privacy.

"No, but lucky for you, that roommate of yours will be heading out soon, because I have a feeling this calendar is going to be getting you some serious revolving-between-the-sheets action."

"You're a sick fuck," I say as Bowie catches my eye and nods to me.

And I can't help but wonder what for.

Because I did the calendar and I didn't fuck it up, or because he knows that Dylan leaving might be a little harder on me than I'm letting on.

My money is on both.

I look at the calendar in my hands again as my feet falter and the guys move on, still razzing the shit out of me as if I was beside them.

And for the first time since I woke up from the accident, I look at a picture of me and realize the scars may not matter as much as I thought.

I stand at the back door and watch her. She's working through lyrics, that much I know from how she constantly repeats the same set of lines over and over. The only difference in how she normally works is this time she's doing it giving Petunia a bath. Both are covered in suds as Dylan works her hands up and down Petunia's back. Her laughter floats into the window and catches my attention just as much as the way she swings her hips.

I watch the two of them and wonder when it happened. When did Dylan seamlessly work her way into my everyday life so that something like this—her washing my pig—feels so goddamn natural that I don't question it?

"I can say I don't care.
That I'll walk away without fanfare.
But you know it's a lie.
This is so much more than goodbye."

My chest tightens when I hear the lyrics. I need to see her. But the minute I put my hand on the doorknob, I hesitate. There is so much I want to say, *need* to say, but know I can't.

Should I show her the calendar? Let her see for herself the words I can't bring myself to say? The emotions I feel but struggle to permit myself to have.

We both have our own lives to move on with when our playing

house comes to an end. We both have promises we made to ourselves we need to keep.

I have promises I need to keep.

Then why is it so hard for me to let go of the doorknob and leave her be without saying a word?

If we're simply enjoying each other and our time left, why does this feel so complicated?

Because it is.

FORTY-THREE

Dylan

"CAN'T SAY ALL OF SUNNYVILLE DIDN'T SHOW UP IN support of the calendar sales," Betsy Malone says and shakes her head as we both stare at the same person. *Her son.*

"Let's just hope Grady walks away without his ego so big he can't fit through the front door." He's all smiles as he sits and patiently talks to the ladies who have waited in line to get their calendars signed.

They run the gamut when they get to Grady—from giggly to flirty, from shy to rambling—but I love that he's patient with every one of them. Taking a picture if they ask. Talking to their kids if they're with them. The perfect ambassador for the station.

And that isn't saying all of the other guys aren't doing the same, but my eyes are fixed on Grady and Grady alone.

They seem to be there a lot these days.

"I'm sure you'll bring him down to earth if it is," she says with a wink. "And if not, he has two brothers chomping at the bit to razz the hell out of him."

I laugh and think of the shit they've given him since the calendars went on sale. Bumper stickers about hose sizes slapped on the back of his truck. A blow-up doll delivered that was some kind of retaliation for something he did to Grant. A box of blow-pop suckers delivered to the station. And the list goes on.

"I'm sure they will."

"Emerson says you're almost done with your songs."

"I have two left to finish, but for the most part, yes." It pains me to admit it.

"So you'll be leaving us?" she asks and then shakes her head with a silly roll of her eyes. "Sorry. Of course you will. I was having motherly daydreams that you'll fall in love with . . . Sunnyville and decide to stay." *And by Sunnyville, she really means Grady.* "Like I said, silly."

"He's a good man, Betsy." I chew the inside of my cheek and fight back the sting of tears as I stare at him. "We're just in different places of our lives right now."

"That's a load of phooey. If you love him, then love him."

I smile softly and am thankful my sunglasses hide the truth in my eyes. "Even if I did, Grady won't allow it. He's made it clear that dating is all he'll ever allow, and I want more than that. Someday I want marriage, kids, the white picket fence." I hate that my voice breaks on the last words.

"Look how far he's come since you've arrived. He did the calendar. He's more comfortable in his skin."

"He is, and I'm so very glad I was a part of helping him get there . . . but there are some opinions I can't sway."

"If you stayed, who knows what could happen."

My heart will be broken. That's what will happen.

But I think of the calendar Grady is signing. The picture of him looking at me. The smile on his lips. The sincerity and warmth in his eyes. And I wonder what *we* might miss out on because he refuses to take a chance.

Because he refuses to face everything and rise.

In an attempt to dispel the conversation in which I know Betsy means well but is pressure applied to the wrong party, I fold my arms over my chest and lean against the wall and take it all in. The event. Grady accepting the enthusiasm of the photo he was so uncertain of in the first place. Even the pang of jealousy as I wonder which of these women will take my place when I'm gone.

"Dylan, there's someone I'd like you to meet."

I turn from where my gaze sits on Grady to find Shelby and Brody standing before me.

"You're right, B-man. She is as pretty up close as she is from far away." Shelby ruffles Brody's hair and looks to me with a shy smile. "It's so nice to finally meet you, Dylan. I've heard a lot about you from Grady."

I smile, suddenly nervous for some reason as if I'm meeting the other woman in Grady's life. "So nice to finally meet you too."

"Quite a turnout, isn't it?" Shelby puts her hands on her hips and turns to look at the crowd.

"It is. Hey, Brody," Betsy says. "I think you should be over there autographing the calendars with the guys, don't you?" His eyes light up and cheeks flush red. "You *are* the first picture in the calendar . . . and you know that's the most important one, right?"

Brody's eyes widen as he looks from me to his mom and then back again. "It is?"

"Absolutely. How about I take you to Grady and let you sign next to him while your mommy and Miss Dylan chat for a bit?"

We watch as Betsy walks an animated Brody across the parking lot to where the tables are set up beneath E-Z Ups. There's an awkward silence between us, because I'm really not sure what to say but feel like I need to say everything. *I'm sorry about the loss of your husband* really doesn't feel like enough, though.

"Grady is a very special man," Shelby says eventually. She doesn't look my way, and her voice is soft, but there is so much emotion packed into those six words that I can *feel* them.

"He is."

"He needed someone like you, you know. It's like you've brought him back to life."

I hold back the hiccup of a sob that threatens. First his mom's words and now Shelby's, which are both hard to hear since the one person I want to hear them from hasn't said them. *Won't say them.* I clear my throat and begin to speak when she reaches over and grabs my hand and clutches it tightly in hers.

If anyone else did that to me, I'd yank it away, but with Shelby, I can sense she needs this connection somehow. Her hand trembles and grip tightens as she sniffs back her own tears.

"Those first months after Drew died, I couldn't bring myself to visit Grady. I was so angry with him for not being able to save Drew, but at the same time I understood that I married a man who loved the beast as much as he loved me. Unfortunately, the beast won." She pauses to collect herself and then begins again. "I had questions. Was Drew in pain? Did he know it was happening, or did he pass out from smoke inhalation unaware? Those two things haunted me. And then when I finally had the courage to see Grady in the hospital, I saw the suffering he was enduring as they scrubbed the dead skin from his burns. He tried not to scream, but let tears silently fall because he believed he deserved the punishment. My heart broke all over again. He lived, but it didn't make his pain any less."

"I'm so sorry, Shelby." I sniffle and squeeze her hand as she lifts her free hand to wipe her tears beneath her sunglasses.

"It's been a little over two years since he died. There isn't a day that goes by where I don't think about him. It's impossible not to when I see him in everything Brody does. And I know it's the same for Grady. And I love that about him. His loyalty to his friend. To his unfounded guilt. To keeping the promise he made to my husband that he'd make sure Brody knew everything about his father . . . but that means Grady stopped living too. Sure, he's gone through the motions, but I haven't really seen him light up with happiness . . . until you came along."

She breaks from her commentary when Brody and Grady look our way and wave.

"Why are you telling me all this?" I ask gently.

"Because Grady will never admit to you that you've made a difference. He won't allow himself to acknowledge what he feels for you, but we all can see it clearly in that photo." I turn my head to look at her and she chuckles. "Marcy told me about the shoot. About the only time Grady actually relaxed and showed his true colors was then.

When he was looking at you."

"I have my life to get back to," I murmur in explanation despite my feet feeling perfectly fine where they're planted.

"Uh-huh." She shifts her feet and releases my hand. "And sometimes life changes at the drop of a dime, and you take the chance."

"I appreciate what you're doing here, Shelby, but Grady is the one set in his ways. I'm glad I helped him in some way to find his everyday normal in a sense," I repeat like a broken record.

"You have. And I thank you for that. We all appreciate it more than you'll ever know."

FORTY-FOUR

Dylan

"UMM." IT'S THE ONLY THING I CAN THINK TO SAY WHEN I walk into the kitchen to find candles lit at the kitchen table and a meal simmering on the stove.

I feel like I've stepped into an alternative reality. *Romance*? Is this romance?

And my heart stills in my chest. And then starts again.

Has he finally realized what I have? Has Grady finally decided to give whatever this is a chance between us without his predetermined rules and regulations?

"Hey there."

"Should I leave? Am I interrupting a date you have planned with someone?" I use humor to combat the sudden nerves rattling around inside me.

The look on his face, amused confusion, tugs at my heartstrings as he purses his lips and shakes his head. "No date planned with anyone else."

I take another step into the kitchen. "Oh?"

"I cooked dinner for you."

The simple statement is enough to make this girl's heart melt. "You did?"

"Yep." He hands me a glass of wine and pulls a chair out for me. "I thought it was about time I tell you."

"Tell me what?" A lump forms in my throat.

Can we try this? Try to make whatever this is work?

Don't go. Please stay.

My head swirls with possibilities, as his eyes remain locked on mine. He sits on the chair beside me, his knees framing mine, as he places his hands on my thighs. He rubs them up and down their length causing chills to chase up my spine.

"Thank you." His smile is shy, the look in his eyes generous, and his voice is almost a whisper.

And my hopes still hang on.

"Grady?"

"Thank you for making me see what I was denying." I lay my hands atop his and squeeze. "You talked me into doing the calendar. You keep reiterating the guilt is okay, but it can't rule my life. You . . . you made me realize the scars on the outside aren't the problem, but it's the ones on the inside I need to work on. This is the new normal, and I have to accept it."

"Not so much accept, but *live* with it."

"You always say things so much prettier than I do." He smiles.

"It's an occupational hazard, but honestly, Grady, I didn't do anything different from what anyone else has. Maybe it was just the new voice that made you listen."

"Perhaps. Regardless . . . I owe you a huge thank you." He twists his lips and looks at our hands. "I know you're on your last song and will be leaving soon, and I wanted to take the time to let you know how much your encouragement means to me, how much *you* mean to me."

Ask me to stay.

I bite back the words because they're silly and not possible, but, God, how I'd try to make it work if he asks.

"Thank you."

"I bet you can't wait to get back to Los Angeles. Your daily routine. Your life without a pig rooting around and a police scanner going off every five minutes reminding you of your dad."

My smile is soft, and my heart is heavy. The hopes I'm creating in my mind—that he's made this dinner to ask me to stay—sink slowly. One by one. My foolishness crashes with a big *thud*, making me feel more stupid than anything. Grady said we were *enjoying each other*. That's it. I am the foolish one who let Betsy's words, Shelby's comments, and the picture in the calendar make me think there can be more.

But I'm wrong.

"I'm used to them now. I think I'm actually going to miss them." I swallow over the twinge in my heart and force a smile.

"I doubt it. Without you, I wouldn't have done the calendar. And without the calendar, I wouldn't have stepped outside of myself to see how others view me. How the scars fade away after the initial shock. For that, I owe you so much." That shy smile graces his lips again and steals my heart. "And what I thought an hour ago was a good idea—cooking for you—I've now realized is a subtle form of torture considering my cooking is not always the best."

I laugh. "That bad, huh?"

"Let's just hope you're standing when we're done with the meal." He squeezes my thighs and stares at me in silence for a beat. I try to tell myself his eyes aren't saying the words to me that my imagination is making up, but it's so hard not to.

The sincerity in his smile. The emotion in his eyes. The hum from our physical connection.

Stop thinking, Dylan. Just enjoy.

So, I do. I push everything out of my head and focus on the playful banter we share over dinner. On the casual brushes of a hand on my back or when we both reach for the bottle of wine. On the undeniable, slow simmer of sexual tension so frustrating and exhilarating at the same time.

Grady tops off my glass of wine and sits back on the couch beside me. "So . . . you're still alive. That's always a good thing."

"The food was great. It's hard to screw up pasta."

"You'd be surprised the things I can screw up when cooking. The guys razz the hell out of me over it."

"Well, I thought it was excellent. Thank you." I take a sip of my wine and give in to the urge and rest my head against his shoulder. We sit and watch the fire crackle and pop in the fireplace.

"What is it with you firefighters? I think you're all secretly pyromaniacs."

He chuckles, and his shoulders move with it. "We are. We all love to play with fire. It's a job requirement."

"That explains why we have a fire going when it's at least sixty-plus degrees outside."

"I've got to get my fix somehow," he murmurs and then fades off. Without having to look at him, I know what he's thinking. It's his only fix. There have been wildfires around us in neighboring communities but none have touched Sunnyville. And Grady's station hasn't been one of the departments called on to help during them.

The question is, if his station had been called, would he have been able to fight the fire? Does the realization he talked about earlier pertain to his career as well, or only his own physical scars?

"I like the song you've been working on," he says softly, and I can't help but wonder if this is his way of changing the subject he unexpectedly shifted to.

"It's been a hard one to get right."

"Maybe it's because you secretly don't want to leave," he jokes and laughs without a clue as to how close his words ring true for me.

"Maybe," I murmur.

"I've only heard it in bits and pieces. What's it about?"

"Love." I chuckle. "Isn't that what most songs are about?" It's the only way I can answer without telling him the song is about him. If he hears all the lyrics together, he'll know.

"I'm still waiting to see you write one of those songs for yourself." *If he only knew*. "And sing it in public."

"And I'm still waiting for you to fight a fire that isn't in your fireplace," I tease.

"Touché," he says and links his fingers with mine. "Am I supposed to go outside and light a fire just so I can hear you sing?"

"You've already lit one," I murmur as I look up and then brush my lips over his.

His chuckle is deep, and it rumbles against his lips and onto mine. "Then maybe it's time I play with it awhile before I help put it out."

Just like that, we slip into whatever this is with each other.

And later, when Grady is cuddled against me, the heat of his body against my back and his arm holding me possessively as he does in his sleep, I pretend this will become something. A future. A tomorrow.

Our tomorrow.

FORTY-FIVE

Dylan

I STARE AT MY COMPUTER SCREEN—AT THE COMPLETED SET OF lyrics for my last song—and a part of me wants to purposely forget to save it.

Because if I don't save it, I'll have to rewrite it.

And if I have to rewrite it, I'll get more time here.

More time means more Grady.

More Grady means less heartache.

Less heartache is always better.

I close the lid of my laptop without saving. Almost as if I'm asking fate to make a decision for me—lose the song and tell me it's worth staying. Save the song and let me know it's time to move on.

Jesus, Dylan. You're going out of your mind.

I flop back on the bed, sigh, and try to forget about the ten emails from the label I need to return. The ones verifying that I will be present for the studio time booked in five days. The time that can't be pushed or rescheduled because it's with the hottest producer in town.

Then there are the texts and voice mails from Jett asking me why I haven't sent him the last two songs. The songs that are about getting over him and falling back in love again, only it's him instead of me who's going to be singing about it.

I put my arm over my eyes and try to shut it all out.

"You okay?" Grady's voice from the doorway scares the crap out of me.

I bolt up from the bed with a little yelp. "Argh! I didn't know you were home yet."

He laughs. "Yeah. I'm off shift and on time. It's a miracle."

"Slow day in Sunnyville emergencies?"

"Yep. By the lack of crumpled paper all over the floor . . . it's true then? You're really done?"

"Yes." It pains me to admit it.

"When are you leaving?" His voice rings hollow, reflecting how I feel. In all honesty, I should be jumping for joy right now, because this last song is the key to the handcuffs keeping me locked to Jett and the label.

"The end of the week," I say because it sounds so much longer than three days.

He chews the inside of his cheek, and I wonder if he's counting the days left like I am. "This kind of sucks." Only *kind of?*

"Yeah . . . it does."

"I have somewhere I want to take you."

"Where?" I laugh at the sudden change of topic. "The last time you said that I ended up winded, climbing up a mountain."

"That wasn't the only reason you were winded," he says and winks. My body reacts to the statement and thinks of our scenic sex atop the mountain.

"True." I chew on the word as I angle my head and study him. He's still in his Class A's. His brown hair is styled, his eyes are alive, and that smile of his seems so much more at ease than when I walked in here a few months ago.

And he's definitely still sexy as hell.

"Do you trust me?"

I laugh. "Famous last words."

Grady doesn't give any hints as to where we're going as he drives a meandering route through Sunnyville. He talks about a few of the medical calls he had during his shift, but nothing of significance.

And then we pull into the parking lot of the strip mall.

"What are we doing?" I ask as I look over to where Marcy's photo studio sits.

"I have something for you to—"

"Grady . . ." *What the hell is going on?*

"Just hear me out."

"Why do I not like the sound of this when you haven't even told me anything?"

"You forced me to stand in front of the lens so I could see how everyone else sees me. So I could step outside of my head and my insecurities and realize that the things I focus on aren't what everyone else sees when they look at me."

"Okay?" I draw the word out, my pulse racing as ideas twist in my mind.

"So, I'm returning the favor." I laugh, but he just grabs my hand and squeezes to get me to listen to him. "I've booked a photo shoot for you. A boudoir shoot to be exact."

If I had water in my mouth I'd have spit it all over his dashboard. "Are you crazy?" My voice screeches as I try to slide away from him, but he just clasps my hand tighter so I can't physically reject his idea.

"Hear me out. *Please*."

"These photos are not for anyone but you. I don't care if they never see the light of day other than your eyes . . . I don't." He shrugs. "So long as you see them. Because I think once you look at them, you might actually see what the rest of us see when we look at you."

"Grady." My mouth opens. Closes. My eyes flicker to the studio and then back to him. My heart swells at the absolute thoughtfulness of this gesture. *And then shrinks when my self-esteem tells me to run and hide.*

"There's a makeup artist, a stylist, a whatever else you need waiting for you in the studio." My eyes widen, and he laughs. "It may not be Hollywood but, yes, even in little Sunnyville we have those."

Stuck in a mixture of indecision, fear, and disbelief, I just sit there when Grady leans forward and brushes a kiss to my lips. The kind that makes all parts of my body tingle and ache and want to stay in this suspended state of desire.

"Let me do this for you, Dylan. I can't give you much. Even with all you've helped me learn over the past few months, I can't give you more . . . but I can give you this."

Tears well in my eyes, and I know he understands why. The fear. The unknown. The insecurity. And yet I bite my bottom lip and nod. That small reaction causes his lips to spread in a huge grin and light up his face.

"You're always more than welcome to share the photos with me too." He laughs as I swat at him. "It was worth a shot." He laughs.

"Grady Malone." I sigh. "What am I going to do with you?" I smile softly at him, feeling sad. The real question is, *what am I going to do without you*?

FORTY-SIX

Dylan

"SO? WAS IT AS EMBARRASSING AS YOU THOUGHT IT WOULD be? It would be a great present for Grant, but not with this prego body." Emerson laughs as she rubs her belly.

I purse my lips and think of yesterday's photo shoot. The first hints of mortification. Then the glass of wine that slowly put me more at ease with each sip. The chatter of the stylist and makeup artist, and then when I was finally in front of the camera—when it was just Marcy and me—how it wasn't as bad as I feared.

But that isn't to say the pictures will be anything worth looking at.

"It was . . . it was something I think every woman should do at least once in her life—a face-your-fear thing—but mind you, I'm saying that before I see any of the photos."

"I'm sure that they will turn out wonderfully. How can they not with you as the subject?"

I roll my eyes. "Like I said, I've yet to see any pictures."

Petunia comes into the kitchen and pushes her snout against my leg. My eyes sting with tears, and I keep them aimed down at her as I try to rein in the emotion.

Emerson reaches over, puts her hand over mine, and squeezes. "You doing okay?"

I nod and swallow over the lump in my throat and the unexpected emotions overwhelming me. "I'm good," I lie. How have these people, this family, become so important to me when four months ago I didn't know them at all?

"So what? You're going to leave just like that? Pack your stuff and walk out without ever looking back?"

"I didn't say that."

"You didn't say anything at all, actually."

"I have a life to get back to, Emerson." I hate sounding like a broken record—pun unintended. Or maybe it's only broken in my head, because that's what I keep telling myself every time I hope Grady will ask me to stay.

"That's such bullshit, and you know it."

"What?" I laugh the word out in defense.

"This pregnant woman is moody and emotional so don't play the innocent game. I pushed Grant away. I know what it's like to want more but terrified to ask for it."

"It isn't the same thing. You two knew each other before."

"And? Are you telling me that just because you didn't know Grady before you can't want to be with him now?"

"It isn't that way."

Her chuckle is low and borderline incredulous. "Then if it isn't that way, why didn't you leave today? Why are you waiting until he's off shift tomorrow to spend one last night with him before you go?"

"Because I want to see him." I scratch the top of Petunia's head, still avoiding Emerson's gaze. She'll see right through me, because a woman in love can always see when another woman is denying their own.

"You're actually going to sit here and lie and tell me that when you leave here, you're not going to leave any part of yourself behind, aren't you?"

"Emerson." Her name is a sigh. A plea. A question.

"Whatever." She scoots her chair back, walks across the kitchen to the counter, and grabs the calendar. She's back at our table in a second, flipping through the months until she gets to August. She tosses it on the table and jabs her finger at it. "You're telling me you're actually going to walk away from this? Look at that man, Dylan. What do you see in those eyes of his? I know what I see. I see a man who's in love and can't admit it. I see a man who needs a bit more patience and then maybe he'll realize it."

"I can't live my life in maybes, Em."

"Oh, sweetie, I know, but you also can't live your life in *what could have beens* either."

Her words strike me to the core and cause the foundation I've been standing so defiantly on to tremble and crack.

"Why are you being so adamant about this?"

"Because I almost threw love away. I tried to run, hide, lie to get out of it . . . and damn it if Grant wasn't persistent. And thank God he was. If he hadn't been, I would have made a huge mistake. And I can't stand by and watch someone I love miss out on living that same dream with you."

"Whoa." I hold my hands up. "No one said we were that serious."

"No one had to."

"It doesn't matter if he loves me or doesn't love me. He's told me he'll never change his mind. He's never going to settle down and bring the burden Brody and Shelby live with upon someone else."

"Then fight for him, Dylan. If he's worth it, fight for him."

"How?" There is so much frustration in that one word, and I'm not sure what else to say.

"Just fucking fight."

I stare at the ceiling. I'm surrounded by everything that smells of Grady—his sheets, his pillow, his T-shirt I'm wearing—as Emerson's words ring in my head.

Over and over.

Grady is worth fighting for. But do I give up my life in Los Angeles on a wing and a prayer? Do I step away—step back—from my life once again for a man and put mine on hold?

It would be so easy to. Simple really.

But what does that say about me?

What does that mean when I put my career second again because of a man?

I close my eyes and try to sleep. But all I see is Grady.

All I want is Grady.

And I know this is going to be one of the hardest things I'll ever do—walk away—and not because I don't love him, but rather because he doesn't love me enough to ask me to stay.

FORTY-SEVEN

Grady

"WHY THE FUCK ARE YOU HERE WHEN SHE'S LEAVING tomorrow?"

"Because I'm here," I grumble. Because if I go home then this is real, and she is leaving, and right now I don't want that to be fucking true.

"You come straight from shift here? Don't you think you should be somewhere else? Man the fuck up, Grady. You'll figure it all out, but just ask her to stay. Or tell her to go, but add that you want to keep this thing going. Something. Anything. Just don't let her walk out that door without saying a word. Quit being such a goddamn pussy, will you?"

"I'm not being a pussy. I'm being realistic."

"Realistic? Do you know the odds of being in a plane wreck twice?"

"Can't be too good considering most never survive the first crash." I sit on his couch and take the beer he offers me.

"Exactly. And you did survive the first one. So why the hell do you keep thinking you're going to crash again?"

I sigh and sink into the cushions and rest my neck on the back of the couch. "Spit it out, Grant. I'm not in the mood for one of your lectures so the least you can do is save me the wasted words."

"I'm a cop."

"No shit."

"Don't be an ass."

"What do you want me to be?" I push his buttons so he stops trying to manipulate mine.

"I want you not to be so stupid and open your ears and listen to me."

Without looking at him, I raise my hand and gesture a give-it-to-me motion. "I'm a cop. I'm married. I have a kid on the way. Do you see me shying away from Emerson? You bet your ass there are times I'm scared and worry about leaving them behind . . . but this is us, Grady. We're Malones. This is who we are. We are public servants, and risk comes with the territory. We don't have a choice in the matter. We were born to do this, but that doesn't mean we should miss out on our lives because of it."

"You weren't there." My voice is a whisper.

"You're right. I wasn't. But that didn't stop you from falling in love with her." I chuckle out a nervous laugh. *It's all fun and games until someone brings up the L-word.* "You do love her, don't you?"

"Does it matter?"

Grant leans over and slaps the back of my head like he used to do when we were kids. "Did I not teach you anything?"

I grit my teeth and fight letting my clenched fist fly. "What were you supposed to teach me oh-holier-than-thou one? We aren't you and Em, so stop making it be that."

"Then let's look at Grayson."

"He's a single dad," I refute. "I don't think we should compare shit to him since I don't see anyone in his life besides Luke."

"Fine," he grumbles, throwing his hand into the air as if he's fed up with me. "I'm still not sure why you're here, Grady."

I look at my oldest brother for the first time and speak the God's honest truth. "Because it's easier this way."

"Easier?" He snorts. "For who? You have seen the calendar, haven't you?"

"Jesus Christ, can we stop with the goddamn calendar already?"

"Then tell me what or who you were looking at when that photo was taken."

And here we go again. The same question he's asked me over and over again during the past few weeks. "I was looking at Dixon. You happy?"

"Yeah. Right." He shakes his head in frustration. "Okay, if that's the truth, then let's call up Mallory. Get her to stop by and have a little no-strings-attached fun."

I glare at him. *Mallory*. Known her for years, fucked her many times, but right now, calling her is the absolute last thing I want to do. Not when every time I think of who I want to see, talk to—fuck—I think of Dylan.

Fuck. Fuck. Fuck.

I lean forward and put my elbows on my knees and shake my head. "I'm scared, man."

"Aren't we all, brother?" He pats me on the back and squeezes my neck. "Aren't we all?"

The lights are on in the house. Dylan is in there. Her bags are probably packed, and she's ready to head back to her life, free of fucked-up firefighters.

I sit in the cab of my truck and debate whether or not I can do this. Ask her to stay. Go to work every day and wonder if I'll be coming back home to her. Put her through the constant state of worry and stress.

Brody's sad eyes flash through my mind. Shelby and her never-ending mourning.

But does lightning really strike twice?

Does Dylan want more?

Fuck.

I slide out of the truck, grab my workbag, and head into the house. The television's on. I can hear it from the back door. It's a low hum, but I realize why it sounds so different. There's no Dylan singing. No random strums of her guitar. No laughing as she talks to Petunia as if she's a person. The foreshadowing of what my life is going to hold in the coming months without her.

When I clear the family room, I drop my bag with a *thump* and that's when I hear her startled gasp.

Dylan whips her head over to face me, and I can see the tears coursing down her cheeks and the grief in her eyes.

"What's wrong? What happened?"

My thoughts fly as I walk toward her. Did something happen to her family? Her brother? To I don't know who?

My hands are on her arms, and I bring her into me. She clings to my back as she hiccups out a sob. I don't know what to say, but I have to say something.

Then I see the television. The images. The running headlines across the bottom. And I get it.

"The city of Boston is in mourning tonight after four firefighters died when the roof of a Boston factory collapsed. Two more are in critical condition."

Just when I think I can do this, reality slaps me in the face and reminds me why I can't.

Goodbye, Dylan.

FORTY-EIGHT

Dylan

"TURN IT OFF," I MURMUR AGAINST HIS CHEST AS HE PULLS me in tighter against him.

"This is my reality, Dylan. My choice. This is my life."

Make me your choice. "I'm so sorry."

He doesn't meet my eyes. He doesn't see the devastation in mine. Instead, his lips find mine.

I taste the salt from my tears and beer on his lips as they slant over mine, and I welcome the taste. The comfort. The reassurance they provide that he is home now from his shift. Safe. Whole. Well.

I'm not sure how he knows this is what I need, but he does. Maybe he needs it too. I don't know. All I know though is I'm devastated. For those firefighters' families. For their brothers who had to rescue them. For me, because I know he'll think my reaction proves what he's said all along.

So I start the process of saying goodbye to him.

In soft sighs and sips of lips. In the slow intimate entanglement of my tongue with his. In the gentle thud of my heartbeat against his chest. In the quiet urgency of our hands as we slip our clothes off where we stand so we can feel each other's skin one last time.

We come together, and there is no frenzy, only the need to connect, to memorize the feel of each other.

There are no fancy words. No dirty talk. No empty promises as we drink each other in. The feel of his dick sliding into me. Satisfying me. Marking me with his indelible touch. Worshipping me one last time.

It's such a contrast from the times we've had sex before.

Maybe because this is so much more than simply sex.

It's soft sighs and measured moans when it's normally carnal groans and desperate demands.

It's whispers of touch instead of the nails down his back free-for-all.

It's silent words but screaming hearts.

It's a goodbye not an invitation to stay.

And later, when I lie in his arms and hear his even breathing, I cry some more. Tears slide down my cheek and onto my pillow. For the man I do love but know I'll never be able to tell. I can't hurt him any more than he's already been hurt. And telling him would hurt him . . . not because he doesn't want it but because he can't give it to me in return.

When dawn comes and the sky is as gray as I feel, I slide out of the bed and stare at Grady. There are no more words to be said. Everything was said when we made love last night.

Because yes, that was what we did. Grady may not be able to verbalize it, but what we shared was so much more than simply sex.

It was everything he can't give me but wants to.

It was my goodbye.

With a sob, I lean over and press the most tender of kisses to Grady's lips. "Goodbye, Grady Malone. I love you."

FORTY-NINE

Grady

I JERK AWAKE.

Just like I do at the station when a call comes in and the alarm goes off.

But there is no call.

No alarm for an emergency.

Just the empty bed beside me.

No request to save someone.

Just the scent of her perfume lingering in the air.

There's no note on the nightstand. There's no text on my phone. There's nothing left of her anywhere.

Except for my fucking heart.

I run a hand through my hair and sigh as I stare at the ceiling.

Dylan's gone.

The woman who was slowly saving me disappeared.

Christ.

She's really gone.

FIFTY

Dylan

My need to work is paramount. To keep busy so I don't think of Grady.

But who am I fooling? It's been a week since I left Sunnyville—since I left *him* with the note on the counter and a kiss on his sleeping lips—and I feel like a piece of me has been left behind.

Emerson was right. I did leave my heart there, but hell if I'll tell her that. And I can't bring myself to answer her texts, either, because I miss her too.

Who knew going to Sunnyville to escape Jett would make me find a whole different life I'd want to keep?

I roll my shoulders as I stare out the conference room windows at the bustling city below. The city I had missed like crazy. The one full of broken dreams and rising stars. The one in which I thought I belonged but now feel like an imposter.

There is no pig wandering around to make me laugh.

There is no constant hammering of Grady and his brothers as they work on the playroom.

There is no scanner going off sporadically in the night.

"Dylan, love. So great to see you. I hope your trek in the country did you well."

I rise from my seat when Callum Divish strides into the room, hair pulled back into a ponytail, and trademark tinted lenses hiding the truth in his eyes. "Good to see you again, Callum." We air-kiss each other's cheeks, as is his fashion, before sitting. "And it did."

"Jett's late. So we'll start without him." He shakes his head. "I'd say the country was good to you and, in turn, me. The songs you wrote . . . Dylan, they are spectacular. I'm going to have a bloody hell of a time picking which ones to put on the album. You really outdid yourself."

"Thank you." I nod, my pride brimming while my heart knows most of those songs are about Grady. They're true and heartfelt.

"We'll get the last few recorded and then meet again with Kai and the team and start deciding which ones we want to use."

"Sounds great."

"In the meantime . . ."

Exhausted is the only way I can describe how I feel.

Everything is draining. From Jett and his bullshit in the studio—the things I now see as complete immaturity—to my lack of sleep. The nights feel like endless bouts of tossing and turning. Grady wasn't the only one who found solace in our sharing the same bed.

Grady.

My heart twists in my chest as I sit at the computer like I have almost every day since I left. I head to the Sunnyville Gazette and read about what's happening in the town I've left. I open up a blank email, type Grady's email address, then delete it. Then I begin to type him an email but don't know what to say. He hasn't reached out to me since I left. He hasn't texted or called or sent up a smoke signal. So maybe I made this all up in my head. Maybe I was still so fresh and raw from my breakup with Jett that I saw things in Grady that weren't there.

Maybe he came into my life just to teach me how to let go.

That's such crap.

I know it was real. I know how I felt.

How I feel.

So then why haven't we talked?

The cursor blinks as my email alerts my incoming messages. I tab over and scan through the new ones. My first thought? There are none from Grady.

I open the one from my brother to see the new pictures he had taken of the twins, and I contemplate flying out there when Callum gives this album the A-okay. I need some family time. A connection with someone I know won't hurt my heart.

My computer pings again, and I hold my breath when I see the sender is Marcy Holden. I can pretend all I want that I forgot about the photo session Grady set up for me, but I didn't. I just chose not to think about it.

But now I can't. Now the photos are on the end of this little link.

I click it.

Hold my breath.

When the screen populates with pictures, a nervous laugh escapes from my lips. And then tears spring to my eyes.

These can't be me. They can't. I scroll through the pictures. One after another. I see the smile on my face. The sass in my expression. The guarded caution in my eyes.

But I don't see the dimples in my thighs. I don't see the fullness to my cheeks I try to contour out. I don't see how big my arms look when they're pressed against my sides.

I don't see any of that. I see a woman trying to accept her sensuality. I see a woman in the chiffon robe with lace camisole underneath, a little uncomfortable in her skin but who is trying to own it. I don't see how big her feet are in the high heels but rather the definition in her calves and the strength in her legs.

I see fit where I usually see flabby.

I see curves and sexy where I usually turn my head and cringe.

I see the beauty where I've always seen ugliness.

When I finish the first scan of the photos, of the four outfit changes, of the gamut of expressions she captured—flirty to feisty to shy to demure—I start all over again, trying to comprehend that these are really me. That I am *her.*

She must have airbrushed them.

That's my conclusion when I go through them with a more scrutinized eye and try to pick them apart. Sure, there are little things I hate, but the big things I have hang-ups about are not there.

She must have airbrushed them.

I repeat the thought as I flip back to the text of Marcy's email, the words and instructions I overlooked because I was too anxious to see what the pictures looked like.

Her words strike me to the core.

I hope you like them. I think they turned out beautifully. And before you refute how gorgeous you are with some smoke-and-mirrors nonsense, know that I didn't airbrush a single one of them.

The tears that were threatening moments before escape in a single tear that slides down my cheek. I flip back to the pictures.

This is the woman Grady saw. The one he was determined to get to believe her worth. Her beauty.

This is the woman he let walk away without telling her to stay.

It's a bittersweet feeling, and one I can't seem to shake.

I pick up my phone, needing to say something—anything to him. My fingers shake as I dial. A soft sob escapes my lips as his voice comes over the connection.

"You've reached Grady. I'm probably at the station and that's why I'm not picking up. Leave me a message and I'll return the call when I get off shift."

Beep.

"Hi. It's Dylan. I just wanted to say I understand now. How you felt when you looked at your picture in the calendar. Thank you for that. I hope you're doing well." *I love you. I miss you. Do you miss me? Stay safe.* "Bye."

I end the call and allow the tears to fall. Hearing his voice was almost worse than not hearing it at all.

Almost.

Because hearing it reminds me what we shared was real.

It was.

FIFTY-ONE

Grady

"WHAT WAS MARCY HERE FOR?"

It takes everything I have to look up from what's in my hand and over to Bowie—but I do for just a second. "She wanted to drop something by for me."

"Don't tell me she's giving you preferential treatment now after the calendar? What? You get a modeling contract?" He rolls his eyes, and I laugh at how ludicrous he sounds.

"Not hardly." I'm distracted so I'm not fast enough when Bowie snatches the photo from my hand. "Give it back, Bow," I warn with venom snapping in my tone.

"Whoa!" He holds his free hand up as his eyes grow big before handing it back to me and whistling. "And you let that go . . . why exactly?"

I don't answer him. I can't. Because my eyes are back on the photo Marcy gave me.

It's Dylan. Her smile is wide. Eyes alive. Expression sincere. There is a hint of some kind of silky thing from her shoulders down that my dick is begging to know what it looks like, but it's her face that holds my mind. And my heart.

The picture is equivalent to mine in the calendar.

Except she isn't looking at me like I was her.

She's happy on her own. She's seeing her worth on her own.

Who am I to ask her back here, to pull her away from her life and everything the confidence in her eyes says she will succeed at? Hold her back when fuck if that look on her face says she's about to fly.

"I didn't let her go. She wasn't mine to keep," I murmur, my fingers itching to touch the picture as if I can feel her skin when I do.

"And sometimes men are dumbasses who don't see what's right in front of their faces."

"Oh. Wow. Look how far you've gotten on this place."

I knew I heard tires crunch on the driveway, but when I look over to where my mom stands, she is by far the last person I expect to see standing in my backyard.

She walks around the playroom. It's been framed, drywalled, and stuccoed. The roof is papered and shingles are loaded.

"It's almost done," I say and step back from where I'm working and stare at her. "That's how long it's been since you've been here."

"I've been staying away," she says as she runs her hand over the wall.

"And why's that?" I chuckle, although I'm pretty sure I know.

"I was just trying to make sure you had your space."

"Space? You mean privacy so I'd fall madly in love with Dylan, right?"

"No. I never—"

"C'mon, Mom." I tip my beer to my lips and shake my head. "You're about as subtle as a flying brick." I walk to the mini refrigerator I have plugged in and am surprised she accepts when I offer her a beer. "I'm sorry I've disappointed you once again, but she's gone now."

"Well, of course, she's gone. Did you ask her to stay?"

"That's the question of the day, isn't it?" Jesus Christ. First Bowie and now my mom. But even with the thought, the photo flashes through my mind and twists up my insides.

"I don't know about that. It's my question, though." She falls silent. "I saw Mallory at the store today."

"Great." Not sure why she's telling me this.

"She said she hasn't seen you in some time."

"I've been a little busy." I turn my back to her and pick up my tape measure.

"I know she's typically your temporary bed partner, and I thought since—"

I choke on air. "Christ, Mother." I turn to face her. "*Really*? You really want to go there?"

"I'm not going anywhere. Don't think I'm dumb. I was young once and liked to have a little fun." She blushes a bit, and as much as I abhor the thought of thinking about my mom having sex, I also love the shit out of her for trying to talk to me and get on my playing field. The woman has a heart of gold despite being determined to expand the Malone clan. "There's nothing wrong with a little companionship now and again . . . so long as you're safe. But Mal said she called you last week, and you didn't return her call. She just wanted to make sure you were okay."

"So what's the question here? Am I okay? Why am I not sleeping with Mallory? Am I not sleeping with Mal because I'm still stuck on Dylan? What, Mom? Give me a roadmap here so I can figure out what your question is?" I run a hand through my hair and walk over to sit on the porch steps.

"You don't need to be rude." She traces the label on her beer before meeting my eyes. "I know you turned Mal down because she was temporary and Dylan was permanent."

"Can't be too permanent since she isn't here." There's more bite to my tone than she deserves.

"I hate to see you hurting, Grady."

"I'm not hurting. I know hurt. This is just . . . this is how it has to be."

"Says who? Says the gods of guilt you're living your life by?"

"Says the four firefighters who lost their lives a few weeks back.

Says their wives and kids who will never see them again. Says Brody and Shelby. Who am I to make someone go through that?"

"You listen to me, Grady Scott Malone, and you listen good. All that talk is nonsense. This is the job you love. The person you are. Any woman who is good enough for you, who loves you, accepts this possibility when she decides to be with you. I accepted it with your father. Emerson accepted it with Grant. Families accept it every day when their son, brother, father, daughter, sister, mother, goes off to serve our country. So, I love you, but I'm sick of you hiding behind your profession. It's an honorable profession. One that makes me proud to be your mother. Stop demeaning it by using it as your excuse."

I stare at my mom, eyes blinking, ears rejecting her harsh rebuke that I more than deserve but still don't want to hear.

"Dylan isn't going to wait around for you forever."

"Who said she's waiting around at all?"

"Seriously?" she asks wryly with a shake of her head. "You men are blind as damn bats. Take a week, Grady. Men do better with deadlines, so take a week to get your head together and figure out what you want. Whatever you decide to do after that week, do it. Move forward, because you can't keep doing this to yourself."

She walks over to me and presses a kiss to the top of my head like she used to do when I was little.

"You don't drown by falling in the pool, Grady. You drown by not trying to swim out of it," she says before running her hand up and down my back and walking off.

I hear the clink of her beer bottle as she tosses it into the trashcan.

I hear her engine turn over and the crunch of her tires as she backs down the driveway.

And I sit and stare at the moon above, the same moon looking down upon Dylan somewhere, and wonder how to start swimming when I've been treading water for what feels like forever.

FIFTY-TWO

Dylan

"WHAT'S GOING ON?" I ASK AS KAI WALKS INTO THE conference room behind Callum and shuts the door. "Where's Jett?"

There's a sinking feeling in the pit of my stomach.

"We wanted to talk to you about something," Kai says. "It doesn't pertain to Jett, so we decided to keep him out of this."

"Okay." I draw the word out.

"I want you to listen to something," Kai continues as Callum sets down his laptop on the center of the conference room table.

A few seconds pass as nerves rattle around inside me, that sense that I've done something wrong all too present. Especially since Jett isn't here.

And then without warning, my voice fills the room. I close my eyes to escape it, but I can't help but be moved by it.

It's the last song I worked on in the studio. I remember it clear as day. Jett on the couch. Kai and Henry in the booth. The song I wrote about how I felt about Grady.

I feel like I'm not breathing the entire time the song plays. My eyes eventually open and stay locked on my hands as I listen to myself sing about love and loss and hope and want. All the things Grady made me feel. That I still feel.

And when the song ends, the room is quiet. Riddled with

discomfort, I finally lift my eyes to see both Callum and Kai staring intensely at me.

"What's going on here?" I ask. Although, the thunder of my pulse in my ears tells me I already know.

Callum looks over to Kai and nods.

"When you sang that song in the studio, Dylan, every person in that booth, including me, had chills. It was that stunning. What you just heard was that one take with a few tweaks to the background. Jett was on the couch, so absorbed in himself he didn't even lift his head, and I remember wondering why he couldn't recognize that a number-one hit was being sung when the rest of us did? But not a hit for him, no. A hit for you, Dylan. With your vocals. So raw and haunting and emotional. *Christ*. I knew you were going to be mad at me, but I had to turn it in to Callum. I had to let him hear what I heard."

I stare at Kai, every part of my body feeling like it doesn't belong to me as I listen to his words, hear his praise, and still want to ask if he's really talking about me.

"I don't know what to say," I finally stutter out.

"Say you'll let me release that single on our label." Callum enters the conversation for the first time. I start to speak, and he holds up his hand to stop my protest. "I know you hate the limelight, Dylan. That's more refreshing than you could ever imagine, but I can't let that demo go without begging you to keep it first. Is it a great song for Jett's album? Yes. Will it be a hit? Yes. But it won't be the same without your voice sounding like it just did. It will be good, but it won't be that."

I stare at him, my eyes blinking, my rationality warring with my insecurities. "I-I don't know what to say."

"Say yes," Kai pleads. "Jett doesn't deserve this song."

"Look, think about it. That's all I'm asking. I'll send the contract to your agent. I'll work with whatever terms you want. You want to release the song and never perform? That's fine. You want to release this single and write more to release a full album? That's even better. The song is so incredible, your voice so perfect for it, that I'm willing to work with you. You know I'm not one to budge on many things."

"I'm flattered." *Stunned*. The world is spinning off its axis. "But I've never wanted the spotlight. I do better behind the curtain."

"We know," Kai says with a reassuring smile. "But, God, Dylan . . . this is worth it."

I leave the conference room feeling like I'm in an alternate reality. I have to be. And yet, I can hear the song in my mind. The clarity of my voice. The raw emotion threaded through it. The possible creation of texture, the layering of harmonies. And I know they're right.

It's a hit.

Not with Jett's voice.

But with mine.

It looks to me as if I owe someone a phone call.

"Dylan? Is that you?" There's what sounds like a flood of relief in his voice and every part of my body reacts to him saying my name. The swell of my heart. The widening of my nervous smile. The ache in my lower belly. The way my fingers grip the phone as if I let it go he's going to slip through my fingers.

"Hi." My voice is shy, quiet, but some of the nerve it took me to actually hit send dissipated as soon as he picked up.

There's silence. Then we both try to talk at the same time. Then we laugh as we both say, "You first."

"The connection is shitty. Is that you?"

"I'm here. Can you hear me?"

"Fuck, it's good to hear your voice, Dylan. Really good."

"Same here. You're well?" I ask, uncertain what to say but knowing I will recite the phone book to prevent him from hanging up.

"Yes. Yeah. Kind of." His chuckle sounds as nervous as mine. There's a loud roar overhead that's almost deafening.

"It's a borate bomber. I'm on scene. The Santa Rios fires. We just got here and are about to gear up."

The exhilaration I felt calling him comes crashing down and shatters all around me when I recognize the fear in his voice. The uncertainty tingeing its edges.

I know about the fires. They're all over the news, their rampage devastating. Maybe I was just being naïve to think Grady was at the station, covering the other units that had been dispatched like he had all summer.

"Grady." A sudden surge of panic reverberates through me.

"God, I needed to hear your voice." Chills race over my skin, and the way he says those words tells me all I need to know. He's struggling. Every part of me wishes I could race to his side, look him in the eyes, and reassure him . . . but I can't. "I'm not . . . I don't . . . I can't let the guys down, Dylan." His raw honesty is heart-wrenching.

"You aren't going to, Grady. I know you won't. You've changed so much since I've met you. You've grown. You've faced your fears. You've realized—"

"I don't know if I can do this."

"You can. I have faith in you." And then my synapses fire all at the same time and my thoughts align. "Grady, we made a deal."

"Yeah?" He sounds distracted.

"I fulfilled my end of it. That's why I'm calling you. I wanted to tell you *I did it*."

"Did what?"

"I sang a song. *For me*. The label wants to record it and release it as a single."

"*You did*?" There is so much pride in his voice, and in lieu of what he's facing now, I almost feel guilty for talking about me. But I have a reason. "You actually went into the label and asked for studio time and recorded a song for yourself?"

"Yes." The white lie rolls off my tongue. My need to give him encouragement is more important than the semantics of how it all went down.

"God. I'm so proud of you, Dyl. You did it. You really did it."

"And I know you can do it, too." I wipe the tear away that slips down my cheek. “This is what you love more than anything, Grady. Your job. Your calling. This is the last step you need to take to get back to the new and improved Grady Malone.”

“I wasn’t aware I needed improving.” His chuckle this time is warmer.

“I’m a fan of you however you are.”

“Malone. Gear up. We’re heading out in five,” a voice calls in the background, and I want to beg for just one more minute.

“You gotta go.”

“I’ve gotta go.” He sighs.

“Be safe, Malone.”

“Always.” I’m not sure who he’s trying to convince more, himself or me.

“Grady.” I’m not sure why I say his name, but I can’t let him go just yet.

I miss you.

Come back to me.

I love you.

“*Two-in. Two-out.* Promise me that.”

“Two-in. Two-out,” he murmurs. “When this is over, McCoy, you and I need to have a talk.”

And then, before I can say another word, before I can tell him I agree, the call drops.

FIFTY-THREE

Grady

"If this shit was easy, Malone, everyone would do it."

I look at Veego as the rig we're on bumps and jostles while it heads up the mountain. The fire rages on the ridge in front of us. She's a mean, nasty bitch, consuming every piece of brush she can find. The wind serving to add gasoline to her fury.

I don't respond other than a nod because I don't have the words. How can I when I've spent every call, every minute, scared of the one thing that makes me feel alive. *Putting out fires.*

My fear and my salvation are one in the same.

The rig stops at a makeshift basecamp that is ready to go on the fly should the wind switch and the fire swing, and we unload in one big mass of equipment and anxious energy.

The next hour or so is spent double-checking our gear and stocking up on any supplies we're going to need in order to keep a line up on the ridge above us.

When we get the go-ahead, we begin the climb into the belly of the beast to be tried by her flames.

My fears are eaten by the adrenaline.

My doubts are eroded by each cut we make into Mother Nature to stop her progress.

My hesitations are nonexistent as I slowly lose myself to the concentration it takes to stay alive.

As I do what I love.

FIFTY-FOUR

Dylan

I'M RESTLESS AS I WAIT FOR EMERSON TO ANSWER MY QUESTION: *How is Grady*?

I pace the confines of my condo, phone pressed to my ear as the news drones on about the fires in the background, doing nothing to calm my irrational fears about his well-being.

It's been four days since I talked to him. Four days of listening to the newscasters talk about the worst fire in California's history and seeing the haunting images of burned-down houses, fire engines, and acres of scorched earth. It's been four days of putting all the craziness in my life—contract negotiations, studio time for Jett, and then studio time for me—on the backburner because my thoughts are first and foremost with Grady. If he's safe. If he's alive.

Radio silence does this to you. It eats at your resolve when you think you're strong. It dredges up doubts when you know you have nothing to worry about.

"Grant is using back channels to get information, Dylan. You know I'll call you the minute I have more."

She makes the statement, but there's hesitation in her voice that causes alarm bells to sound off.

"What are you not telling me?"

"Nothing."

"Emerson, ask yourself this. If it were Grant, would you want me to tell you?"

"Christ," she says, and the single word has my heart jumping into my throat. "There's a crew up on the ridge they've lost communication with. The wind switched and cut off their access route. The last they heard, they were climbing down the backside from where they had been, but they haven't heard from them nor have they seen them from the chopper."

"Oh God." My hand is on my mouth as I sink to the couch.

"That isn't to say it's Grady's team," she hurries to say. "Grant says crews lose communications all the time in rough terrain, lack of service. Hell, lack of being able to charge anything since there's nothing to plug into."

But I know.

Somewhere deep down, I know.

I told Grady a white lie to give him the courage to face his fear. In turn, regardless of how irrational it may sound, did my encouragement push him when he wasn't ready?

And if he's hurt . . . oh, God, if he's hurt . . .

"Sure. I'm sure he's fine." My voice is hollow.

"I'll let you know as soon as I know more."

"I feel like I need to be there." Mentally, I've already packed and am in the car driving to Sunnyville.

He's going to be fine.

"I know you do . . . but if you drive here, you're going to be passing where he is. He's somewhere between Sunnyville and Los Angeles." And yet, I walk into my bedroom and open my closet door to look at my suitcase. "You're welcome to come here and sit and wait with us, but by the time you get here, we're going to get the news that he's fine."

He has to be fine.

"Who's taking care of Petunia?"

"Brody and Shelby."

God, please let him be fine.

"Oh." I try to think of another excuse for me to be there but can't find one other than I didn't tell him I loved him.

Because I do.

FIFTY-FIVE

Grady

F*IVE MINUTES.*

This blanket will only protect me for that long.

Drew's screams echo in my ears. The fear. The pain. The desperation.

It's not real, Grady.

The fire snaps around us. I concentrate on its crackle. On the sound of it marching through the grove surrounding us. I use its roar as my anchor to reality. To remind me that this isn't the warehouse. This isn't a repeat of before.

Three hundred seconds.

The heat.

It's so fucking intense.

PASS alarms go off. One after another. They sound off around me. Sirens of immobility. I squeeze my eyes shut as I battle the memories. As I will the nightmare away.

It's not real, Grady.

But it is. This *is* real. Seven of us are trapped in the fire's vortex. Taking cover in this clearing as the world around us burns.

But it's not just Drew this time.

It's all of us.

Two hundred forty seconds. That's all the time we have left.

It's like the inside of hell, like the nightmare has been brought back into reality.

All the air I'll have.

"Grady?" It's Bowie's muffled voice. I can barely hear him above the roar of the fucking fire. Not Drew screaming for help. Just Bowie asking me to check in. To let him know I'm hanging in there.

"Good," I shout when in reality I feel as if I'm suffocating.

"Dixon?"

"Good," he sounds off.

"Veego?"

"Ten-four." I can barely hear him.

And he continues on through the crew. One by one.

I wait for one of them not to answer. I wait to hear silence.

But there isn't any.

One hundred eighty seconds and counting until the blanket will give way to the extreme heat.

My back feels like it's on fire again, itchy and slick with sweat that burns in rivulets as it slides over my skin. A branch cracks somewhere overhead and I wait for it to fall on me. I brace for the impact.

For the weight of the beam as it pins me down.

You're not there, Grady.

I strain to hear Drew's screams. I brace for the words he's going to say next.

But there's nothing. Just the whoops of the guys around me as anxious adrenaline takes hold. Just the roar of the fire as it eats the vegetation and sucks the oxygen.

One hundred twenty seconds left.

I'm not going to die.

Drew, I'm not going to die.

I tense when the explosion hits. The water truck's gas tank just went. And then I scramble through the shock to hold the fire blanket around me. Pin it to the ground with me between it and the ground that's heating underneath me.

The wind howls. It's the eeriest sound I've ever heard.

My fingers burn in my gloves as I pin the blanket down.

Eighty seconds left. I'm not going to die.

Someone shouts out a curse to combat the feeling of suffocation.

But it has nothing on my pulse pounding in my ears.

My adrenaline coursing through my blood.

My breath labored and desperate.

Forty seconds. I'm not going to die.

Dylan.

I repeat her name over and over and over. I use it like a second hand on a clock as I wait out the terror. As I pray for the fire to blow through. As I put my faith in these blankets protecting us. As I tell myself, that when I see her again, I'm going to put it all on the line.

I'm not going to die.

There's a whoop of excitement. Someone yells, "Fuck you, bitch," to the fire. Another shouts, "Go back to hell, you cunt!"

I laugh. We're sick fucks.

And then the words, "All clear."

Motherfucking music to my ears.

I shove the blanket off me and gulp in air. It's hot and thick, because everything on the edges of the clearing is still on fire. Bright oranges and deep yellows and hues of blue on the burning metal of our vehicle . . . but I'm alive.

I'm alive.

So is the rest of my crew.

We did it, Drew.

And so I lie on my back in the middle of the High Sierras and try to stop my body from trembling. The ground beneath me is hot and the ashes suffocate what's left of the vegetation, but I don't move. The adrenaline takes over, owning every part of me as I stare at the small glimpses of stars in the night sky above trying to break through the smoke. As the eerie orange glow lights up everything around us.

I know I need to get up. I understand the fire is still raging around us and we have a job to do. I realize that our tanker—our only transportation—is now gone, and so we have a shit-ton of work and trekking to do before we're in the clear.

But I don't move.

I can't.

A fucking tear I fight back finally escapes. Too much emotion. Too much everything.

I close my eyes to process it. To accept it.

Just one more minute.

I'm alive.

"You good, man?" I open my eyes to see Bowie. He's standing over me, looking down, hand extended to help me stand.

Our eyes meet and he nods ever so slightly to let me know he knows the hell that just went on in my head. And that he's proud of me for holding on.

I don't trust myself to speak, so I nod in return and let him help pull me up.

"Seven-in. Seven-out," he says as he lifts his chin over his shoulder to where the guys are gathering the supplies we have left that the fire didn't incinerate so we can work our way out of this gorge.

And we do. We work hour after hour. Our bones hurt and muscles ache and chests burn, but we do what we love. We cut prevention lines should the wind switch and bring the fire back this way.

No matter how hard we work, hot spots flare around us.

"Keep that line," I shout to Veego and his crew as I turn to look over my shoulder.

We're in the depths of hell. At least that's what it looks like all around us. The smoke is so thick that the ash falls like a downpour. The orange flames lick the perimeter around us. With our tanker, food, and communication devices taken by the fire, it's up to us to get the fuck out of here.

Out of habit, I look at my cell again, knowing there is no battery left but hoping anyway.

"Where are the goddamn Hotshots?" Dixon asks, referring to the elite team of wild-land firefighters as he stops and takes a conservative sip from what little is left in his canteen.

"My bet is they're on the eastern ridge. That's where they're needed the most," I say as I look over to him. My face probably looks like his, black with soot but streaked from sweat, eyes red and exhausted.

"It looks like our sorry asses could use them right now," he says with a delirious laugh as he holds his arms out and does a mini-spin.

"You pussying out on us, old man?" I ask with a matching laugh. "I'm the only one who's allowed to do that."

It's my pseudo-apology. In the middle of a firestorm. It's my way to let them know I know I've let them down. That I'm not going to let them down this time.

No matter the cost.

Dix walks over to me and puts an arm around my shoulders. "You kicked ass, Grady. We never doubted you, but hell if it doesn't feel good to have you back." He squeezes and then lets go, nods, and goes back to holding the line.

"How much farther do we have?" Mack asks.

"Ten miles. Fifteen. Just depends if we get out of this gorge on our own or if they find us first," I guess to the groan of the guys. They're exhausted, starving, and want to be anywhere that isn't covered in rocks to fall asleep, even if it's just for thirty minutes.

"My stomach's growling, boys. Quit the yacking and finish cutting this line so we can head out," Johnson says. "Food's calling my name and a hot shower is the only other thing I want."

"Me too," I murmur. *And Dylan.* The only other thing I want is her.

"Balls to the wall, boys," Bowie says and all six of us repeat it back to him.

"Let's do it."

FIFTY-SIX

Dylan

"DYLAN?"

"*Grayson*? What is it?"

"He's out. They made it out." Grayson's voice is gruff, swimming with emotion.

I try to bite back my cry of relief, but it's useless. It's out, and with it comes the tears of joy. "He's okay?"

"Yeah." He clears his throat. "Yes. He's at base camp. His cell is toast, but he asked me to call you and tell you he made it out. He said to tell you, *two-in. Two-out.*"

I smile through the tears and nod like he can see me. "Thank you." My words are barely audible.

"He's going to be there for a while until the blaze is contained. If he can't get through to you, we'll let you know when his crew is on their way home."

"Okay." For the first time, the silence that fills the line is a positive thing as we both breathe easier.

And when we hang up moments later, I slide down the wall and cry with the phone clutched in my hand and Grady's stamp on every part of my heart.

FIFTY-SEVEN

Dylan

I scrub my hand over my face and exhale a frustrated breath.

My guitar's in my lap, my three notebooks are on the table in front of me, and the clock is telling me I've been at this way too long.

But I can't sleep. It seems like sleep is few and far between these days.

And so I work.

It's all I can do to keep my mind busy and my stress to a minimum.

And I wait. To hear from Grady. To hear the story that his brothers told me—how fire overwhelmed his crew and they had to take cover and then hike their way out. To know he's home safe. To have that talk he promised we'd have.

It's been ten days. Ten long ones.

They've been packed with new experiences. Me, behind the mic to record for the first time. Me, giving creative input to my own songs. Me, taking a step into facing my fears and realizing that singing my own song in a studio isn't terribly different from when I'm directing Jett on how to sing a new one.

I pull my guitar onto my lap, tuck my pencil behind my ear, and begin again.

The knock startles me, and my first thought is that Jett's drunk and coming over as he's done in the past. But when I look through the peephole, I can't get the door open fast enough.

Because it's Grady standing on my doorstep.

It's Grady looking completely exhausted and more handsome than any man I've ever set eyes on. He has an unshaven scruff. His hair is longer than normal, curling over his ears, and his clothes look like he's been outside camping for days on end without washing them. But he is the best sight I've ever seen.

It's Grady representing every single damn thing I want, and I can't wait to tell him I intend to have it. Because this time I am going to fight. This time I'm not going to let him walk away without knowing how I feel about him.

But that can wait because within a heartbeat, I am in his arms. Legs wrapped around his waist. Lips against his. Hands running over his back and cheeks and face. Laughter sounding off in the space against us.

"You're here," I murmur against his lips.

"I'm here," he repeats back to me.

"How are you here?" I laugh wondering how he knows my address.

"Your brother gave me your address."

Simple enough and too much explanation that doesn't matter right now.

"God, I missed you."

Our tongues meet, and our bodies press against each other's as we physically reconnect. He walks us into the house, and I stay attached to him like a spider monkey because there is no way I'm letting him go yet.

Not when he stumbles backward. Not when he sits on the couch. Not when he breaks his lips from mine, hands framing my face, and his lips saying, "Let me look at you, Dylan."

My heart melts. There is so much swimming in his eyes. So many unspoken words. So many unnamed emotions.

He leans forward, kisses me, and then rests his forehead against mine as his thumbs brush over my cheeks.

"What are you doing here?" I laugh and whisper and press another kiss to his lips.

"I told you when I was done with the fire we needed to have a talk."

"A talk? Is that what we're going to do? Talk?"

His dick is hard and tempting where it presses between my thighs, and every part of my body aches for it as much as every part of my heart needs to hear what he has to say.

"Yes." His voice is strained, and he kisses me again so that when our lips part he has to hold my head in place to prevent me from taking more. "We need to talk. We've gone on too long without talking." Another brusque kiss. "And then we'll communicate in other ways." I can feel his mouth spread into a smile against mine.

"Are you okay, Grady?" I'm not sure why I ask the question in this moment, but it feels so very important that it just comes out. I lean back from where I sit astride his hips and study him, needing to see his eyes when he answers.

"I am now." It's a struggle to fight the tears that threaten because those three words are almost as meaningful to me as another set of three. It means he finds solace in me. Comfort.

"Good. I'm glad."

"I was finally able to listen to the song you sent me in my voicemail. It was incredible, Dylan. You are incredible. I'm so proud of you."

"It's because of you I could do it."

"No. It's because of you."

"I—"

"You're going to be a star." His smile is shy and warms every part of me. "And I'm going to tell you 'I told you so' every single day."

"Every single day?"

"I have a few things I need to say—"

"Grady—"

"My turn, Dylan." He presses a lingering kiss on my lips. "There were some things I should have said before. A lot of things. And I need to say them now."

"It doesn't matter what you say, it only matters that you're here."

"It does matter. Words always matter." He shakes his head and looks down for a minute before meeting my eyes again. "Just because I let you go doesn't mean I wanted to. In fact it was quite the opposite . . . but how could I ask you to stay and put you through this life I live when you have your own?"

"Isn't that my choice to decide?"

"The protector in me was trying to prevent you from being hurt."

"The protector in you is appreciated, but I can make my own decisions, which is why you're not fully to blame. I have a voice, and I chose not to use it. I figured you were so set in your opinions that nothing was going to change them, so why try?"

"Sometimes it takes something—or someone—to make you see the error of your ways. A man can only call himself a man when he's willing to admit he was wrong." Grady angles his head and stares at me. "I was wrong, Dylan."

"I was wrong too."

He laces his fingers with mine, offers me a shy smile, and then explains everything about what happened to him and his crew from the wind shift to the firestorm they had to endure under their space blankets to their long, arduous hike out.

"You see, when I was under that fire blanket, all I could think about was you. How I wanted to come home to you. How I want you waiting for me, missing me. I know that's selfish, but what is all this for if there isn't someone willing to take the risk with me? What does all of this mean if I can't go home and share the ups and downs and sideways days with someone?"

My pulse races, and every part of my body surges with an immeasurable pride in him. "I don't know what you want out of life, Dylan. We never talked about shit like that. Kids? Dogs? More pigs? I don't have a clue. But I'd love to. I want to know what you want, what you need, what you dream of. And I'd love to be the one to help you get it."

"Grady." I can't speak over the emotion clogging up my thoughts. "I—"

"I'm not asking to be your whole world, Dylan, I just want to be a part of it. I want to be the part that revolves around you. I want to be the one who grounds you so we're forced to come home to each other, even when we're mad. I want to provide the arms that hug you and the hands that hold yours through whatever adventure awaits us. I want you and whatever the two of us decide we want for our future."

I press my lips to his as my tears fall. There is the taste of salt in our kiss. The sweetness of love in it. The sprinkle of hope mixed in.

"Can I talk now?" I laugh.

"Mm-hmm."

"I love you. Plain and simple. *I love you, Grady Malone*," I murmur against his lips.

"Why didn't you say so?" He laughs.

"Because you never asked me to stay."

"I'm asking you now. Stay with me, Dylan. Please stay."

"I never thought you'd ask."

"I love you too. More than you'll ever know."

EPILOGUE

Dylan

HOW IN THE HELL DO THEY DO THIS EVERY DAY?

How?

I look at my brother's twins asleep on the couch—at Tessa, who less than an hour ago had spaghetti smeared all over her face, and then to Mia, who I'm sure still has noodles somewhere in her hair. Then I turn my attention to Grant and Emerson's daughter, Gwen, who's in her swing, and I repeat the thought, how in the world do they do this on a daily basis?

And why in the hell did I think I could handle watching all three of them at the same time?

The inadequacies of my mothering skills are clear.

But the chaos that was a cacophony of squealing and refusals to go to bed was worth it now that they're asleep.

Now they're so peaceful and sweet that I want to stare at them for hours on end so they don't grow bigger during the night.

I continue to sing little lullabies that my mom used to sing to Damon and me. Songs I've written for others. The song I wrote for myself that's still on the Billboard Top 100.

I think about how all of this started with needing to write a set of songs and how much has changed since then. I'm now signed as an artist to the same label that let Jett go. My mom is going on ten months sober—the longest stint she's gone yet. And I now live in

Sunnyville where I get to live with my best friend, who just so happens to be the man I love.

I wouldn't change any of the heartache because it all led me here. To Grady.

Just as I begin a new song, I shift, catching sight of Grady standing there with his arms crossed and shoulder leaned against the doorjamb.

"Hi." His smile is wide and eyes full of amusement.

"Hi." I walk toward him and hold a finger to my lips for him to be quiet.

"How'd it go?"

I laugh. "Crazy. Chaotic. Exhausting. Incredible." I smile and lean in to press a kiss to his lips. But once my lips are there, I don't want to leave his just yet, so I draw out the kiss a bit more.

He leans back and smiles. "You have spaghetti in your hair," he says as he reaches out and pulls a noodle from the top of my head.

"I'm sure that isn't the only place I have it," I say and then catch the humor in his eyes the same time I think back to him using the same phrase the first time we met. My smile widens and I shake my head a beat before I step away to begin picking up the tornado of toys.

But Grady puts his hands on my arms and keeps me put. His eyes hold mine with an unspoken intensity I don't understand.

"What is it?"

His smile is soft. The shake of his head subtle. "It's you."

My hands are patting down my hair immediately, looking for more noodles but he just laughs. "What?"

"I like seeing you like this."

"Like what? Frazzled? A mess? Feeling like I have absolutely no clue what I'm doing? What?"

"All of the above."

"Gee, thanks."

"Add to that gorgeous."

"Have you been out drinking with your brothers?" I tease.

"No. Not at all."

"Are you feeling okay? Feverish?" I narrow my eyes and study him. In the past year I've learned how to decipher his expressions, but this is one I've never seen before.

"Perfectly fine, why?"

"Then what are you talking about?"

"I like seeing you like this," he reiterates. "You. Singing to babies with a messy kitchen and pasta in your hair and that smile on your face. I know I love you. I know I told you that us living together was all I could give you . . . but damn it, Dylan, I can't do this anymore."

Panic strikes and whiplash hits as I try to figure out the contradiction in his words. "Grady?"

Then it's as if he realizes what he's said. He frames my face with his hands and leans in to kiss me. A physical reassurance to stop the sudden panic he's caused. His kiss is slow and methodical and packed with so much sensuality that I'm kind of wishing the kids weren't here so we could continue this where we stand.

"I lied to you, Dylan." He brushes his lips to mine. "It wasn't intentional, but I did. I told you I couldn't give you more, but you know what? I don't think there's any way I can give you less."

"What do you mean?"

"I want to walk into our house and see you like this with our kids. I'd give anything to come home from work and have them run out and meet me on the driveway like we used to do with my dad. I want to have nights where the house is a mess and we're stressed to the gills from them crying and fussing. I want the good, the bad, the ugly in life . . . and *I want it with you*."

My eyes sting with tears—the good kind—as I look at him. I think I know what he's saying.

"You compromised with me, Dylan. You have given me time to work through my fears and doubts. You moved here and gave up your Hollywood life to prove to me this could work when I gave you no promises in return."

"You didn't have to give me anything to stay other than your heart. That's all I wanted, Grady, and you've given me that and then some."

"But you deserve more, Dylan. You deserve the white picket fence and sticky-faced kids and nights where a glass of wine once they're in bed is the only type of satisfaction you need."

It's my turn to laugh and press a kiss to his lips. "Wine is good, but you are much better at satisfying me."

"Good," he says. "Because I want to give you all of those things. I told you once I didn't want to be your whole world, but rather the part you were in. I lied. It isn't enough. It'll never be enough with you. I want to be your whole world, Dyl. I want to make the rest with you. I want to fill it with love and laughter and kids and pets and late nights and early mornings. I just want you."

I reach out and run my fingers down his cheeks, my own words escaping me in the moment.

"I can't promise you I won't make you worry. That my job won't have you worry. But I can promise that you are who I'll happily come home to each night. That you are who I *want* to come home to every night. *No matter the cost*. Marry me, Dylan. Be my wife. Make my life. Make me complete."

I'm nodding. My mouth is open, but no words are coming out. My tears are falling and still no words are coming out.

And he's slipping a ring on my finger that I can't see through the tears and the shock and the love.

Because he's right. I was willing to settle. To give him what he needed because I didn't need a piece of paper or his last name to know he loved me. I just needed him. I needed us. And that was more than enough for me.

And now I'll get the cherry on top. The unexpected dessert.

I get to be a Malone.

"Yes, Grady. Yes," I finally say.

He lets out a whoop and lifts me into his arms so he can kiss me senseless.

We sink into the kiss and right as our bodies react with want and need, Gwen starts to cry.

Grady rests his forehead against mine and starts to laugh.

"You did say you wanted the crying and fussing," I murmur against his lips.

"That I did." He sighs.

But we take a moment longer to breathe each other in.

In a messy kitchen.

With a crying toddler.

And with our hearts as one.

We let our scars fall in love.

We let our hearts heal each other's.

And now we have the rest of our lives to live.

No matter the cost.

THE END

STAY TUNED

Want more of the Malone brothers? Stay tuned for the final standalone book in the Everyday Heroes series. Medevac Pilot and single father, Grayson Malone has a big challenge on his hands—how not to fall in love with *off-limits* Sidney Thorton. *Cockpit* is coming late spring, 2018. It's available for exclusive preorder on iBooks.

And in November of 2018, you'll learn a little bit more about the ever quirky and equally loved best friend in the Everyday Heroes series, Desi Whitman in *Control.*

Control is something Desi Whitman abhors. Why live life in black and white perfection when you can messily color outside the lines? But when she comes face to face with SWAT officer Reznor Mayne, he's about to show her just how good control can feel.

***Control* can be preordered on Amazon.**

ABOUT THE AUTHOR

New York Times Bestselling author K. Bromberg writes contemporary novels that contain a mixture of sweet, emotional, a whole lot of sexy, and a little bit of real. She likes to write strong heroines, and damaged heroes who we love to hate and hate to love.

A mom of three, she plots her novels in between school runs and soccer practices, more often than not with her laptop in tow.

Since publishing her first book in 2013, Kristy has sold over one million copies of her books across sixteen different countries and has landed on the New York Times, USA Today, and Wall Street Journal Bestsellers lists over twenty-five times. Her Driven trilogy (Driven, Fueled, and Crashed) is currently being adapted for film by Passionflix with the first movie slated to release in the summer of 2018.

She is currently working on her Everyday Heroes trilogy. This series consists of three complete standalone novels—Cuffed, Combust, and Cockpit (late spring 2018)—and is about three brothers who are emergency responders, the jobs that call to them, and the women who challenge them.

She loves to hear from her readers so make sure you check her out on social media or sign up for her newsletter to stay up to date on all her latest releases and sales: http://bit.ly/254MWtI

Connect with K. Bromberg

Website: www.kbromberg.com

Facebook: www.facebook.com/AuthorKBromberg

Instagram: www.instagram.com/kbromberg13

Twitter: www.twitter.com/KBrombergDriven

Goodreads: bit.ly/1koZIkL

CPSIA information can be obtained
at www.ICGtesting.com
Printed in the USA
LVOW13s1815220318
570811LV00014B/1362/P